SWEETEST SURRENDER

THE SERAFINA: SIN CITY SERIES

Katie Reus

Sweetest Surrender by Katie Reus Copyright © 2014
Killer Secrets by Katie Reus Copyright © 2011

All rights reserved. Except as permitted under the U.S. Copyright Act of 1976, no part of this publication may be reproduced, distributed, or transmitted in any form or by any means, or stored in a database or retrieval system, without the prior written permission of the author.

Cover art: Jaycee of Sweet 'N Spicy Designs

Publisher's Note: This is a work of fiction. Names, characters, places, and incidents are either the products of the author's imagination or used fictitiously, and any resemblance to actual persons, living or dead, or business establishments, organizations or locales is completely coincidental.

Sweetest Surrender/Katie Reus. -- 1st ed.
ISBN-13: 978-1497319714
ISBN-10: 1497319714

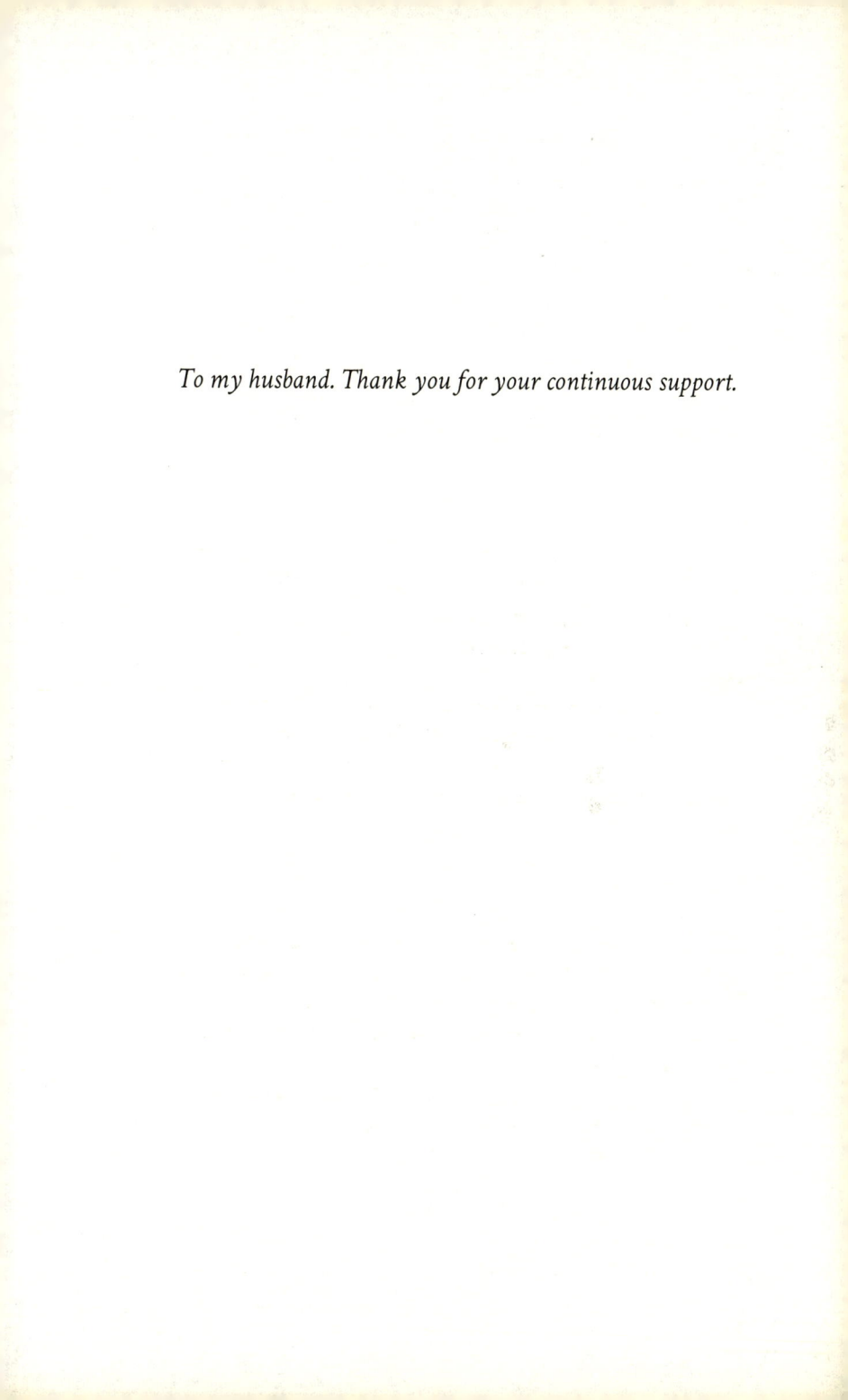

To my husband. Thank you for your continuous support.

Praise for the novels of Katie Reus

"…an engrossing page-turner that I enjoyed in one sitting. Reus offers all the ingredients I love in a paranormal romance." —Book Lovers, Inc.

"Has all the right ingredients: a hot couple, evil villains, and a killer action-filled plot. . . . [The] Moon Shifter series is what I call Grade-A entertainment!" —Joyfully Reviewed

"I could not put this book down. . . . Let me be clear that I am not saying that this was a good book *for* a paranormal genre; it was an excellent romance read, *period*." —All About Romance

"Reus strikes just the right balance of steamy sexual tension and nail-biting action….This romantic thriller reliably hits every note that fans of the genre will expect." —*Publisher's Weekly*

"Prepare yourself for the start of a great new series! . . . I'm excited about reading more about this great group of characters." —Fresh Fiction

"Nonstop action, a solid plot, good pacing and riveting suspense…" —*RT Book Reviews (4.5 Stars)*

CHAPTER ONE

Angel clutched the brown paper bag filled with the boxed up leftover food she'd planned to take home tonight. It didn't matter that it would have been thrown out, what she was doing was stealing. Something she'd never thought to do. Ever. Stealing was wrong. Something she'd learned before kindergarten.

In the last two years, however, she'd learned to live in shades of gray, not black and white. The world simply wasn't so nice and tidy—those who thought it was viewed life with rose-colored glasses. Okay, that sounded a little bitter. But it was how she was feeling.

She hated that she'd gotten to a point where she was actually stealing from one of her employers. She paused at the back door of the restaurant that would lead to a long hallway on out to the dumpsters behind The Serafina Hotel. No, she just couldn't do it. She turned and headed back to the main kitchen. She'd planned to leave the bag out there and grab it after she'd clocked out. Pretty much no one was left at Cloud 9 this late. She'd been the closing server; the bartenders had already gone home while she finished cleaning up the kitchen.

As she stepped back into the galley of the main kitchen, she froze. Sierra Archer was standing there cataloging salad dressing. The petite woman had her long black hair pulled into a ponytail; she wore plain clothes, not her normal chef's jacket. Normally she didn't work on Thursdays and it was after hours so Angel was more than surprised to see her.

Sierra glanced up, smiling. "Hey, Angel. You getting out of here?"

Unable to find her voice, she nodded, clutching the bag.

Sierra lifted a dark eyebrow, her smile faltering. "You okay?"

"Yeah," she managed to rasp out, hating the guilt suffusing her.

"You want me to ring you up?" her boss asked, nodding at the brown bag. "I've still got a register open. Haven't gone through the night's drink reports yet and it's gonna take forever." She made an annoyed face.

Before Angel could respond, Hayden, Sierra's fiancé and also one of the heads of security at the Serafina, strode in. "Hey, sweetheart," he murmured to Sierra.

Without his normal suit and tie and wearing just a T-shirt and jeans he should have looked casual and unintimidating. Unfortunately the huge man with the tattoos always made her feel nervous. Both he and his brother did. They were nice and Angel knew Sierra wouldn't be with a loser, but still, in her experience she stayed away from men that big. She knew what fists could do.

Sierra gave him a quick kiss before turning back to Angel. "I'll get you now."

"No, it's okay. This isn't..." Oh God, she didn't even know what to say. She hated confrontation and always clammed up when she felt cornered. Only Sierra wasn't cornering her. She was just being nice. But Angel felt so guilty and it must have shown on her face because Sierra turned to her fiancé.

"Can you meet me out front? I need to talk to Angel alone."

Hayden's eyebrows rose, but he nodded and left after giving Sierra another quick kiss on the forehead.

When Sierra faced her again, she leaned one hip against the metal countertop they put hot plates on for the servers to deliver. Right now it was buffed and shiny. "What's going on? Is that the throwaway food?"

Swallowing hard, Angel nodded. "Yeah. It expires tomorrow and I was..." She was going to tell Sierra she'd been bringing it back but didn't think she'd believe her or that it would matter. Angel had packed it up and had been ready to take it. That was damning enough. "I'm sorry."

Instead of condemnation, Sierra looked concerned. Which just made Angel feel even crappier. "I just need to inventory the loss before we throw it out, but...you can have it. You should have asked me though." She rubbed a hand over her face. "You've been such a great employee, but..."

Angel knew that even small infractions like this were cause for being fired. Especially at a restaurant in a casino. If she took something small, who was to say she wouldn't skim elsewhere? Her face heated up with shame, but she forced herself to hold the other woman's startling green gaze. "I know and I'm really sorry. I'll grab my last paycheck next week but...I get it." Angel knew the other woman would have to fire her over this and there was no point in trying to convince her not to.

"Angel—"

Sierra turned at a slight scuffing sound to find Hayden and Vadim entering the big galley kitchen. What the hell was Vadim doing here? He was part of the hotel's security team, but she hadn't even thought he was working tonight.

Right then Angel wanted the floor to open up into a giant hole and swallow her. For a brief moment she met Vadim's pale blue eyes but quickly looked away. To say she had a massive crush on him would be an understatement. So many of the wait staff were afraid of him but she didn't understand why. He was so sweet and gentle and right now she simply couldn't bear to have him witness her getting fired.

"Sierra." She tried to keep her voice steady as she dragged the other woman's attention back to her. With the bright lights of the kitchen overhead she felt as if she was under a giant spotlight. When her boss looked back, Angel said, "I'm going to go, but I really am sorry. Please don't…" What? *Don't fire me in front of them? Them, meaning Vadim Sokolov, the man she'd been lusting after for months.* She could feel her face turning even redder and thanks to her Irish coloring, she probably looked like Rudolph's nose.

Sierra took a step forward, closing the distance between them. "Let's just talk about this in my office," she murmured, motioning toward the back of the kitchen.

"Is everything okay?" Vadim asked, still standing in the entry with Hayden. The slight trace of his Russian accent was ever present, the delicious sound rolling over her like a warm, all-enveloping embrace.

Angel swallowed hard. "Fine." She gave Sierra a beseeching look. She seriously doubted the other woman wanted to call the police over some food, so she was going to make her exit before Sierra could tell her fiancé what Angel had done. For all she knew, the head of security had protocol to follow. Setting the bag on the metal countertop, she clutched her purse to her side. "Sorry, Sierra," she muttered before making a beeline for the exit. She mumbled a quick goodbye to Vadim, who looked oddly hurt by her getaway, but she couldn't think about that now. She just needed to get home and away from here.

And figure out her next move. She'd been lucky enough to find work in Vegas but she'd been here months already. It was time to move on. Tonight was just a sign that she'd stayed in one place too long.

Vadim wanted to rush after Angel, but needed to find out what the hell was going on first. "What's wrong with Angel?" he asked Sierra.

The petite woman bit her bottom lip nervously. For a moment he thought it was because of him and he bit back his annoyance. At six feet tall, he wasn't overly large, and he was good looking enough. Not hideous at least. He simply did not understand why women seemed fearful of him when he would literally cut off his own arm before harming a female. But then he realized Sierra was watching Hayden nervously.

"If I tell you something you have to promise not to get involved or try to fire Angel."

Hayden frowned, shoving his hands in his pockets. "What's going on?"

Sierra stuck out her chin mutinously. "Promise."

At that moment, Vadim found himself liking the chef even more. What the hell had Angel gotten herself into?

"Fine. I promise. Now what's up? She looked like she was about to burst into tears."

Vadim had seen that too and the thought of Angel crying raked against his insides like jagged glass. He'd known her for five months, but it felt like a lifetime for how attracted he was to her.

"It's not a huge deal, but I caught her taking food." Sierra motioned to a brown bag on the counter. "It's going to be thrown away since it expires tomorrow, but it's more than fine to eat. We just have standards…and that's not the point. She was taking it without telling me, but I wasn't going to fire her. I just wanted to talk to her to see if she needed some extra help or wanted more shifts, but she hurried out of here after telling me she'd get her last paycheck next week. I think…" Sierra looked at Vadim, her face flushing. "I think she was embarrassed you were here."

Vadim blinked, not sure what Sierra meant. If Angel had a problem she could come to him. They were friends and Angel knew that. Or he thought she did. He was more worried about why she'd had to steal food. The thought of her not having enough to eat pained him. "I think you're mistaken, but I'm going to check on her. Does she still have a job?"

Sierra half-smiled. "Of course. I just want to talk to her so we can straighten this out."

Vadim nodded at her and Hayden, then hurried from the kitchen. He made his way through the closed restaurant, the lobby of the hotel and got caught in a rush of people by the valet parking outside. He knew Angel must have come this way.

She always took the same bus home every night. A quick glance at his watch told him he might miss her, spurring him into moving faster. Not bothering to be polite, he plowed his way through the thickening crowd of partiers and gamblers making their way into the hotel and casino. The place was busy most of the day but at ten o'clock at night it was always the busiest. Ignoring a few protests, he elbowed his way around people and bounded between the idling cars waiting to be parked by the dozens of working valet drivers.

As he raced down the exit to the main road, he spotted Angel's normal bus pulling away from the curb—and saw that familiar flash of red hair as she sat at a window seat. Biting back a curse, he turned and headed back the way he'd come. He knew where she lived and even though he knew it would annoy her, he was going to see her tonight.

For some reason she always refused to let him drive her home after work, even though he offered practically every night. She didn't live in a safe neighborhood and he was almost certain she was embarrassed by her place of residence. He'd been there before to check on her, but he'd never told her, knowing it would bother her. Now he didn't care if she got annoyed with him.

If she knew where he'd grown up, she'd have nothing to be embarrassed about.

Tonight he'd planned to ask her on an unofficial date after she got off work. Hayden had said that they could join him and Sierra at one of the bars for drinks. Vadim sucked with women and relationships, but Hayden had told him to stop being a pussy and just ask her out. So he'd planned to do just that, but under the guise of friendship, so if she rejected him, things between them wouldn't be strained afterward.

He didn't have many friends, but he valued his relationship with Angel. She was kind and giving and one of the few women who didn't look at him like he was an un-caged tiger. And he planned to find out why the hell she needed to steal food. Because whatever she needed, he would give to her.

CHAPTER TWO

Angel stared blindly out the window of the bus as she neared her stop. Because of the fluorescent lights all she really saw was her reflection. And right now she didn't want to look at herself. Still reeling from that entire embarrassing situation where a woman she respected now probably thought the worst of her, and a man she liked way too much... Ugh, Angel mentally shook herself. She didn't have time to worry about stuff like that. She needed to get home and check on her neighbor's kids.

The woman she only knew as Dee left her fourteen year old boy and six year old girl alone more often than not because she was hooking up with losers or scoring drugs. Mark, the boy, hadn't told Angel that directly, but he'd alluded to it in so many words. And it broke Angel's heart. He'd also warned her not to call social services—and she'd been planning to—because he'd said they'd end up in a worse situation than at home. The fear in his eyes when he'd told her had been real too, so she'd listened. She understood that he didn't want to be separated from his sister or dumped somewhere even worse.

Sometimes the devil you knew was better than the alternative.

Angel knew they weren't her responsibility, but she didn't care. She couldn't turn her back on two innocent kids in need. So she'd been looking after them when she wasn't working, buying them food and making sure they got to the bus in time for school. It had been exhausting and she knew she should probably ask someone for help, but she hadn't known who to turn to. And she'd been doing fine balancing everything—until someone broke into her place and took most of the cash she'd saved. She couldn't believe they'd found it. She'd hidden it in a box of baking soda in her refrigerator, making sure it was buried in the white powder. Hadn't seemed to matter because whatever jerk had robbed her had found it.

As the bus shuddered to a halt, she jumped up and called out that it was her stop, knowing from experience that this particular driver would keep going if she didn't stand within five seconds. Hating that she didn't have any food for the kids, she hurried off the bus. Luckily the stop was right in front of her apartment complex. Which wasn't exactly in the best part of town, but it wasn't terrible either. She reached into her jacket pocket and pulled out her keys and her pepper spray. Holding each in one hand, she made her way to the second building down. Her apartment was on the second floor.

She could hear and see a couple teenagers who sometimes like to harass her on one end of the long balcony walkway, so she used the stairs on the opposite side before heading to Dee's place. Shivering against the cold January air, she knocked once and was surprised when the door swung open.

"Hello?" she called softly. It was late and she didn't want to wake the kids, but if their mom wasn't here she wanted to make sure they were okay. Dee had never seemed to mind Angel's presence; she'd almost appeared to feel guilty that Angel was helping out her kids. But at least she'd never stopped Angel from giving them food.

When no one answered, she stepped farther inside. Frowning when she didn't see any of Chloe's toys scattered in the hallway, she shut the door behind her and clutched her pepper spray tight. "Mark? Dee?"

"They're gone," a familiar male voice called out. Mr. Botkin, her landlord, peered around the corner at the end of the hallway and smiled warmly at her. He was Russian, like Vadim, and had taught her a few words, which she'd tried to impress Vadim with.

Vadim had simply smiled at her attempts to converse with him, amused. And she loved making him smile. She shook herself, not needing to think about the sexy Russian now. "What happened?" she asked, hurrying down the short, tiled hallway to find him already repainting the living room. Plastic sheets covered the hardwood floors of the empty room.

Even though this place wasn't in the greatest part of town, Mr. Botkin took great care to keep up the interiors of the apartments.

"They left this afternoon," he said. "The boy called his grandparents and told them what was going on with their mother. They had no clue about their daughter and came with a moving truck. They give her…" He paused and she knew he was trying to figure out the right word. "An ultimatum. She go to rehab, they take the kids while she does." He patted his coveralls almost absently then reached into the pocket and pulled out a small envelope. "This is from the boy for you."

Angel was speechless as she took the card. Clearing her throat, she found her voice. "They just left? Did the grandparents seem nice? How were the kids?"

Mr. Botkin nodded. "I think they're good people. They were worried over the kids. The boy, he's smart and protective, he'll watch out for his sister."

Angel nodded, knowing that much was true. At fourteen Mark was already taller than her five feet six and was vigilant about looking after Chloe. She tore into the envelope and quickly scanned the card, fighting back tears as she read. Mark told her that he'd found his grandparents contact info and called them himself. He'd also thanked Angel for everything she'd done and left a contact number for her to check up on him. God, he was such a man, so responsible. She swiped at her eyes. "Thanks, Mr. Botkin."

He nodded, then motioned toward the hallway. "Let me walk you to your door. I don't like those punks loitering around here lately."

She wasn't going to argue. Even though Mr. Botkin was older, she knew he carried at least one gun on him. Once she was safely inside her apartment, she pulled her cell phone out of her purse and texted Mark as she walked down the hallway to her kitchen. It was late and she wasn't sure when they'd left or if he'd be awake so she didn't call.

He responded moments later. *G-parents nice, mom embarrassed by where we ended up but it's all good now. Chloe's happy she has her own room. I'll call u 2morrow with deets. Thank you for everything Angel. I know what a pain it was to watch out for us.*

Smiling even though her chest ached at how grown up he sounded, she texted back. *It was never a pain. I love you guys. Keep in touch no matter what but if you have a problem with anyone let me know.*

I will but I don't think they're freaks or anything. Mom's okay leaving us w/ them while she's in rehab and she wouldn't if they were weirdos.

And there was the fourteen year old shining through. Angel shook her head as she shot off a quick goodnight response. When she reached her small kitchen she set her purse on the counter nearest the refrigerator and opened the door even though she didn't have much in there except some fresh fruit. Almost on cue her stomach growled so she grabbed an apple. Biting into it, she started unbuttoning her Oxford-style black shirt as she headed to her bedroom. Right now all she wanted was a hot shower and to crash. She'd worry about her lack of a job tomorrow. She wasn't even sure if she wanted to stay in Vegas anymore. She'd been here too long as it was and the longer she stayed, the better chance he had of finding her.

Yeah, she definitely didn't want to think about *that* tonight. As she rounded the corner of the built-in counter in her kitchen she came face to face with Vadim striding in from her living room. His movements were impossibly silent.

And he looked pissed.

On instinct she jumped, but stopped herself before she stepped back. Her breath caught in her throat as she stared at him, apple between her teeth and the front of her shirt completely gaping open. Stunned, she pulled the apple from her mouth. "What are you... How the hell did you get into my apartment?" she shouted, feeling suddenly vulnerable. Not because she thought Vadim would hurt her but because she'd just replaced her locks and added extra alarms to her windows. She didn't feel very safe anymore.

His jaw clenched once, his pale blue eyes seeming almost darker in her dim apartment. She'd never thought of him as intimidating but at six feet tall, she was suddenly aware of how much bigger he was than her. He rubbed a hand over his short blond hair in agitation. "Why didn't you tell me you needed food?"

"I don't. And don't change the subject. Why are you here and how did you get in? And how did you even know which apartment is mine?"

He took a step closer, his gaze briefly flicking down to her open shirt and her face burned even hotter. Hell, what was she thinking? She set the apple on the counter and wrenched her top together. She was just wearing a plain utilitarian white bra. She was more embarrassed about him seeing her in something so boring than flashing him skin. She'd had plenty of fantasies involving him and in all of them, the first time he saw her in any state of undress she was wearing lace and silk. Not a cotton bra she'd snagged in the dollar bin at a discount store. She hurriedly buttoned her shirt, her fingers shaking.

"Your address is in your employee file."

"Which you shouldn't have access to," she snapped, nerves and embarrassment threading through her. Though she wasn't surprised he did. The man was a computer genius from what she'd heard. He didn't talk much about his work to her, just in generalities, but she'd picked up enough from other employees to guess that he was gifted when it came to security measures. They were friends but she was pretty sure he'd signed a non-disclosure agreement or something since he didn't talk about what he did.

He made a scoffing sound, his expression almost arrogant. Then he frowned again and took another small step closer so that there was only a foot separating them. "You should have come to me. I would have helped you. And I still will. You still have a job. Sierra doesn't want to fire you." He lifted his hand a fraction, as if he would touch her, then dropped it back to his side.

Relief slid through her that she still had a job. Angel was going to get back to how the heck he broke into her place, but for now, she motioned behind him in the direction of the living room. With him this close, his subtle spicy scent teasing her, it was hard to think straight. She needed some distance between them if she wanted to talk in coherent sentences.

His jaw clenched again, but he nodded and turned toward the small room. It had come pre-furnished and now she was thankful she'd bought slip covers to hide the hideous seventies-style flower pattern on the couches. When she'd bought them she'd felt guilty for spending money on something frivolous but those colors had just been too ugly to look at day in and day out. The light cream color slip covers were much easier on the eyes. The rest of the room was decorated in plain earth tones, which was fine with her.

"Would you like something to drink?" she asked as he perched on the edge of the loveseat. The polite question was ridiculous considering he'd broken into her place, but manners had been drilled into her at a young age. It was that Southern upbringing.

He was tense, his entire body coiled and ready to pounce. For the first time she understood why some of the other waitresses were nervous around him. Not that she was afraid of him, but she could see that deadly edge now. It was jarring to her senses to see him this way. With her he'd always been so sweet and gentle.

"No. I want to talk. Now sit," he said gruffly.

She was so surprised by the command in his voice that she did. As soon as her butt hit the couch though, she wanted to smack herself for doing it. Friend or not, the man had broken into her home and she wanted to know how and why. "Vadim—"

"I came in the front door. Picked the lock in less than fifteen seconds. It's a piece of crap," he said, guessing her train of thought.

"I just replaced it." She'd installed it herself.

His lips pulled into a thin line, his expression disapproving. "It's crap. And the reason I'm here should be obvious. I want to help."

Some of her steam faded at that. "You could have called."

"And you would have ignored me. I eliminated that problem before it happened." His voice was so matter-of-fact and it sounded just like him. He liked to look at problems from every angle.

Considering how embarrassed she'd been at the restaurant, he was right to have guessed she'd have ignored a call from him. Still, it annoyed her that he'd broken into her place. But she could put that on the backburner.

"Now tell me why you were taking food. Are you not making enough money?" he asked in that blunt way of his. Normally she appreciated it but now she just wanted to die of embarrassment.

"It wasn't for me. My neighbor has two kids and she wasn't taking care of them so I've been buying food for them. And I've been doing fine. More than fine actually." She'd managed to save a couple thousand with the tips she'd been bringing in even though she'd been feeding Mark and Chloe. She'd almost felt like it was karma rewarding her. The more she helped them the better she'd done at work. Of course that theory had been shot to hell when she'd been robbed. "But then I was robbed and—"

"What?" He shifted slightly, his hands clenching the edges of her couch so tightly they turned white.

She stared at his knuckles and long fingers and for a brief moment wondered what it would feel like to have those hands stroking over her breasts, cupping her face and...other parts. She quickly shook herself. Now was not the time to indulge in that particular fantasy. "Yeah, couple weeks ago. They took my TV and the cash I had hidden. Honestly, I've been doing great. It was just a setback. I know I should have just asked Sierra for the food, but I was embarrassed. She gets so many sob stories from the employees and me telling her I needed to feed two kids sounded fake. Even if it is true." And Angel had been embarrassed. Sierra was so young and had her whole life together. Angel hadn't even finished college and thanks to circumstances, she was on the run and living from paycheck to paycheck.

"Fuck that. You should have told *me* you needed help." The possessive note in his voice took her off guard. She wondered if maybe she'd imagined it. Either way it did strange things to her insides.

Her cheeks burned again as she swallowed hard. She didn't want Vadim's freaking charity. But she couldn't tell him that—it would make things worse. "I know. I just..." she shrugged, not knowing how to continue. "Sierra really doesn't want to fire me?"

"No, which you would have known if you'd stuck around."

Another burst of relief slid through her. Sure it would be awkward and embarrassing to see Sierra that first time but with her cash savings gone, the thought of leaving Vegas had been scary without a backup fund. And the truth was, she didn't want to leave Vadim, even though she knew that was stupid. He saw her as a friend and nothing more. He'd made that perfectly clear. She'd dropped enough hints that she would be interested in more back when they'd first met and started hanging out, but he'd friend-zoned her months ago. Which was probably just as well. She didn't have time for any entanglements. "Well it gave you a chance to show off your B and E skills."

His lips twitched slightly, the closest he ever came to a smile. "Did you report your robbery to the police?"

She shook her head. No way was she putting her name in the system more than absolutely necessary.

He seemed angered by that, but didn't respond. "Why isn't your money in a bank?"

Angel glanced at a spot over his shoulder and bit her tongue. She wasn't going to tell him anything about her past. Setting her jaw, she waited for him to continue. If he expected a response, he'd be waiting a long time.

Finally Vadim sighed and scrubbed a hand over his face. "I need a favor. It's why I came to see you earlier tonight."

Her eyebrows rose. "You need a favor from me?"

He nodded, his expression still so unreadable. Something that irritated her about him. "I'm going out of town for a few days for work and my house sitter cancelled at the last minute." He let out an annoyed sounding word in Russian. "I don't like to kennel Charlie and I wanted to ask you to house sit. It won't be long and you can use my car while I'm gone so you won't have to worry about learning a new bus schedule."

Her first instinct was to say no, but she didn't have a reason to deny him.

"You're one of the only people I'd trust to stay at my place." The sincerity in his words took her off guard and touched her.

"Even after I just stole from the Cloud?" she asked wryly. What everyone who worked at the Serafina called Cloud 9.

His lips pulled into a thin line again. "For kids. Which..." He trailed off frowning.

"What?"

"Should I go out and get food for them or is it too late?"

In that moment Angel was pretty sure she had more than just a crush on Vadim but she ruthlessly shoved all her emotions back into a tiny box, locked it, then threw that key in the deepest, darkest ocean of her heart. Swallowing back the strange tightening in her throat, she shook her head. "No, they're staying with their grandparents now. I just found out from my landlord when I stopped by their place. I hope everything's going to be okay for them now. But thank you for asking."

His shoulders relaxed as he stood. "Okay, good. Then it's settled. You'll stay at my place."

She frowned at him. "I never agreed to that."

"We both know you're going to. You're too nice to say no and Charlie loves your belly rubs. And if you say no, sweet Charlie will be put in a kennel and she gets anxiety if she doesn't get to sleep in her own bed."

She gritted her teeth to keep from smiling. His dog's name was Charlotte, Charlie for short. He brought her to work sometimes and Angel had fallen in love with the beautiful dog. The German Shepherd was better behaved than most humans. The way she listened to Vadim's commands was impressive. And she was incredibly adorable. "You're a master manipulator."

His shoulders lifted casually, but the glint in his pale eyes set her off balance. She felt like something had shifted between them but wasn't sure what.

"So when do you need me?" She really wished he needed her on an entirely different level than dog sitting.

"Tonight."

Her eyes widened. "You weren't kidding about last minute."

"I know and I'm sorry for asking like this. I leave in the morning, so you should stay with me tonight. It'll be good for Charlie to see you sleeping in the guest room."

Angel would rather sleep in *his* bedroom, but knew that would never happen so she ignored what that thought did to her traitorous body. Or she tried to, but her nipples tingled as she imagined what it would be like to be stretched out naked under Vadim's lean, powerful body. When she realized she'd been staring, she nodded and glanced away. "I'll go pack a bag then. Should I shower here or would it be easier if I did at your place?"

For the briefest moment, his eyes went molten—which just confused her. But then his expression went completely blank as he nodded. "My place is fine."

That hungry, needy sensation she experienced every time she was around Vadim welled up inside her as she hurried back to her small bedroom. Vadim had looked almost turned on, affected by her. *Her*. But that couldn't be right. Could it? He'd never looked at her like that before, but...she didn't think she'd imagined that look in his eyes. Or hell, maybe it was just wishful thinking.

At least they wouldn't be sharing a roof. Well, tonight they would be, but he'd be leaving in the morning. Then when he returned, she'd go back to her apartment. Which was good, because she was pretty sure she couldn't handle sharing a living space with him without making it painfully obvious how attracted she was to him. She didn't want to suffer rejection from him on top of everything else.

CHAPTER THREE

Vadim leaned against the doorway of Angel's bedroom, watching her pack a bag. His small lie didn't make him feel an ounce of guilt. He was going out of town, but only for one night. And as soon as they reached his home he'd text his friend, letting him know it would be unnecessary to watch Charlie.

While Angel was out of her place, he planned to set things into motion so that she wouldn't be coming back here. No, she could stay with him until he found her a decent apartment. It was underhanded, but he didn't care. He constantly worried about her living there and after seeing just how easy it was to break into her home, he couldn't stand it any longer. The woman brought out his protective instincts to the point where he couldn't think straight sometimes. He'd never felt like that about anyone and it was jarring. Sometimes he wondered if he got a taste of her if it would slake the need he always seemed to have for her.

"You don't have to stand guard," she muttered as she opened the top drawer of the only dresser in the small room. "I'm not going anywhere."

"Maybe I just want a peek at your panties too." His teasing words surprised him.

She looked up, those dark green and brown hazel eyes wide with shock. Then her full lips curved, her megawatt smile like a punch to his chest. "I always knew you were a pervert." Laughing, clearly not believing he was serious, she went back to digging through her drawer. Surprising him, she pulled out a skimpy green thong and waved it once. "Happy now?" Laughing to herself, she shoved it into her bag before heading to her closet.

He was glad she wasn't paying attention to him as she grabbed her clothes because he'd forgotten how to breathe. The thought of Angel in a thong—or any state of undress—was enough to give him a heart attack. They'd been friends for almost five months and up until recently he'd been sure she'd had no sexual interest in him. Until Hayden had told him he was a dumbass and to start paying attention more.

Vadim was good with computers and a lot of things, but not women. Well, not women like Angel. She was sweet, giving and incredibly beautiful. And she always saw the best in people. That he didn't envy, but he still liked it about her. Who was he kidding? He liked everything about her, from the way her eyes crinkled at the corners when she laughed to—

"Vadim?"

He blinked, realizing she was talking to him as he stared off into space like an idiot. "Yeah?"

She stood near the edge of her bed, her shiny red hair still pulled into a ponytail as she fingered the soft grips of her bag. She looked even younger than normal, reminding him of their ten year age difference. Another reason he'd held off on making a move. "I'm ready if you are."

He nodded once, not trusting his voice as he strode over and grabbed her bag. She started to protest but he took it anyway. It wasn't much, but he wanted to take care of her any way he could. Starting now he planned to do just that. Even if he had to be underhanded about it. She was independent, something he liked, but she was too stubborn about asking for help when she needed it. Clearly, or she would have told him about her neighbor's kids.

Vadim exited the apartment first, placing himself in front of her in case there was a threat. He doubted there would be, but he didn't like the looks of the teenagers hanging out near her place. While she locked the door behind her, he saw her landlord exiting her neighbor's apartment carrying a paint can. Late to be working but Vadim understood that a man in his position was on call 24/7.

Vadim nodded once at the man he'd met before—without Angel's knowledge.

Mr. Botkin was in his mid-fifties, in shape, and right now he looked wary as he eyed Vadim. His expression softened though when Angel looked up from her door.

"Hi, Mr. Botkin. You done for the night?" she asked.

He nodded, flicking another glance at Vadim. "Yes. Is everything okay?"

Angel nodded, then glanced at Vadim before looking back at her landlord. "I'm just house sitting for my friend. This is Vadim, by the way. He's my friend, the one I told you about who's Russian."

Vadim was beyond surprised she'd mentioned him, but smiled politely at Mr. Botkin, as if he'd never met him before. In Russian he told the man he'd be visiting the day after tomorrow about some business so to expect him.

The older man's eyebrows rose in clear surprise, but he just nodded. Then in English he said, "Nice to meet you."

Angel playfully poked him in the arm as they headed down the stairs. "You're going to teach me more Russian. Mr. Botkin said I was pretty good."

Vadim hid a smile. Her attempts had been awful, her sweet, normally very light Southern accent seeming to get stronger every time she tried to speak the first language he'd learned. He might have been born in the United States, but his mother had been a Russian immigrant and she'd barely spoken any English. He'd learned

English from a neighbor and then in school, but he'd never lost his mother's language. And he'd picked up a couple more languages over the years. "I'll teach you whatever you want." All the better if he got to spend more time with her.

When they reached the bottom of the stairs, he placed himself in front of her again. "Stay behind me," he murmured as they headed to the end of the sidewalk. He'd had to park in front of another building because there hadn't been space in front of hers.

"Vadim, is that really necessary? I walk through here all the time." She sounded annoyed.

He grunted, not responding because he knew he'd say something he might regret. As they reached the end of the sidewalk, he glanced to the left, down the next one. Two men loitered next to the driver's side of his car. Something he'd been concerned about. Without turning around, he reached back and handed her bag to her. "Stay here."

She made a frustrated sound, but took it. He walked quickly down the sidewalk, immediately making eye contact with the taller of the two. They were in their late teens or early twenties, both with dark brown hair and brown eyes. Possibly related. Not that he cared. "Can I help you with something?" he asked, stepping off the sidewalk and crowding right into their space.

The slightly shorter one moved back a step, but the taller one stayed where he was—then had the audacity to lean against the door. "Nice ride," he said as he lifted up the front of his shirt to reveal a silver revolver.

It was a good piece. Too bad the shithead was about to lose it. The instant display of the man's weapon was all the provocation Vadim needed to eliminate these two threats to Angel. He had two weapons strapped to himself, as he always did, but he didn't bother with either of them. Without warning he struck out, punching the taller man in the throat with a force just shy of being a killing blow. Before the man could even think about reacting Vadim punched him in the solar plexus, in the nose, then slammed his boot into the man's balls for good measure. Out of the corner of his eye, he saw the shorter man scrambling for his weapon, but it was too late.

Gasping and wheezing, the taller man fell against the side of Vadim's car. As he slid down, Vadim pulled the man's weapon free and aimed it at the other man's head before shorty could draw his own weapon tucked stupidly down the front of his pants. Would serve him right if he shot his own balls off.

"Go for it and see what happens," Vadim said calmly, kicking the other man in the stomach as he slid to the ground.

Out of the corner of his eye he watched the fallen man continue to struggle for breath as he curled into a tight ball. Right now his brain was confused, trying to come to terms with the pain and rapid assault his body had just received. In Vadim's experience it would take the man roughly thirty seconds to regain some of his bearings. But he planned to be long gone before then.

The standing man raised his hands in the air, leaving his weapon still tucked away. "Man, I don't want any trouble."

"Good. Neither do I. Angel," he called out. "Get in the car." With his free hand he reached into his pants pocket and pressed his keyfob, unlocking the doors. Then he stepped over the still wheezing man, pressed the weapon to the standing man's chest as he took the guy's revolver. He'd get rid of these, but he wasn't leaving them behind.

"Back up, over there. Keep your hands in the air." As Vadim motioned to another row of parked cars on the opposite side of the street he heard the passenger door open then close. Keeping his gaze on the man walking backwards, he reached over and opened his door then slid behind the wheel. Without having to insert the key, he pressed the engine button and quickly reversed before tearing out of the complex. In the rearview mirror the standing man raced to his friend's side but he wasn't even paying attention to Vadim's exit. Good. Meant he wasn't concerned with his license plate. Not that it would do him any good if he tried to track him down with it.

"What the hell was that?" Angel asked as Vadim put the weapons in the back seat.

He glanced over at her. "They had weapons and weren't afraid to use them. The guy I punched showed me his gun immediately, telling me he had no problem escalating into violence very quickly."

She blinked at him, wide-eyed and not full of fear exactly, but she looked wary. He turned away, not wanting to see fear or anything akin to it in her expression. Ever. And especially not directed at him.

"You didn't just punch him. You massacred him and made it look as if you'd barely done anything. That was insanely awesome. I've never seen anyone move so fast. You were like…a ninja. Where did you learn all that?" The awe in her voice surprised him.

He shot her another glance before pulling out onto the main road. She didn't seem wary now, just maybe a little overwhelmed. "The Marines."

"Well, you're officially a badass. No wonder—" She abruptly cut herself off before shifting uncomfortably against the plush leather seat.

"No wonder what?"

"Nothing. Thanks for what you did. I didn't realize that guy, well both of them, had freaking guns." She turned around in her seat to look at them, then looked forward again. "That was crazy," she muttered, almost to herself.

Vadim knew he should let go of whatever she'd been about to say, but he couldn't. "What did you stop yourself from saying before?" he asked as he pulled up to a stoplight.

She bit her bottom lip. "I don't want to hurt your feelings."

"Say it."

"I was just going to say no wonder some of the girls—and guys—at the restaurant are a little afraid of you." Her teeth pressed into her bottom lip even harder as she watched him, clearly concerned for his feelings. Which wasn't exactly surprising. She was always looking out for anyone, not just him. It still touched him that she cared.

Half-smiling, he turned back to the road. "I already know they're afraid of me." Frowning, he looked at her again as another thought occurred to him. Even though their wariness annoyed him, he didn't truly give a shit what anyone thought of him—but Angel's opinion mattered. "Does this change how you feel about me?"

"Uh, yeah. Now that I know what a badass you are I'm never going to piss you off," she said laughingly, the sound pure music rolling over him.

The tension that had started to build inside him immediately dissipated. As long as she didn't look at him differently, he was fine.

Glancing at his GPS, he frowned as he steered his rental car into the apartment complex. He was following the information his private investigator had given him, but this didn't seem like the type of place where Angel would be living. Still…he looked over at the thick manila file he had on Angel, ready to scan his notes again, but decided against it.

He had all the information memorized and this was definitely the correct address. The woman had proven more resourceful than he'd given her credit for when she'd run from him. She didn't have a bank account in her name, didn't use any credit cards and as far as his investigator could find, she wasn't using her social security number for work anywhere. She also hadn't been in contact with any of her friends since she'd gone on the run. Had even deleted all her social media accounts.

It was as if she'd literally vanished into thin air. But he knew that wasn't the case and his very expensive investigator finally had a lead on her place of residence.

Slowly cruising by the apartment building that was supposed to be hers, he was surprised by the level of activity this late at night. The place was older, set up almost like a motel with visibility of the front doors from the parking lot. An older man stepped out of the apartment next to hers carrying a bucket in one hand and a folded up plastic sheet in the other. He set the supplies next to a paint can before returning inside the apartment, but he left the door open. On the other end of the upstairs balcony three teenagers were smoking cigarettes and talking.

Since there was a parking spot open, he slid into the space. They didn't appear to be marked for guests or residents, but he wouldn't be staying long anyway.

Taking a gamble that the man with the plastic sheet was in maintenance, he pulled a few bills from the center console and shoved them in his jacket pocket as he exited the vehicle. Instead of his normal suit he was wearing jeans, a plain T-shirt, a nondescript windbreaker and a ball cap. Nothing to make him memorable. It was one of the reasons he'd rented a standard four-door car with no bells and whistles. Just a plain, domestic car that wouldn't stand out anywhere.

Scanning his surroundings as he made his way up the stairs, he breathed a sigh of relief when the older man exited the apartment again, this time locking the door behind him. He didn't want to wait around to talk to this guy, didn't like being in this neighborhood.

He smiled as he approached the older man. "Hi, you got a second?"

The man just watched him, his body tensing.

So he hung back a few feet, not wanting to crowd the maintenance guy. "I'm just looking for someone." He pointed to the apartment door behind him, the one that should be Angel's. "My friend's sister has gone missing and we're just trying to find her." He had a picture of her, but didn't pull it out yet. "She's got red hair, dark green eyes, about this tall, really cute looking in that girl-next-door way." He held up a hand to measure her height and kept his smile friendly. When the guy didn't respond, he reached into his pocket, figuring he wanted money.

Everyone did. It was how the world worked. You could buy any damn thing you wanted with the right amount of cash.

He froze when the man spoke, his words harsh and guttural. In another language. He watched the older man who started talking to him in rapid-fire…was that Russian?

When the man took a breath, he said, "I don't understand."

Shrugging, the man shoved the plastic sheet into the bucket, then picked it and the paint can up before striding past him, muttering under his breath in the same language.

He stood there for a moment, debating his options. He could just knock on her door and surprise the hell out of her. It wouldn't be hard to take her off guard. Just punch her in the face and barrel his way into her apartment. If she even lived here. But that left open too many variables.

When he realized the teenagers had stopped talking and were watching him curiously, he turned and headed back to his car. That was exactly the variable he didn't want to deal with. Witnesses.

He'd been patient for two years, he could wait another night before he started scoping out her place. First he'd figure out if Angel even lived here. Then he'd learn her schedule, terrorize her like she deserved, then destroy her. He was going to make her regret the day she'd ever betrayed and humiliated him.

CHAPTER FOUR

Angel couldn't believe how gorgeous Vadim's home was. Huge, in the desert with no neighbors for miles, it was all glass, stone and high ceilings with exposed beams. It was an architectural masterpiece as far as she was concerned. That aside, it was a little cold, with very few personal pictures. Although she had seen photographs on a small table behind his couch of him wearing some kind of military fatigues with his arm wrapped around another man's shoulders. They were both sort-of smiling. But nothing full-on because Vadim just didn't do that. Apparently not even for pictures.

She knew he'd been in the Marines for twelve years before coming to work for Wyatt. But he'd always been so cryptic about what he'd done while in the Marines and why he'd left. The man was such a mystery. A very sexy one she wanted to figure out. Even if she knew she'd get hurt since she'd be leaving Vegas eventually, something she hated thinking about.

Constantly moving was wearing on her in ways she hadn't counted on. She missed all her friends from back home, friends she hadn't talked to in two freaking years because the moment she reached out to any of them, they could become a target. Or it would give *him* a way to find her.

Lord, why was she even thinking about that right now? Shaking her head, she quickly undressed, stripping out of her standard work uniform of a fitted black button-down shirt, black slacks and black heels. She thought the heels were stupid for waitresses to wear, but it was part of the image, even if they did kill her feet. She was allowed to wear a black skirt, but she never did.

Setting her clothes on the shiny marble countertop of the luxurious guest bathroom, she made her way to the huge stone enclosure of the clearly custom-made shower. It was done all in stone—or maybe tile that looked like sandstone—but there were little sparkly pieces of glass intermixed throughout that made the whole space seem to shimmer.

The shower itself was heaven, the powerful jets massaging her shoulders and back in a way she hadn't realized she'd needed. And Vadim had given her new shower gel, shampoo and conditioner. Really expensive stuff too. Not that she was surprised after seeing this house and knowing him for five months. Whatever he did for his billionaire boss, he was very well compensated.

As she turned to face the jets, the water cascading over her breasts, stomach and legs, she tried not to remember how incredibly hot it had been to watch Vadim disarm those two men. She hadn't even realized something like that would turn her on but apparently she was a freak because it had. Way too much.

He hadn't talked much on the way over to his place, which was fine with her. She'd been so caught up in her own thoughts. Namely about him. And what it would feel like to have those very capable hands sliding all over her body, cupping her mound...She shuddered as she slid a finger over her clit, barely brushing over it with her middle finger.

But she pulled back, stopping herself because it felt wrong. Even though she knew it absolutely wasn't. But she felt weird fantasizing about a man who was her friend, a man whose house she was currently staying at. Even if she'd thought about him before while stroking herself, she was in his house now.

Turning the water a few degrees cooler, she quickly finished washing. After blow drying most of the dampness out of her hair, she pulled the green thong out of her bag and put it on. She couldn't believe she'd actually shown it to Vadim. Afterward she'd felt ridiculous and hadn't been able to meet his gaze. She slid on a warm pair of black fleece pajama pants then slipped on the thick robe Vadim had left for her and cinched it tightly around her waist. It was too big and too long and incredibly comfortable. But it was so soft and thick she didn't bother with a top.

And it smelled like him a little. Something she shouldn't care about. Oh, but she did. Way too much. Shaking those thoughts free once again, she set out to find him.

The layout of the house was simple. The three bedrooms were on the east side and the central living room linked the kitchen, dining room and library—he had a library!—on the other side. There were a couple other shut doors that she wondered about, but figured one was probably his office.

She found Vadim in the oversized kitchen at the sink with his back to her—shirtless. Sure the house was warm enough, but did he have to walk around without a shirt? All she could see was his broad, muscular back, but he'd turn around soon enough and she'd get to see what she'd been fantasizing about for months.

"How was your shower?" Vadim asked without turning around.

She nearly jumped, impressed that he'd even heard her, but she stepped farther into the room, the tile surprisingly warm beneath her feet. "Wonderful, thanks. I can't remember the last time I had a shower that amazing. The water pressure…" She trailed off as he turned, her gaze traveling down the length of his lean, muscular, perfectly cut body.

A computer geek who was ripped. Though that word seemed too weak to describe him as she hungrily devoured every dip and ridge of the muscles along his eight pack. It dipped into a V below the waistband of those loose cotton pants and all she could do was stare for a moment, imagining what was underneath there. He also had a few scars that surprised her. They were long, jagged and clearly old given the white hue of them against his lightly tanned skin.

At the sound of Vadim clearing his throat, she snapped her gaze to his guiltily. That was when she realized he had a mug in his hand. He held it out to her. "I made you hot tea. Earl Grey."

Her favorite. "You made me tea?" she asked, sounding surprisingly accusing. Why did this insanely attractive man—her *friend*, she reminded herself for the tenth time that night—have to be so damn thoughtful? So sexy?

He faltered and she wanted to kick herself. "I thought you liked it."

"Thank you. And I do, a lot." Oh my god, she sounded like an imbecile. Her gaze kept straying back to the beauty of his body and she felt like the biggest asshole. Vadim was her friend, she couldn't ogle him like...like...She blinked again as her brain short-circuited and somehow found the strength to meet his gaze while reaching for the cup. There was no hiding the flush on her face now. Absolutely no way. She couldn't stop staring at his body and now he knew what a pervert *she* was.

"Is there something wrong with the water pressure at your place?" he asked as he handed her the simple brown mug with light tendrils of steam rolling off the top.

"What...oh, no, it's fine. But your guest bathroom shower is amazing." It was definitely spa quality and she'd loved the different showerhead options. One directly above and one on the wall. But she didn't want to stand around talking about his freaking shower. Because it made her think about being naked and how she'd almost stroked herself to orgasm not long ago.

He started to respond when a light scratching at his kitchen door made them both look. Vadim smiled. "That would be Charlie."

Angel put the mug down on the long rectangular island top as Vadim opened the door. A moment later, his German Shepherd trotted in. As he shut the door behind her, the dog stopped in her tracks, watching Angel carefully for all of one second. Then she bounded over to Angel, before whining softly and falling to the floor where she rolled onto her back, revealing her belly.

Vadim snorted. "She's shameless."

Grinning, Angel bent down and rubbed Charlie's belly. "She can be as shameless as she wants. I wish you brought her to the hotel more often." She paused in rubbing as she looked up at Vadim. "So what's the deal with her schedule? I don't work tomorrow." Even though she still needed to call Sierra and apologize. Again. "So should I take her for walks or do you have a schedule you like to keep her to? I know you like to take her to the park sometimes." She'd met Vadim and Charlie at a park near the casino on multiple occasions. Vadim would try to get Charlie to exercise but she mainly flopped on her belly and soaked up the sun.

Vadim snorted again and motioned to the pantry door. He opened it and pointed inside. "You don't have to worry about the park. There's plenty of room around here. She's spoiled and does whatever she wants all day long. She prefers to stay inside and she's got a doggy door I leave open when I'm at work. However, I lock it at night. She goes outside when she has to. All you have to do is fill up her bowl of food in the morning and then again in the afternoon. She eats when she's hungry. Her water is set for the next couple days, but check on it. And she'll try to convince you that she's allowed to have as many treats as she wants." He pointed to a bag filled with green bones. "She's not, but…I indulge her sometimes."

Angel grinned at Vadim. "You're such a softie," she murmured.

To her surprise his ears flushed red. "Yeah well, don't tell anyone. As far as sleeping, she usually sleeps on her bed, which is in my room. But she might want to stay close to you at night. She likes human contact. If you're comfortable with that, you can bring her bed in with you and she'll push it wherever she wants to sleep."

"Okay. Sounds good. Oh, what about furniture? Is she allowed on it?" Angel didn't think so because all of his stuff was leather and in pristine condition, but she wanted to make sure.

"She has a beanbag in the living room that's hers," he said as he pulled one of the green bones from the plastic baggie.

Angel turned from the pantry doorway to find Charlie sitting there patiently and quietly. Dang, the dog was as stealthy as her master. She hadn't even heard Charlie move. The second Vadim gave her the bone, she ran off, this time making plenty of noise as she bounded from the room.

Vadim chuckled lightly. "She hides her treats under her beanbag." He cleared his throat almost nervously as he stepped out and shut the door. "You've got my cell number and I'll leave the name and number of my hotel on the kitchen counter when I leave in the morning. I've got a taxi service coming to get me at the crack of dawn, so I'll leave my keys on the counter too. Use my car for work or whatever you need. It's yours while I'm gone. And the refrigerator is stocked and you're welcome to everything in it."

She shifted uncomfortably, but nodded. She didn't know much about vehicles, but she knew enough that his Mercedes S-Class was pricey and one of the newer models. "Okay, but I don't work the next two days so unless you're gone longer than that I probably won't drive anywhere."

He nodded, watching her for a long moment with those unreadable pale eyes. Feeling unsettled, she shoved her hands in the pockets of the robe.

Taking her by surprise, he reached out and lightly fingered the lapel of the thick robe. On instinct, she stepped closer to him, not wanting any distance between them. Then he froze and she realized from his expression that he'd surprised himself too. But he didn't back up like she expected. Her heart rate kicked up a notch being this close to him.

His next words nearly made her knees buckle. "You look good in my robe."

His? She was wearing his robe? Okay, she might not be able to read the sexy Russian all the time, but the fact that he'd given her his robe to wear had to mean something. Didn't it? Taking a chance, she reached out and traced one finger along a particularly ugly scar that ran from the bottom of his neck across one of his pecs.

He shuddered at her light touch, but didn't attempt to move. No, his grip tightened on her robe. He wasn't touching her at all and his breathing was unsteady and erratic, but he was holding onto that robe for all he was worth.

A wave of desire slammed into her. "What's happening?" she whispered, feeling almost stupid for asking, but needing to know what the heck was going on between them. She'd always been attracted to him but had known—well, clearly her knowledge was wrong—he only saw her as a friend. Now it was like things had changed in one night. And she wasn't sure what had happened to push the change.

He didn't answer, just bent his head to hers, giving her plenty of time to pull away. Hell no. Clutching onto his shoulders, she met him halfway, feeling dazed that Vadim was actually about to kiss her. That the man who starred in all her fantasies had given her his robe to wear. How sexy was that?

The second his lips touched hers, she moaned into his mouth. It was like that sound set something off in Vadim. He jerked against her, a ragged sound tearing from him as one hand fisted her hip and the other tugged on the robe, pulling her closer.

Stroking her tongue lightly against his, her nipples tightened when he shuddered against her. She was vaguely aware of him guiding them backward and when his big hands clasped both her hips she realized why. He lifted her up onto one of the high swivel chairs at the island, making her closer in height to him.

As their tongues danced, gently teasing and learning each other, one of his hands slid slowly, smoothly, inside the lapel of her robe. He moved slow enough to give her time to stop him. Instead her fingers dug into his shoulders. She wanted to explore every inch of him too, but all she could seem to do was clutch onto him for dear life. She'd wanted this for so long.

Her senses were going into overload as Vadim lightly nipped her bottom lip. He made the sexiest sound, a groan of pure pleasure that told her he didn't want to be anywhere else. When his hand finally cupped her breast, his big body shuddered again.

And she could barely think as his thumb stroked over her nipple. It was already hardening under his touch, but when he slowly rolled it between his thumb and forefinger, she gasped and let her head fall back a fraction.

He took it as the invitation that it was, immediately nuzzling her neck in the sweetest way. She wrapped her arms around his neck, spreading her legs wider for him as he stepped closer against her. A rush of heat flooded between her thighs and she cursed all the clothes between them. His erection pressed insistently against her lower stomach, letting her know he was just as affected as she was.

"Do you know how often I've fantasized about the color of your nipples?" he growled against her neck before feathering soft kisses up to her jaw.

He'd fantasized about her too? "You don't have to fantasize anymore," she murmured as he lightly tweaked the hard bud. She couldn't wait for him to slide the robe fully off so he could completely look his fill—and touch and taste her everywhere. She moaned loudly, arching into him, but froze at the sound of a loud bark.

Vadim whipped around, withdrawing his hand as he swiveled to face Charlie. If dogs had expressions, Angel would swear Charlie was frowning at Vadim. She barked again then made a low growling rumble that almost sounded threatening.

"Crap, I think she got jealous," Angel whispered.

"It's not that...I think she thinks I was hurting you," he said before murmuring soothing sounding words in Russian, still keeping his body in front of Angel's.

After spinning around in circles a couple times, Charlie sat down, but still made a soft whining sound. As soon as she sat, Vadim stepped away, still keeping his gaze on the dog. "Get down so she can see you're okay."

Angel slid off the seat and immediately Charlie lunged for her, tongue hanging out as the dog loudly sniffed and nudged her hands with a cold, wet nose. Even though the sharpest sense of disappointment punched through her that their kiss had been interrupted, she found herself smiling. She petted Charlie's head with both hands, bending down to nuzzle her. "I'm okay, you adorable mutt. Though I think I might have to kidnap you later," she said as she looked back up at Vadim.

He didn't respond, just watched her with a gaze so hungry there was no mistaking what he wanted. Abruptly he turned from her, taking her off guard. "I'll leave the instructions for the alarm code, but there's an alarm fob on my key chain with four buttons. They're all self-explanatory." His voice was brusque as he pulled a pad of paper and a pen from one of the drawers.

"Okay." She wrapped her arms around herself, confused by the sudden change in his demeanor. She wanted to continue right where they'd left off and hopefully end up with both of them naked, sweaty and satisfied.

"I need to get her settled for the night and pack." He didn't look up as he scribbled on the pad of paper. His jaw was clenched tight; she couldn't read his expression or even guess what he was thinking.

But she recognized the tone enough to realize he was dismissing her. It hurt more than she could have imagined. Almost like a physical blow. "Oh...okay." She floundered, willing him to look at her, but he didn't, he just continued writing. She could feel her face turning red and something even more horrifying, tears burning at her eyes. "Hope you have a good trip," she said softly before hurrying from the room.

She wasn't sure what had happened. He'd initiated that kiss and he'd been into it—that much she knew. His erection left no doubt in her mind. But something had clearly happened to make him pull back from her.

Once she made it to the safety of the guest room, she shut the door and headed directly for the inviting bed even though she knew she wasn't going to sleep. Not with the memory of Vadim's hot lips on hers and the way her nipples still tingled from his touch. If she was braver she'd ask him what had happened to make him do such a one-eighty on her, but she felt too raw to even contemplate asking him. Sighing, she turned off the bedside lamp and closed her eyes. After all these months she was finally in Vadim's bed—his guest bed—and now she was worried that she'd lost her chance with him before it had even started.

CHAPTER FIVE

Angel stared at her cell phone, willing herself to stop being such a coward and simply make the call she needed to. Vadim had left early that morning just like he'd said, leaving all the necessary information she could want, including how to arm and disarm his alarm system. She'd been with Charlie most of the day, reading, relaxing and despite the cold, she'd played outside with the dog for a couple of hours.

But Angel couldn't get the kiss and Vadim's bizarre reaction afterward out of her mind. A couple years ago she'd have had plenty of girlfriends to call and they could dissect his behavior over glasses of wine. Now? Not so much. And it sucked. Maybe she only attracted psychos and Vadim sensed there was something wrong with her. Or maybe he sensed her reluctance since she'd have to eventually leave Vegas. Just like every other place over the past couple years.

She sighed, shoving those thoughts away. She could play the 'what if' game for hours and make herself crazy. Not to mention she had other important things to take care of, like apologizing to Sierra.

"Screw it," she muttered to herself. Charlie looked up from where she was dozing on her beanbag—Vadim hadn't been joking about her loving that thing—but just as quickly lost interest when Angel held her phone up to her ear. Biting her bottom lip, she hoped Sierra wouldn't answer.

Of course the woman picked up on the second ring. "Hey, Angel, I'm glad you called."

She swallowed hard. "I didn't get a chance to really apologize and explain myself last night."

"It's okay, Vadim called me this morning and explained what you were doing."

"He did?" That was news.

"Yeah, freaking early too. He called from Wyatt's jet before they took off."

The other woman knew more about Vadim's trip than Angel did. Which shouldn't bother her, but it did just a little. And she was surprised he'd called Sierra on her behalf. "I might have had a good reason but I still should have asked you."

"You were bringing the food back though, weren't you?" Sierra asked.

"Yeah." But she'd thought telling her that would sound like a lie.

"I figured that out after you'd left. Listen, any time you want to take any of the throw away food home, for you, your neighbors, whoever, you can. Just let me know first."

"I will, I promise. And thanks for being so understanding."

"Of course, you're a good employee. Probably the best I've ever had...And I'm not just saying that because I need a little favor."

At this point there wasn't much Angel would say no to. "What is it?"

"Can you come in tonight? I know it's last minute, but—"

"Yes," she said quickly, not needing any convincing. Charlie would be fine and Angel could use the money and distraction. Anything to get her mind off Vadim. Which was hard to do when she was at his place.

"Great, thanks. Can you be here by six? I need an opener, but you won't have to close. I'll cut you as soon as we have a lull, but it's Friday so expect to stay until at least eleven."

"That's fine and the time works too. I'll see you soon." Once they disconnected, Angel turned on the television for Charlie, hoping it would keep her company the next few hours, then she checked the dog's food and water.

She'd already showered so she changed into casual clothes and sneakers, put on makeup, then pulled her hair into a ponytail and braided it. She needed to run by her place to get her work clothes but it would take her less than a minute to change once she got there. Knowing she'd be cutting it close, she grabbed her purse, Vadim's keys and headed out only once she was sure Charlie was okay. Angel felt bad leaving the dog, but she hadn't even seemed to notice Angel getting ready to leave as she snored softly in front of the TV. Plus she was clearly used to Vadim being gone for work. Once Angel was in the garage she set his alarm to stay mode using the keyfob—which was incredibly nifty.

Driving his Mercedes was like driving around in an insulated cloud. The leather was butter soft, the interior sleek, and even the seats had warmers. Still, it was hard to enjoy the luxury car when she was terrified she'd get a ding in it or something. Things were already weird between her and Vadim and she figured that scratching this baby would make things even more strained. Sticking to the speed limit, she made her way to her place, scanning for the men Vadim had taken on the night before.

Even thinking about that impressive display made her feel warm all over. But clearly she'd overthought things with him. He probably regretted kissing her and now didn't know how to deal with it. She'd noticed that sometimes his social skills were a little off and figured he just hadn't known how to tell her last night that he regretted their kiss. Instead, he'd simply shut down.

Which was seriously depressing when all she wanted was a replay.

Shaking away all thoughts of Vadim, she pulled into a spot right in front of her building. She couldn't believe she'd gotten such a great one, but she wasn't going to question her luck. Racing up the stairs, she hurried into her place, changed into her standard uniform and black Mary Jane slingbacks and ran back down. The complex was quieter than normal, especially for a Friday night.

Glancing at the row of cars, she rubbed the back of her neck, feeling almost uneasy, as if she was being watched. For a moment her throat tightened as that familiar panic surged through her. But just as quickly it was gone as she took a deep, steadying breath, forcing herself to remain calm. Rolling her eyes at herself, she slid into Vadim's car and steered out of the parking lot, thankful her hands were steady. With thoughts of Vadim and her cash problem on her mind it was no surprise she was on edge. When she'd first gone on the run she'd seen the man hunting her in every corner, in every shadow, waiting to strike her down.

It had been two years. Still, she knew she could never let her guard down. Not after that monster had killed her brother. She might not be able to prove it, but deep down Angel knew he'd been behind it. Hell, he'd confessed to her that he had and she didn't think he was lying. He'd had no reason to.

Blinking back the sudden tears that always formed when she thought of her brother, she steered out of the parking lot and tried to think of happier things. She couldn't act depressed while serving people tonight. It was time to get her game face on.

His heart beat erratically as he watched Angel slide behind the wheel of the newer model Mercedes. What the fuck was she doing driving something like that when she lived in this shithole?

After sitting on her place most of the day he'd been about to give up and leave when he'd seen that flash of brilliant red hair. The woman was like a beacon, calling to him. She always had been. From the moment he'd first seen her.

And she'd loved him too. He just knew it. But something had changed between them and he didn't know what. Didn't care at this point. He hadn't decided how much he planned to make her suffer before he killed her, but seeing her in the flesh again after so long he was going to keep her around for a while first.

Shifting uncomfortably, he rubbed a hand over his crotch as he steered his rental car out onto the street after her. Oh yeah, he was definitely keeping her around.

Keeping an eye on his surroundings, he tailed Angel as best he could without seeming too obvious. It was easy with the steady flow of traffic. So many vehicles were heading in the same direction as she was. When she turned into the main entrance for the Serafina hotel, his anger grew.

Maybe she was meeting a lover there. Probably the man who owned the car she was driving. Because there was no way in hell that was hers. His investigator had assured him that she hadn't registered any new vehicles in the last two years. No, she'd been a ghost.

Until now.

Staying four cars behind her, he slid on his ball cap when she stopped in front of the valet parking. She talked animatedly with one of the drivers for a couple minutes. The conversation seemed longer than normal for a patron of the hotel. Maybe the whore was planning to meet up with him later.

She'd always been like that, flirting with everyone. He'd hated it as much as he'd loved her. She was so vibrant and full of life but she should only be like that for him. Only with him.

Needing to see where she went—and who she was meeting—he continued through the line, stopping when it was his turn.

A man in his early twenties greeted him with a smile. "Welcome to the Serafina. How long will you be leaving your car?"

"I'm not sure," he said as he slid from the rental, keeping his hat pulled low.

"No problem. Stay as long as you like." The man rattled off the daily rate before asking if he had any questions.

He started to say no, but paused. "Where do you keep the cars you valet? Are they secure?"

The guy nodded, as if he was asked that all the time. Pointing past the hotel, he said, "See the offsite parking garage? The bottom two floors are valet and the rest of the garage is for spillover. But we've got a guard stationed there 24/7 so the cars are secure."

"Thanks." After getting his parking stub, he headed up the stairs to the wide doors of the luxurious hotel.

Once inside he was stunned by the marble floors and huge fountain in the middle of the lobby. Definitely first class all the way, which was what he was normally accustomed to. At least the dress varied. There were people wearing track suits while others wearing thousand dollar suits milled about so he'd be able to blend in.

Unfortunately the place was huge. Angel's hair might be a beacon but he'd never find her in this place. Especially if the whore had already gone up to a hotel room to meet some guy. Fighting his anger, he made his way across the lobby, deciding to do a sweep of the main floor. He knew where she lived so he could always just go back there and wait, but he wanted to learn everything about her schedule.

As he passed the open entryway for a restaurant called Cloud 9, he almost stumbled. Standing next to a cocktail table of three men, she was smiling at something one of them said as she jotted down a note on her pad of paper. Shit, she worked at the restaurant.

It still didn't explain her car, but knowing she worked here made all the difference. Keeping track of her movements would be a lot easier now that he knew where she lived and worked. The restaurant was huge, a mixture of cocktail tables, fine dining tables and a roped off area of modular couches where it looked like people were only drinking cocktails.

He scanned the area in seconds, but couldn't stop being drawn back to her. Of average height, she gave the appearance of being taller because of her slim legs. And she was stunning. The kind of woman a man did an automatic double take for.

He would have given her everything too, if only she'd stayed. If only she hadn't involved the police in their business. She never should have gone behind his back. And she never should have tried to leave him in the first place. Then he wouldn't have had to hurt her, to remind her who was in charge.

"May I help you, sir?" A pretty woman wearing a simple black dress and heels asked him, her smile polite.

That was when he realized he'd stepped inside the actual restaurant and wasn't hovering outside anymore. Like an idiot, he'd started walking toward Angel without even thinking. But he couldn't let her see him yet. No, his appearance in Vegas would have to be a complete surprise. That didn't mean he couldn't mess with her head. He shook his head quickly at the hostess, stepped back out and hurried away.

If Angel was working she'd likely be at the restaurant for a few hours. And he planned to fuck up her car while she was occupied. If there was only one guard in that lot, it should be easy enough to get in undetected. It wasn't as if he wanted to steal the thing, just vandalize it.

What he wouldn't give to witness Angel's expression when she saw it.

CHAPTER SIX

Vadim finished his second drive around Angel's apartment complex before parking in front of Mr. Botkin's two-story building. He knew the man lived there with his wife and that his three daughters all lived in the other apartments with their families. The job Vadim had been on with Wyatt had been cut even shorter than he'd expected. Instead of coming by tomorrow he'd decided to stop by tonight, after a call to Mr. Botkin had assured him that it wasn't too late.

As he exited one of Wyatt's company vehicles, Vadim automatically scanned the area for trouble. When he didn't see anyone, he headed for the walkway. Before he'd reached the curb the landlord was already striding toward him.

Vadim nodded once as he met him on the sidewalk. "Thanks for meeting with me," he said in English.

The older man grunted. "Russian?"

Vadim nodded, knowing it would be easier on the man to converse in his native tongue so he quickly switched languages. "I need a favor." When Mr. Botkin didn't respond, just watched him carefully, Vadim continued. "I don't like Angel living here. It's not safe for her with no male protection." He knew what he was saying was archaic, but he also knew this man was old school and would like, or at least understand, the sentiment, especially since he had three daughters. And Vadim needed this guy to do what he was requesting. It wasn't like he could force him. "Early tomorrow I want you to call her, tell her there's a flooding problem at her apartment but you've packed up her belongings. You'll also tell her you have no idea how long it will take to fix the pipes or the flooring and that there is no other apartment open right now. Be very apologetic, offer to help her find another place, and be believable. I'll come by later tomorrow and pack up her stuff."

Mr. Botkin watched him, his eyes narrowing a fraction. "Is this because of the man asking about her?"

At the man's words, Vadim went still. Someone had been asking about Angel? He flicked a glance around them again out of habit. "What man?" he asked, turning back to Mr. Botkin.

"A man came by her place late last night, stopped me as I was leaving another apartment. He said his friend's sister was missing and he was helping look for her. I didn't like the look of him." The man's lip curled in clear distaste.

"What did you tell him?" Vadim's voice was steady, but a low grade panic hummed through him. Angel had been quiet about her life before moving to Vegas and he'd respected her privacy. Her background check the hotel ran for all new employees had come back clean. Now he wondered if she was running from someone.

"Nothing. Pretended I couldn't speak English and he left."

"What did he look like?"

Another shrug. "White, tall like you, dark hair, dark eyes. What my daughters would call Hollywood handsome." He rolled his eyes at that. "He looked fucking shifty to me though."

Vadim filed that away for later. "What was he driving?"

Mr. Botkin reached into his pocket and pulled out a folded piece of paper. "Looked like a rental, I tried to get all the numbers, but he left too quickly. Missed the last one." He gave him the make and model as Vadim took the paper.

He slid it in his jacket pocket then pulled an envelope from one of his interior pockets. He handed it to Mr. Botkin.

The older man glanced inside at the cash and lifted his eyebrows as he met Vadim's gaze again. "You care for this woman?"

Vadim nodded.

"She'll have a place to stay? With you?"

He nodded again. He didn't care how underhanded this was. He wanted—needed—Angel somewhere safer.

Preferably with him. Especially now that some man was sniffing around her place asking about her. He was going to get to the bottom of that too.

For a long moment he worried the other man would reject his offer, but when Mr. Botkin tucked the envelope under his arm, Vadim knew he'd won.

"I'll make the call tomorrow at seven," the landlord said.

"Thank you."

Another grunt, then the man turned and headed back to his place. Knowing things were taken care of, Vadim quickly left the complex. He had one more errand to run before heading home. He'd be home late, well past one or two in the morning, but it would give him more time to figure out what the hell he'd say to Angel about that kiss. He knew he should have called her while he was gone, but that kiss had jarred him far too much.

She made him want to lose control, something he never did. She also made him want things he'd never imagined for his own life, like a family and someone to come home to every night.

Angel stood next to the valet stand where the keys were hung on pegs, half-listening as one of the guys spoke in hushed tones into his radio. She'd been waiting over twenty minutes for Vadim's car and didn't understand what the problem was. It was after eleven and even though the casino was slammed, the valet station was slow.

She wrapped her arms around herself, shivering against the slight breeze that kicked up. All she wanted was to go to Vadim's place, kick off her shoes and wash the restaurant smell off her. And sleep. Tonight had been busier than she'd expected, which was good because she'd made double what she had last night, but she was still tired. At least she'd had a few missed texts from Mark letting her know that he and Chloe were settling in nicely. She'd already texted him and had heard back almost immediately with him reassuring her they were doing well.

When the man, whose name she didn't know, put down his hand-held radio and glanced over Angel's shoulder almost nervously she tensed and turned around.

Iris Christiansen was striding down the stairs coming straight for them. Angel immediately straightened at the sight of the Serafina's head of security—and billionaire Wyatt Christiansen's wife. Crap, what if they thought she wasn't supposed to be driving Vadim's car? Angel couldn't imagine why Iris was here. The tall, slender woman was nice, but she was also intimidating as hell.

"Vadim is letting me use his car. You can call him and ask," Angel blurted when Iris stopped in front of them.

Iris blinked, her mouth pulling up into a half-smile. "I know. You mind coming with me to the parking garage? I need to talk to you."

A thick block of ice settled in her stomach, numbing her from the inside out. Had Sierra told Iris about what Angel had done? Maybe now she was going to lose her job. Tongue-tied, she nodded and fell in step with the taller woman as they headed down the sidewalk. Angel's heels clicked loudly while Iris's shoes were silent. She knew the tall woman had been in the Marines, just like Vadim.

"Have you been having any problems at work lately with customers?" Iris asked.

She glanced at her, surprised by the question. "No. I mean, I get the typical pervs and creeps who ask me out but no harassment or anything if that's what you mean."

Iris nodded thoughtfully. "No one hanging around after work waiting for you?"

Angel shook her head again, starting to worry about this line of questioning. "No, but I take the bus. Why are you asking?"

"What about a…boyfriend or ex-boyfriend? Any problems there?" Iris completely ignored Angel's previous question.

Angel frowned. Had Iris somehow found out about Angel's past? Maybe they'd started digging into her life after the food-stealing incident. She'd been so careful, but maybe not careful enough. "What's going on?"

"Someone keyed Vadim's car while it was in valet. They scratched the word 'whore' on the hood. Since you're driving it and whore is typically a word used to insult females, I'm trying to figure out if this message was meant for you or Vadim."

Angel could feel the blood drain from her face. A chill snaked through her as they neared the lowest level entrance to the garage. Behind the electronic arm that let people in and out of the structure, one of the valet guys was talking to a man wearing a button-down black shirt and black slacks. Clearly security. When the security guy saw them he nodded at Iris.

Following Iris, Angel walked along the outer sidewalk that lead into the garage, on the other side of the arm so they wouldn't have to duck under it.

"Called the cops to make a report, but they won't be here for an hour since this isn't a priority," the security man said to Iris.

Lips pulled into a grim line she nodded before glancing at Angel. "You don't need to stay for the report. For now I'm going to let you use a company vehicle so you can get home."

"What about Vadim's car?"

"Since this happened on hotel property we'll be taking care of it. This shouldn't have happened." There was a sharp bite to Iris's words as she cut an equally hard look at the security guy.

No doubt someone was definitely in trouble over this. "Can I see it?" She felt terrible that this had happened to his car while she'd been the one driving it.

"Ah..." Iris frowned again, as if contemplating it, then shook her head as an SUV pulled to a stop near them. "You don't need to see that. This is your SUV for now. How comfortable are you driving one?"

"I'm fine with it." She wanted to push Iris about seeing Vadim's car but knew there was no point. She wouldn't gain anything by seeing the vandalism. But she still felt terrible about it. She pulled her cell phone from her pocket and glanced at the time. It was almost midnight, but Vadim should know about this. She'd call him as soon as she had some privacy. "Have you told Vadim about this yet?"

Iris shook her head.

"I'll let him know."

"Thanks." The other woman handed Angel a set of keys. "Whoever did this, we're going to figure it out, okay?"

Angel nodded, palming the keys. She still didn't know what to think about the vandalism. In the back of her mind she wondered if this had something to do with her past, but if the man from her nightmares knew where she was working and about her driving Vadim's car, he'd have likely already come after her. He was violent, with a hair-trigger temper. Something she'd found out too late. "Okay. Do you need me to stick around for anything?"

"No, but be careful on your way home, check to make sure you're not being followed. I know you're house sitting for V so make sure you set the alarm as soon as you're inside. And text me when you get to his place so I'll know you're there." Iris wasn't asking.

"I will." Anxiety threaded through her veins, making her numb all over. She really wished Vadim was in town. At least she could go to his place, which had a great alarm system and a dog. It was the only thing that made her feel better about this whole situation. After saying goodbye and getting another demand to stay safe from Iris, Angel slid into the driver's seat. She pulled out of the garage, but idled for a moment while she called Vadim. She knew him well enough that he wouldn't care how late it was, especially not when it concerned his car.

After his cell phone went straight to voicemail, she tried his hotel. The perky woman who answered immediately transferred Angel to his room.

"Hello?" A groggy, husky, feminine voice answered. Angel froze, her throat tightening. "Hello?" the woman asked again.

When she heard a muted male voice in the background, she hung up. The sharpest sense of betrayal sliced into her, which was stupid. She didn't have a claim on Vadim. They were friends who had shared a kiss. Well, a really hot kiss with a little groping action. Then he'd immediately rejected her after their interruption, making it clear he thought it was a mistake and that it wasn't happening again.

None of that mattered now. Setting the phone down on the center console, she headed to his place. She'd been looking forward to spending more time at his place with him, now she was just counting down the hours until she could leave. At least it would give her something else to focus on other than the bizarre vandalism.

It was impossible to completely dismiss that whoever had done it was from her past. Still, she was having a hard time wrapping her mind around that. Not when she'd been living like a ghost. She didn't have an online trail for anyone to follow. But if her past had caught up with her, it was time to run again. She'd already escaped a monster once. She'd do it again.

CHAPTER SEVEN

Angel's eyes opened with a start and she glanced around Vadim's guestroom. According to the digital clock on the nightstand it was almost two in the morning. She'd left one of the lights from the bathroom on so she could see in the unfamiliar place. A faint illumination streamed through from the cracked open door. Charlie's head popped up when Angel moved, but she sniffed once, then laid back down. Angel paused at the dog's lack of reaction. Maybe she hadn't heard anything after all.

Vadim's house was a lot quieter than where she lived and that took some getting used to. Not that she'd be getting used to it. As soon as she could leave, she was gone. Still, she could swear she'd heard something.

Sliding out of bed, she crept to the bedroom door, her bare feet silent against the hardwood floor. Her heart pounded an erratic tattoo against her chest as she eased the door open. It was all because of that vile vandalism. It had her on edge.

Slowly, she stepped out into the hallway, and nearly screamed when she saw Vadim making his way down the hall, a gun in hand. Her eyes widened and she froze.

What was he doing here with that? Was someone in the house?

"Are you okay?" he whispered as he came to stand next to her.

"Yeah. Why wouldn't I be?" How the hell had he gotten home already when she'd only heard him with that other woman in the hotel room a few hours ago?

At her words, he relaxed a fraction and sheathed his gun in a hidden holster under his suit jacket. Before she could ask more questions, he continued. "I saw an SUV. Are you alone?" There was an edge to his question that took her off guard.

She rubbed her eyes and shook her head. "Well, no—"

Vadim stepped past her, moving lightning fast as he stepped into her room. He flipped the overhead light on and Charlie whined, covering her face with her paw.

Now it made sense why Charlie hadn't reacted. She must have realized it was Vadim in the house. Angel snapped the switch down and the dog stopped fussing. "Vadim, what's going…oh my gosh," she bit out, keeping her voice low. "You thought I had someone in there with me."

His jaw tightened once and he didn't deny it.

Which lit the fuse on her temper. "First, I would never bring someone into your home without asking you first. Second…you have no business caring if I sleep with anyone else," she said hurriedly, unable to hide the bite of anger to her words. Normally she didn't have much of a temper, but she was incredibly hurt and it was making her edgy. After hearing that woman in his bed she felt more than a little crazy with jealousy. Even thinking about it made her stomach twist in knots.

He seemed surprised by her words. "I don't have any business caring?" he asked her, that edge to his voice still firmly in place.

She wrapped her arms around herself, suddenly very aware that she was just wearing a long T-shirt and panties. She hadn't expected him to be home so early. "No," she ground out. "What are you doing back so early? Is everything okay?" She hoped he would let her change the subject.

His pale blue eyes narrowed a fraction, still watching her in that careful way of his. Almost as if he was trying to figure something out. "Finished the job early."

And clearly he wasn't going to expand. Sighing, she rubbed a hand over her face. She still wasn't fully awake and just wanted to go back to bed. Not stare at the deliciously sexy man who'd just left another woman's bed a few hours ago. "Good, I know Charlie will be happy to have you back. Listen, something happened with your car."

"I saw the SUV in the garage."

"I picked up an extra shift today—last night—and was really careful with your car. I even used valet." She wrung her hands together, feeling awful about his car. "I don't know what happened but someone vandalized it. They keyed the word 'whore' on the hood while it was in the parking garage." As his expression darkened, she hurried on. "The hotel is going to fix it since it happened on company property. That's why I've got the SUV. Iris let me use it so I could get home. Uh, here, your home. I'm sure it's for you to use until they've handled everything."

Vadim was silent for a long moment, watching her intently. When he spoke, his question surprised her. "Are you...okay? Having any problems with anyone?"

She shook her head. "No, but Iris asked me the same thing. I can't imagine why anyone would put that on your car." Of course, she couldn't shake that nagging feeling in the pit of her stomach. Maybe her past had caught up to her. But that seemed impossible. And why would he bother to vandalize her car? No, he'd just kill her.

Vadim's eyes narrowed again, as if he could see her innermost thoughts. "What are you thinking about? You just thought of something. Or someone. I can see it."

Swallowing hard, she shook her head. "Nothing." There was no way in hell she was telling him about her past. Not when she'd used a different social security number other than her own to get a job at the Serafina.

She could tell he didn't believe her, but he nodded anyway. He cleared his throat, almost nervously. "Can we talk about...what happened between us?"

Angel tightened her grip around herself, feeling so vulnerable in just her T-shirt. She needed more clothing as armor if she was going to have this conversation with Vadim. "There's nothing to talk about. We kissed, it was a mistake and I don't want to screw up our friendship." Even though she knew things would never be the same between them. At least not on her end. He'd gone from kissing her to sleeping with some woman on his business trip. She didn't care if she didn't have a right to be angry, she was. But more than anything, it hurt. A lot more than she'd imagined possible.

For a moment she thought *he* looked almost hurt, but then that mask fell back into place, his pale eyes shuttered. "You think it was a mistake?"

She nodded. A big one. Because now she couldn't even look at him without thinking about how wonderful it would be to do it again. Except that it had clearly meant more to her than him. Otherwise he wouldn't have slept with someone else so quickly.

His expression was darker than normal, edgier. Jaw tight, he turned away from her, glancing into her bedroom. Charlie was awake now, watching them curiously. Vadim said something to her in Russian. Clearly a command. Whatever it was, Charlie didn't like it. She jumped from her soft bed into Angel's bed and flopped down at the end of it, still watching them.

Instead of being angry, Vadim looked hurt. Even if she was angry at him, she didn't like seeing him in pain. Acting on instinct, she reached for him, dropping her arms from around herself and touching his forearm. When he glanced back at her, however, she couldn't read him.

"Do you want Charlie to go with you?" she asked, her fingers slightly digging into his arm. The strength under her fingertips was too much. She felt so weak where he was concerned, ready to give into the hunger he made her feel. The man just turned her insides to mush until all she wanted to do was slide her hand up his muscular arm, link her fingers behind his neck and pull him down for another kiss. And this time she wouldn't stop at kissing.

Vadim shook his head, his gaze raking over her in a quick sweep that made her hot and tingly but when he met her eyes again, the heat there nearly singed her. "No. Get some sleep." Then he was gone, turning and striding down the hallway on silent feet.

Vadim sat at his island top staring at his freshly brewed coffee as he waited for Iris to pick up his call.

She answered after four rings. "Hey, V."

"Hey, did I wake you? I thought you'd be up by now." It was only six-thirty but he knew she liked to run early in the morning. They'd been working together for less than a year, but Iris had very particular habits.

"No, been up. Just working on something." She let out an annoyed curse and he heard what sounded like glass breaking. "Stupid computer," she muttered. "What's up? Angel tell you about your car?"

"Yeah. What happened? And how the fuck did someone key my car while it was in valet?" That annoyed him almost as much as the destruction and vicious word they'd used.

She sighed. "We've caught the guy on video doing it. He managed to sneak in a side door to the garage and avoid the guard. Look, our guards are there to make sure cars aren't stolen. We've never had a vandalism problem. And I don't think we do now. From the video it's clear your car was targeted. But I don't think the message was for you." There was a slight question in Iris's voice.

"Yeah, I don't either." But before he discussed anything with Iris he needed to talk to Angel. The vandalism on his car combined with the man asking Mr.

Botkin about her was too strange. "Did you get his face on screen?"

"Not exactly. He was wearing a ball cap and what I'm pretty sure was a wig. But we got part of his face. I didn't want to plug his face into that scary software program you've got though. Figured you could do it when you got back."

He was glad Iris hadn't touched it. She could break a computer simply by looking at it wrong. "What did the cops say?"

"Not much. We filed a report but they're chalking it up to random vandalism. Which, I don't blame them, even if I don't think that tagging was random. What's going on with your girl?"

"She's not my…I don't know what's going on with her." But he planned to find out. And he really wished she *was* his girl. But she'd made it plain last night that she didn't want to be.

"Is she in trouble? She's a sweet kid, but she's kinda skittish. She was all nervous last night, telling me that you'd let her take your car to work. As if she was worried I'd think she'd stolen it." Iris snorted. "I wonder if she realizes you'd give her the damn thing if she wanted."

Vadim gritted his teeth. He adored Iris, but he didn't want to talk about his personal life with her. He started to respond when Angel strode into the kitchen, fully dressed in jeans and a sweater, carrying her overnight bag and purse.

Vadim's heart sank.

She gave him a stiff smile as she set the bag on the floor. Charlie was tagging along next to her, whining as if she knew Angel was leaving. He understand how the dog felt. "I've gotta go. I'll be in soon though. I'm going to get to the bottom of this problem today." He disconnected before Iris could respond.

"Is everything okay?" Angel asked, absently rubbing Charlie's head. The little traitor was soaking it up.

He couldn't believe Charlie had refused his command to come with him last night. Seemed she liked Angel just as much as he did. "Yeah, just has to do with my car. They got the guy who keyed it on video."

Her eyebrows rose in surprise. "That's great news. I hope they catch that jerk."

"Yeah...you want some coffee or tea?" He needed her to stay for at least another half an hour until Mr. Botkin's scheduled phone call.

She shook her head. "No, I should probably get going. I made the bed because I wasn't sure if you wanted me to strip the sheets. And I left my dirty towels in the shower since I wasn't sure where to put them." As she spoke, she avoided his gaze entirely, glancing anywhere but at him.

Fuck. He knew he'd screwed up, but it almost seemed like she was pissed at him. That didn't seem right. Even though she'd said it was a mistake and she wanted to be friends, he didn't. He couldn't go back to being friends with her and the truth was, he knew that after she left his place, she'd be putting distance between them. He could already see the walls she'd erected as if they were physical barriers. "Angel, shit, I'm sorry about the way I pulled back from that kiss. I got..." God, he was so bad with women. But especially with Angel. She was sweet, soft and the exact opposite of him. He might not deserve someone like her, but he wanted the chance. He struggled to find a way to explain it to her without sounding like a jackass. "I didn't want to fuck things up with you and I was ready to take you right on the counter. You deserve better than that—but I'm not sorry I kissed you and I don't want to be just friends."

Her eyes widened and for a moment, her expression softened. Just as quickly a spark of anger replaced it. She wore her emotions right out in the open. She was definitely pissed. But she gave him a tight smile. "The kiss was nice, but...I only want friendship from you."

She was lying. He could see it in her eyes. But he wasn't sure why. "Why are you lying?"

Angel gasped at his question, taking an annoyed step forward. "I'm not lying."

"Bullshit. You want more than friendship. I can see it when you look at me." Now that he could see the truth in her gaze, he was desperate for her to admit it.

"Aren't you just full of yourself?" she asked, her voice quivering. What she probably meant to be cutting didn't come across that way. She seemed nervous and damn it, that flicker of hurt bled back into her eyes. What the hell?

Before he could answer, her cell phone rang. After shooting him another glare she dug her cell out then turned away from him as she answered. "Hello?"

He sat back against the stool, feeling like a dick because he knew what the call was about. But he didn't regret what he was doing. He had to get her the hell out of that place.

"What? Wait...are you kidding me? What about all my stuff...Oh." There was a long pause, then she sniffled. "I can come by and get my stuff today. Are you sure you don't have..." Another pause. "Okay. Okay. Yeah, thanks." She slipped the phone back into her purse and turned to face him.

Tears glittered in her hazel eyes, the sight like a physical blow to his senses. "Angel..."

She blinked them away. "It's nothing. I just...can you take me home?"

He rounded the island, coming to stand in front of her, not giving her a chance to put any distance between them, physical or otherwise. "No. Not until you tell me what's going on. Who just called you?"

To his horror she burst into tears. It was as if she'd been holding them at bay and a dam just broke. *Fuck him.* He was the biggest douche on the planet. Not caring that she was angry at him, he pulled her into his arms and to his relief, she went willingly.

Wrapping her arms around him, she buried her face against his chest. Stroking a hand down her back, he savored the feel of her delicate form pressed so tightly against him—even while he felt like a jerk for being the cause of her tears. Not that it changed his determination to get her out of that place. A few tears would be worth it to have her somewhere safe.

Still remaining in his embrace, she turned her head to the side so that her cheek lay against him. "My apartment flooded. I don't have much there, just clothes, but…Mr. Botkin has no idea how long it will take to fix everything. He says the pipes won't take long but he's going to have to rip up the floors and…" Shaking her head, she stepped back, swiping at the stray tears as she avoided his gaze. "He doesn't have any extra places, but said he'd try to find me a new apartment at another complex. He's also going to refund this month's rent, but still."

"Stay with me."

Her head snapped up, her eyes wide. Was she really that surprised by his offer? That cut almost as deep as her tears.

"I can't do that." Her voice was watery as she wiped away the last of her tears.

"Why not? Charlie adores you and I have the space. We work at the same place so there's no issue with transportation." As if to reiterate Vadim's point, Charlie nudged her hand, whining softly before she darted through the doggie door.

"Vadim..." She trailed off, biting her bottom lip, and he could see the wheels turning in her head. "If you really don't mind, it'll be just for a week. Maximum. It probably won't even take that long to fix." But she didn't sound too sure.

He grunted. "You can stay as long as you like. Listen, I've got to run up to the hotel. Emergency. I'll be there for a couple hours so unless you want to come hang out with me, I'll just grab your stuff on the way back."

She bit her bottom lip again in that adorable way that made him wish she was nipping at his lips. "I guess that's okay. Mr. Botkin said he'd packed everything but can you check the drawers? I really only have clothes in the closet and drawers. And of course everything in the bathroom. Everything else in the kitchen and living room came with the place. Oh, and my laptop. Crap, I hope it's okay."

"If it's not I'll buy you a new one." The words were out before he could stop himself. Hell, he knew her laptop was fine since there hadn't been any flooding. But he couldn't help the offer. She started to protest, but he shook his head. "I've gotta run, but I'll have my cell phone on me." Not giving her a chance to respond, he headed to his bedroom to get changed.

There was no emergency at work. He planned to head straight to her place, pack up her stuff and bring it back here. Then he would figure out who the hell had keyed his car and who'd been asking about Angel. She'd been pretty tight-lipped about her past but that was about to change.

Keeping her safe was his number one priority. Getting a repeat of that kiss was a close second. Damn, he'd fucked that all up. But he refused to believe that he couldn't have a second chance with her. From the moment they'd met, their friendship had been leading to more. He might suck with the opposite sex, but he knew his feelings weren't one-sided. He would win her over again.

CHAPTER EIGHT

Sinking low in his rental car, he watched the fit, blond man carrying another box from Angel's apartment to the back of his SUV. The windows of his new rental were tinted so no one could see him, but he still wanted to be careful. He'd already switched out cars after what he'd done at the casino. He'd been careful, but he liked to keep his tracks covered. Angel couldn't know he was in town yet.

Not until he'd had his fun.

The blond man had been methodical in his work. He'd shown up with folded, clearly new boxes, a roll of packing tape, then had headed up to Angel's place. Five medium-sized boxes later, he seemed to be done clearing out her place. He definitely wasn't a typical mover though.

Wearing cargo pants, a long-sleeved black T-shirt and boots, the man moved with a predator-like quality. Quick and methodical. The entire scene was interesting.

And frustrating. Maybe he was Angel's new lover and moving her in with him. It made sense. She'd probably found some rich guy to take care of her. That car she'd been driving had been proof enough of that because he knew it wasn't hers.

When the blond man pulled out from the parking lot, he followed. As he drove, he jotted down the license plate number of the SUV. If Angel was moving somewhere else, he was going to find out where. He'd just found her again and wouldn't let her get away from him.

He pressed the third speed dial number on his phone.

"Yeah," Glen Humphrey, his private investigator answered on the second ring.

"I need you to look up a license plate for me." He knew the investigator could do it. There was a website that allowed license plate look-ups for a fee. Unfortunately he also knew the site kept detailed records of their registrants and they had to have legal reasons for looking up that kind of information, like skip tracing. And even then, the site didn't always have the necessary data, just basic public records. Sometimes not even that, especially without a name to go with the plate.

"I can try," Glen said. "But you know it may not return anything."

"I understand." He rattled off the license plate number, still following the SUV. This early in the morning he was surprised by the amount of traffic but apparently this city never slept. "Call me when you have anything." After they disconnected, he slammed on the brakes to avoid hitting a motorcycle that swerved in front of him.

Cursing, he watched as the SUV cruised through a yellow light too far ahead of him. Unless he wanted to make a scene and possibly get in an accident, there was no way he could follow. Not with cars boxing him in on both sides and that stupid motorcycle in front of him.

At least he knew where Angel worked. And now he had a possible lead with that guy's license plate. The problem with her work, however, was that he couldn't sit on the restaurant all day without looking suspicious. He'd have to gamble occasionally and hang out at the bar at least a few times until he learned her schedule. Unfortunately that increased his risk of her seeing him. He'd just have to disguise himself. And he knew exactly how to do that.

Vadim typed another command into his keyboard, narrowing down the search parameters to see if he could learn more about the man who'd keyed his car. After watching the surveillance video a dozen times he was convinced it wasn't random. The man had methodically looked for Vadim's Mercedes before keying it. And there was something about the man's body language that had been almost gleeful.

It was the only way Vadim could think to describe it. He'd taken such great care with his destruction. Carving in each letter with determination, with *relish*. And when he was done, he'd stopped and looked at it, placing his hands on his hips as he stared at his handiwork.

A knock on his open office door had him looking up as Hayden stepped halfway inside. "Angel's working and Logan's keeping an eye on her."

"You couldn't get Roman to watch her?" Vadim asked dryly.

Hayden shot him an obnoxious grin. "Sorry man. Wyatt's got him dealing with something else."

Vadim just grunted and turned back to his laptop. Roman and Logan MacNeil were two highly trained members of Wyatt's personal security team. They sometimes did stuff for the hotel, but Wyatt kept them close on hand. Vadim had asked his friend and boss if he could spare one of his guys to keep an eye on Angel, so it wasn't as if he could complain about the man's choice. Vadim just hated Logan as a choice. The man flirted with all females whereas his brother rarely talked to anyone, much less the opposite sex.

But Vadim couldn't think about that right now. He had shit to do and wanted to find out something substantial before he picked up Angel from work. This morning after he'd packed up her things, he'd checked in with Mr. Botkin to let him know he had all of Angel's belongings and would be leaving. Then he'd brought her stuff home and found out she'd picked up an afternoon shift. He'd needed to come into work anyway so he'd brought her.

She'd been quiet most of the drive and he couldn't tell if it was because she was upset about her place, or if she was angry at him. Because he'd definitely sensed angry vibes from her. He just wished he could figure out the anger part. He'd screwed up but he'd apologized and Angel wasn't one to hold a grudge. It was almost like she was pissed about something else.

Sighing, he put that on the backburner as he rolled his chair toward his other desk. He'd already plugged the unknown man's obscured face into his custom-made—illegal—facial recognition software he piggybacked off other legal programs. He'd also put it into the casino's software. Now it was time to check his DMV hack.

He didn't like to mess with the DMV, but he always covered his tracks. There was no way anyone would be able to trace him back to the hotel, not with all the false trails he left, but he still didn't like to use the program more than necessary.

Right now, it was very necessary. He wanted to find out more about the man asking about Angel, to see if the guy was somehow tied to the car vandalism. Unfortunately Mr. Botkin hadn't had the entire plate number so Vadim was waiting for the list of potentials to come up. From there he'd have to narrow down the driver. When he saw the program had finished running and that he had fifteen possible cars, he printed off the list of names and owners. He didn't save a file of it because he didn't want a digital record anywhere on his computers.

After closing down the program, he stared at his PC for a long moment, tapping his index finger against his desk. His gaze strayed to the small origami owl Angel had made for him the first week they'd met. He'd gone down to the Cloud looking for Hayden, and Angel had just been getting off work. She'd told him she'd seen him around the hotel, introduced herself in that friendly way of hers and sat at the bar with him, telling him she'd keep him company until Hayden came out.

Nothing about her attitude had been flirty, she'd truly just wanted to talk with him and she was one of the only women in the damn hotel—and in general—not fucking afraid of him. He'd also seen a hint of loneliness in her hazel eyes, something he understood well. As they'd sat and talked, she'd made him the owl.

Ever since then he'd resisted doing the one thing he always did with people. He hadn't looked deeper into her past. Hell, he'd wanted to, but he'd known it would be the ultimate violation of privacy. Something he'd never cared about before. When he'd been in the Marine Corps, he'd been part of a deeply secret intel unit. He'd done a hell of a lot more than hack, but he'd violated people's privacy every damn day. Just as he did as Wyatt's employee.

The billionaire had hired him for a reason—he was damn good at finding out people's secrets. Hell, his Mercedes had been one of his signing bonuses, which told him how badly Wyatt had wanted him. Vadim scrubbed a hand over his face and pulled up the file Wyatt had sent to him this morning. He could have gotten the info off the system himself, but he'd been upfront with Wyatt about what he wanted and that he planned to look into Angel's past.

Part of him had hoped Wyatt would say no, but his friend hadn't paused, giving him the green light. Wyatt didn't like the vandalism or the fact that one of his employees might be in trouble. If Vadim could figure out who was behind it, then Wyatt was all for more digging, regardless of Vadim's method.

An hour later, he printed off the information he'd found on Angel, then deleted everything from his computer, erasing all of his tracks with more care than he'd shown in a long time.

CHAPTER NINE

"Thanks for the extra shift, Sierra." Angel put her tips into her purse before sliding the straps onto her shoulder.

Sierra snorted. "Thanks for coming in on such short notice..." She glanced over Angel's shoulder at someone shouting near the galley window. "Damn it, I've gotta run. Get out of here before I decide to keep you," she said half-jokingly.

And that was all the motivation Angel needed to exit the kitchen. The dining area was a mish-mash of people. Even though Cloud 9 was considered fine dining, that didn't matter in Vegas. Some people still showed up in their track suits. It was a little ridiculous, but as long as their money was good and people wore shirts and shoes, Wyatt didn't care how they dressed. She quickly scanned one of the two bar areas, looking for a spot to sit. Vadim had told her he'd be ready to leave around six and it was only five-thirty so she had time to kill. She didn't feel like heading up to his office either, even if he'd said she could wait there.

The thought of being alone with him, all cooped up...no thanks. She was still reeling from losing her apartment. It seemed too surreal. But she was also grateful Vadim had stopped by to pick up all her things. She needed to call Mr. Botkin again to thank him for boxing up everything. He'd probably only done it because he felt bad about her losing her place. Even so, she was glad she hadn't had to do it on top of everything else.

When she spotted an open seat at the bar, she waved at the bartender who grinned and grabbed a bottle of wine—Angel's favorite brand—and poured a glass without having to be asked. As she started to slide onto the seat, she paused and looked at the man next to it. There was a couple on the other side of the seat, clearly involved in only each other, but she wanted to make sure he wasn't saving the seat. "Are you saving this for someone?" she asked as her friend slid the glass in front of her.

"Nope. Just waiting for you to get off work," he said.

His words made her freeze and his eyes widened. "Oh, sorry, Vadim has me watching you today. Said there was an issue. I thought you knew and that's why you were here..." He trailed off, as if unsure that he'd said too much. "I'm Logan, by the way."

Immediately she relaxed. Vadim had told her he'd have someone in and out today keeping an eye on her, which was something she wouldn't complain about. She looked at the dark-eyed man with reddish-brown hair carefully. Now that she was paying attention, he looked very familiar. "One of the twins, right?"

Grinning, he nodded and motioned to the bartender who brought him a beer instead of what looked like the ice water in his current glass. "I'm off the clock now so I can join you for a drink. So, you've heard about my brother and me?"

She nodded, trying to remember what she'd heard about them. One of the waitresses had been talking about Logan or...Roman, who was the other brother. But Angel couldn't remember what the conversation entailed. "I recognize your name. You're not regular security though, right? You work directly for Mr. Christiansen." That, she found a little disconcerting. She didn't want Vadim using any special resources, not when she was in a public place surrounded by co-workers. Besides, they weren't even sure that the thing with his car was more than stupid vandalism.

Logan nodded, half grinning at her in a way that was probably supposed to come across as boyishly charming—which it did. This guy was a player with a capital P. "That's right. So what's up with you and V?"

She blinked, unsure what he was referring to. "You mean about the car?" Jeez, did everyone know what had happened to it?

His brow crinkled slightly. "No, I mean you two. How long have you been dating? He's so quiet about these things and I'm nosey."

"Ah, we're not dating. Just friends." She took a sip of her wine, thankful to have something to keep her hands occupied. The restaurant was getting busy, the noise level a welcome and steady hum of distraction.

"Oh, in that case, what are you doing tomorrow night?" he asked, his expression one of perfect friendliness. She'd gotten good at reading people and the man wasn't creepy, no, far from it, but he had that same vibe to him Vadim did. Like a predator waiting to strike. He was likely former military too, she guessed. Which made sense if he was part of Mr. Christiansen's security.

"Why?" she asked.

His eyebrows rose in clear surprise, his lips tugging into a smile that, if she'd been remotely interested, would have likely gotten her hot and bothered. "Because I want to take you out on a date."

She started to tell him no. It was her knee jerk reaction anytime anyone asked her out. Being on the run wasn't conducive to dating or relationships. But then that woman's voice as she answered the phone in Vadim's hotel room came to mind and something inside Angel hardened in anger. There was no reason she couldn't go out on a date. She was young and single and it had been a long time since she'd been out with a man. "Okay."

Logan looked surprised, as if he hadn't expected her to say yes. Which she found odd. "Were you not serious?" she asked, taking another sip.

"I'm *very* serious. Just couldn't decide if you'd been telling the truth about not dating Vadim. Now I know you are." He grinned in that charming way and held out his hand. "I'll program my number into your phone so you can call me. If you want to cancel, no hard feelings."

Yeah, probably because he had a harem of women waiting on standby. She dug her cell out of her purse, typed in her security key, then slid it over to him. "This is just a date. Don't expect anything."

He shook his head, a dimple appearing in his left cheek as he typed in his number. "I'm always hopeful, but never expect a thing. I can pick you up or meet you out some place. Think about it then call or text me later with what you want. I'm easy."

"I bet you are," she murmured before she could stop herself.

He let out a loud bark of laughter that had heads turning their way as he handed her phone back to her. Before she'd put it back in her purse, Vadim was suddenly there, standing next to them.

And he looked pissed, his glare icy and cutting as he watched Logan. "Your services aren't needed anymore."

His slight accent was heavier than normal, as if he was barely containing his rage.

Alarm slid through her at Vadim's reaction to Logan.

"I don't know, I think Angel might disagree with you." Logan's voice was smug.

Dear God, what was Logan doing, poking a rabid beast? She wanted to tell him to shut up. How could he not sense Vadim's anger simmering beneath the surface?

When Vadim looked at her, his expression softened. "Are you ready?" He still sounded pissed though, his voice vibrating with anger.

She nodded. "Yes, but I need to pay first."

"I got it," Logan said. When she started to protest, he shook his head. "If it makes you feel better you can buy me a drink tomorrow night. On our date." He looked at Vadim almost challengingly as he said the last part.

That was when she realized Logan was intentionally trying to rile Vadim up. Maybe that was the only reason he'd asked her out. The fact that she didn't even care told her she should cancel the date. When Vadim actually took a step toward Logan, she slid off her chair and stepped in between them. She placed a hand on Vadim's chest and her traitorous body flared to life. Just like that, her nipples hardened at the feel of all that strength underneath her fingertips. She clearly needed her head examined. "Let's go," she murmured, pushing against him.

She couldn't have moved him if he hadn't wanted to go, but Vadim took a step back, his body rigid. Angel glanced over her shoulder and thanked Logan for the drink before being herded out by Vadim. To her surprise, he placed his hand firmly at the small of her back in a way she knew he meant to be proprietary as he propelled her away from Logan and the restaurant. Why did she have to like his touch so much? Just the feel of his hand on her back, not even on her bare skin, got her hot and flustered.

His behavior surprised her, but maybe it shouldn't. Maybe it was a ridiculous guy thing. Another man was showing interest so he decides to get all macho and stupid. Ugh. This wasn't even about her, she realized, as Vadim steered her across the main lobby to a door she knew led to one of the private, employee parking garages. This was all about male ego.

Vadim slid a key card over the scanner then yanked open the heavy metal door. She stepped into the hallway that would lead to the garage ahead of him, but before she'd taken more than a couple steps, she found her back pinned against the nearest wall.

Vadim's pale eyes were dark with anger as he crushed his mouth over hers, rolling his hips against hers in such a dominant display she knew she should be angry. Knew she should shove him away. But as his tongue danced against hers, she moaned into his mouth, linking her fingers together around the back of his neck.

She truly, utterly needed her head examined. She didn't like this caveman routine, let alone that he'd been with another woman last night. Hell, she hadn't thought Vadim capable of it. But she loved the way he was pressing her tightly against the wall, loved the feel of his thick erection pressing against her lower belly.

Taking her completely by surprise, he eased his hips back then cupped her mound, rubbing the heel of his palm against her clit. Even with her pants and underwear in the way, the friction felt amazing. Her inner walls tightened, heat flooding between her thighs as she imagined what it would feel like to have him pushing deep inside her. But she needed to stop this. What the hell was she doing? Before she could protest, the sound of the door opening made her snap her head back.

Vadim dropped his possessive hold on her most intimate area, but kept his body pressed tight against hers as he glanced toward the door.

Two laughing women entered—she immediately recognized them as blackjack dealers—talking animatedly until they spotted her and Vadim. One of the women's eyes widened. "Sorry," she murmured, grabbing her friend's elbow as they whispered and hurried down the hallway, their shoes clicking loudly against the tile.

Vadim took a step back from her then, putting a foot of distance between them. He was dressed casually in black pants and a thick, cable knit blue sweater. He shoved his hands into his pockets, his expression unreadable. "Why did you make a date with Logan?"

His question surprised Angel, though maybe it shouldn't have. She shrugged, trying to act casual, but the motion was jerky. "Why shouldn't I?"

He rubbed a hand over his face and for the briefest moment, he looked shattered. Which killed her. But screw him, he'd slept with someone else. That rigid mask slipped back into place so quickly though, she could almost believe she'd imagined that streak of vulnerability. "I thought you had feelings for me," he said quietly.

"Yeah well, I thought you had them for me too," she snapped, unable to hide her anger.

"I do." He sounded so convincing. "Did you agree to go out with him to make me jealous? I didn't think you played games," he said stiffly.

She snorted. "I'm not playing any games! You're the one who slept with someone else so blame yourself for—"

"What the fuck are you talking about?" he asked, his angry tone taking her off guard. "I haven't slept with anyone since I met you. Hell, I hadn't slept with anyone in the six months before that." While he seemed embarrassed by the admission, he also seemed impossibly sincere.

Either he was the world's best actor or he was telling the truth. Relief detonated inside her like an atomic freaking bomb. She nervously licked her dry lips, some of her earlier steam subsiding. "I called your hotel room after your car was vandalized. Well, first I tried your cell, but when it went straight to voicemail I called the hotel. A woman who'd clearly just woken up answered and I could hear a man in the background." A man she'd assumed was him.

Vadim smiled suddenly, an actual full-on smile that made her breath catch in her throat. But she couldn't imagine what there was to be happy about when she'd just called him out on being a liar. "That's why you've been so angry at me?"

Frowning, she nodded.

"If you called right after my car was damaged, then you would have called late Friday, long after we'd left. The reason I didn't answer my cell is because it was off—because I was on Wyatt's jet. We finished our business early. We didn't even stay at the hotel a single night. Just checked in that morning, then grabbed our stuff again that afternoon before flying out."

All the anger left her then and she felt, well, she didn't know what she felt other than staggering relief. Now that she thought about it, it actually made sense, especially since he'd gotten home not too long after, scaring the crap out of her with that gun. Not wanting to wait another minute, she pulled her cell phone from her purse and texted Logan, telling him there wouldn't be a date tomorrow night. She knew he'd get over it, if he'd even care at all. When she was done, she looked up to find Vadim watching her with a mix of curiosity and wariness. "I just texted Logan and told him there won't be a date."

When Vadim smiled this time, it was one of his half-grins, the sexy predator back. "Good, I won't have to kick his ass now."

For some reason, she didn't think Vadim was kidding. "I'm sorry I've been so...distant, I guess. I just thought, well, after our kiss when I thought you'd slept with someone else, it hurt me." Way more than she'd imagined it would.

Vadim took a step forward, eliminating the distance between them. Gently, he cupped her jaw and stroked his thumb over her cheek. "I don't want anyone else but you," he said softly, the conviction there making her toes curl in her slingbacks. Before she could respond, he dropped his hand, though it appeared to pain him to do so. "Let's get out of here. I don't want any more interruptions."

The implication of those words made heat bloom inside her, rapid and scorching. Not trusting her voice, she simply nodded and let him guide her toward the parking garage. She really hoped the reason he didn't want any interruptions was the reason she was thinking.

Now that she knew he wanted her as much as she did him—and wasn't screwing around with other women—her imagination ran wild about what he'd do to her, and let her do to him. Suddenly the thought of being under his roof for the next week or so sounded like a lot of fun.

CHAPTER TEN

Angel slipped her sweater over her head and pulled her damp hair through, letting it fall down her back. Vadim had received a work call almost the second they'd gotten in the SUV. Then he'd received two more and had still been on the last one when they'd reached his house. He'd looked so apologetic, but she didn't mind the calls.

She was still reeling from the sharp relief that he hadn't slept with anyone else. That he wanted to be with only her. Because she definitely felt the same way.

Smoothing her hand nervously against her jean clad thighs, she stepped out into the hallway. The house was quiet and after searching most of it and finding it empty, she knocked on the door of what he'd told her was his office.

When no one answered, she cracked it open and peeked inside to see if he was on the phone. He wasn't in there, but a glass door leading to the outside was open. The room was gorgeous, with a full wall of windows. The drapes were pulled back, revealing the dark night and desert stars. She imagined he got a lot of natural light in the day. His desk was in pristine condition, with two laptops on the glass top. The rest of the desk was wood, teak she guessed. It went perfectly with the wall of built-in bookshelves.

He must have taken Charlie out because Angel hadn't seen the dog anywhere either. A cool breeze blew through the room. "Vadim?" she called out, not wanting to invade his privacy, even if he had told her that his office door was always open to her. He didn't answer so she started to leave when another gust of wind swept through.

A manila folder on his desk flipped open, the pages ruffling, a few scattering to the floor. Pushing the door open, she stepped farther in and started to pick them up when she saw her name on one of them. As she started to scan it, her fingers turned numb as it sank in what she was looking at. He'd compiled information on her.

"Angel." Vadim stood in the doorway, his expression grim.

Since she'd already jumped to conclusions once, she didn't want to do it again. Giving him the benefit of the doubt, she stood, one of the fallen papers in hand. "The wind blew these off your desk and I saw my name." She motioned to the others near her bare feet. "Is this work related? Did your boss want you to look into me after I took the food from Cloud 9?" She really hoped that's what it was and could actually understand that. Sierra hadn't said anything about telling Mr. Christiansen about what Angel had done, but for all she knew, the chef had done just that. And she wouldn't blame her.

Vadim paused for a moment and she thought he was going to say yes. But he shook his head and stepped to the side as Charlie came in. He shut and locked the door behind the dog, then picked up a small remote from the nearest bookshelf. He pressed a button and she nearly jumped in surprise when the drapes slid closed, covering the windows.

"I didn't want to do this now, but will you take a seat?" He motioned to a small cushioned chair on the other side of his desk.

It looked a little worn, as if he sat in it often in addition to the ergonomic chair behind his desk. Not that she cared about that. She wanted to know why Vadim had a file on her. She'd been stalked once and was now on the run because of it. As she sat, she placed the paper with her name, address and other employee information on the desk and tried to hide her trembling hands in her lap. Charlie plopped down beside her and nudged Angel's foot, as if to let her know she was there. But she couldn't even look at the dog, her gaze was riveted on Vadim.

He sat on the edge of his chair, but he looked like a caged tiger, wanting to pace. "Until today I've never looked into your past. I never wanted to violate our friendship like that. I hope you believe me." The expression on his face told her that was important to him.

Which eased her fears. "I do."

Vadim let out a sigh and slouched back against his chair, the action disconcertingly uncharacteristic. He scrubbed a hand over his face like he did only when he was upset about something. "I don't talk much about my work, but you know I handle a lot of Wyatt's computer security." When she nodded he continued. "Before I came to work for Wyatt I was part of an intel unit in the Marines. I did a lot of stuff for them in conjunction with other government agencies."

She didn't even want to guess what agencies, though the way he said it, she could. "So now you do similar stuff for Mr. Christiansen?"

He nodded. "Yes. Sometimes legal, sometimes not." After he said that, he watched her carefully, as if waiting for a reaction.

Angel shrugged. "If you're waiting for me to judge you, I'm not going to." She was using someone else's social security number. She had no room to judge. Ever.

Something seemed to shift inside him at her words, even though his body language never changed. Finally he continued. "When I stopped by your apartment complex, I spoke to Mr. Botkin. He told me a man had been asking about you. This just happened, right before the vandalism incident. It feels like too much of a coincidence for the two things not to be related. Maybe I'm overreacting. Do you know why anyone would be asking about you?"

That numbness was back, creeping over her entire body like cold fingers. "Someone was asking about me?"

"Yes. Brown hair, brown eyes, tall and Mr. Botkin said his daughters would have considered him handsome in the Hollywood sense."

Oh, god. She was going to be sick. He'd found her. He'd been asking about her. What if she'd led him right back to Vadim's? Oh, no. No, no, *no*. Angel jumped up from her seat, terror forking through her like jagged slashes of lightning. She had to leave. To run, right now. Panic battered against her insides but before she'd taken a single step Vadim jumped up and had rounded the desk.

He grabbed on to her hips, holding her in place, as if he was afraid she'd bolt. Which was exactly what she was planning on doing. "Who is he?"

She shook her head, her throat tightening. "Vadim, I can't...I need to go. Right now. You could be in danger." Tears burned her eyes, streaking a hot path as they fell down her cheeks in wave after wave. She'd been running for two years and while she didn't feel safe exactly, she'd started to hope that maybe she'd left her past behind.

Angel didn't even realize she was sobbing until Vadim pulled her against his chest. She wrapped her arms around him, savoring his strength for just a moment. She knew it wouldn't last, that she couldn't depend on him. Couldn't put him in danger like that. He rubbed his hand up and down her back steadily, just like he'd done this morning when she'd been crying about her apartment.

Lord, what was wrong with her? It was like her pent up emotions from the last two years were just coming out all at once. She was too upset to be embarrassed though.

She wasn't sure how much time passed, a minute, an hour, but eventually that constriction in her chest loosened and she could breathe again. Sucking in a deep breath, her tears finally dried up, she pulled back and looked at Vadim.

He held her face in both his hands, murmuring words she didn't understand as he wiped the stray wetness from her cheeks. His gentle expression nearly cracked her heart open and she almost started crying again.

Reaching up, she lightly gripped his forearms, not to stop him, but because she needed to touch him, to use his strength. "His name is Emile Glass and he killed my brother."

Vadim filed that name away, knowing he would kill this bastard for Angel if the man came after her. He would do anything to take away the raw agony in her beautiful eyes still filled with unshed tears. Motioning to his favorite chair, he sat, and pulled her with him so that she sat on his lap.

She didn't even protest, just curled against him, bringing her legs up so that her knees tucked into him. He wrapped his arms around her, holding her close, waiting for her to continue. He'd just started his investigation on her and so far all he'd discovered was that the social security number she'd been using belonged to a girl who had died as an infant. And Angel had just started using it when she came to work at Cloud 9. He didn't even know if her name was Angel. He didn't care.

"My name really is Angel," she said, as if she'd read his mind. With her head on his shoulder, she absently traced a pattern over his chest with her fingertips. He hated that his sweater was stopping him from feeling her against his skin. "I'm from a small Louisiana town about an hour north of New Orleans. I grew up with two loving parents and a wonderful older brother. Seriously, we were like the perfect all-American family. I loved them so much and I truly appreciated them. I knew what we had was rare. When I was in my last year of college my parents were killed, along with four others, in a freak boating accident. They'd been on vacation with friends in the Bahamas when a swell came up and..." She sucked in a ragged breath before continuing. "That's not important for this story. After they died I went into a depression. Really bad. I dropped out of school and moved back into their home. Which in hindsight was stupid because of all the memories there. I just couldn't seem to pull myself out of my depression. I was never suicidal, but I wasn't happy. Didn't want to leave the house, didn't want to see any of my old friends, nothing. I was living like a shut-in at the age of twenty-two."

Vadim tightened his grip, hating the pain he heard in her voice, hating that she'd had to suffer the loss of her parents. Whenever he'd asked about her family she'd been vague and he hadn't wanted to push. He didn't like talking about his own past so he understood. His mother had tried hard, but she'd had addiction problems among other issues. He'd been more of a burden to her than anything.

"Eventually my brother got me into therapy and out of their house. I still wasn't working, but at least I was leaving the house and doing normal things like grocery shopping on my own. I was such a mess it was pathetic," she said, her self-disgust clear.

"It's not pathetic to mourn those you love." He'd never been lucky enough to have caring parents—had never known who his father was—but he'd lost many friends in the Marines, and he still mourned them. "I wish you'd told me all this."

"I wanted to, so badly. I almost did when you told me about..." She glanced up at him. "About all the friends you'd lost. You were so open and real and I wanted to tell you, but I knew if I told you they'd died I'd end up telling you the whole truth." She sniffled again then ducked her head back to his shoulder and kept tracing random designs on his chest. He stroked a hand down her long, damp hair as she continued. "Long story short, this guy named Emile befriended me. He was sweet, or so I thought, and didn't mind my weirdness of not wanting to go anywhere or do anything. In hindsight I realize he wanted me all to himself and that's why he didn't mind my anti-social behavior. But as you know, that's not the real me. The therapy started helping and so did spending time with my brother. After about six months I started bouncing back, started seeing old high school friends and even my friends from Tulane had started to visit now that they were done with school and I was actually accepting visitors. And they were encouraging me to go back and finish. I was—am—only twelve credits shy of graduating and I was ready to go back too. I still hurt, but I wasn't that emotional mess anymore and I wanted to live my life again."

When she paused, he knew that whatever she was about to say would be horrible.

"Emile must have sensed my...I don't know, me just getting back to normal. I feel like maybe I should have seen the signs but I was so caught up in my own bullshit I didn't realize that what I thought was just friendship, he viewed as much more. One Saturday night I was at his parents' place for dinner. His dad runs the biggest law firm in the town so he's kind of a big deal. There were so many people there, it was...overwhelming. I didn't know most of them and right before dessert he proposed to me." She pulled back and looked at Vadim, her pretty face a mask of horror and confusion. "It was insane, like I was watching it happen to someone else. When I say we were friends, I'm talking just friends. We'd never kissed or flirted or anything. But he got down on one knee, had a ring and everything." Groaning, she covered her face and shook her head. "It was awful," she muttered through her fingers.

Finally she looked up again, and this time sadness bled into her eyes. "Maybe I should have handled it differently, just told him no right then. But I didn't want to embarrass him in front of so many people. I thought it would be kinder to wait. So the next day I met him at his place and apologized if I'd ever led him on or let him believe that I wanted more than friendship. When I tried to give him his ring back, he punched me in the face. Broke my nose. It hurt, but it was also such a shock. That level of violence."

Vadim jerked in the chair, seeing red at the thought of anyone hurting Angel. Oh yeah, this man was dead if he came after her. He didn't want to hear anymore, didn't want her to continue, but he knew she needed to get the whole story out and he needed all the details if he was going to find this bastard. And he was. Very soon.

"I won't go into all the details, but he hurt me. Would have raped me if a neighbor hadn't intervened and called the cops. I pressed charges, filed a restraining order, did everything I was supposed to. Then I moved almost immediately. We'd already sold our parents' house by that point and school didn't start for another couple months so I went to live with my brother while I was healing. Luckily Emile hadn't broken any bones, except my nose. It was mainly just bruising and..." She trailed off and clutched on to Vadim's shoulders. "Vadim."

That was when he realized he was actually shaking. The urge to kill someone had never been so great. So real it felt like a consuming thing, eating at him from the inside. "Keep going," he rasped out, amazed he could speak when his jaw was clenched so tight.

For a moment she looked unsure, but continued. "A couple weeks later my brother was killed in a mugging gone wrong. The town we lived in was a little bigger than the one we'd grown up in, but the area he was in at the time wasn't known for crime and he still had his wallet and very expensive watch. It wasn't a mugging. I knew it and Emile confirmed it with a phone call on the day of my brother's funeral. He said that unless I came back to him, he'd kill everyone I loved. I told the police, but the number he called me from was a throw-away phone. There was nothing they could do except bring him in for questioning but they had nothing to charge him with. So I packed up and ran. He wanted to fight his assault charges in court, and there was no way I was sticking around as long as his father would have dragged it out. I would have been a sitting duck and it's not like the cops could protect me. So I've been on the move for two years." The pain in her voice sliced at him.

Vadim let out a curse, pulling her into a hug. She twisted in his lap and wrapped her arms around his neck. He had a dozen other questions, but knew now wasn't the time. Now he just needed to hold her, to comfort her, to let her know that he wasn't going anywhere and that he'd help her get through this. Because he'd die before letting that monster touch her again.

"You're the first person I've told," she murmured against his neck. "I've wanted to tell you for so long, but didn't know how. Now you understand why I have to leave," she said as she pulled back.

He forced his jaw to work. "There's no way in hell you're leaving. I'm going to kill that bastard."

"Vadim, don't say that." She sounded horrified, but he didn't care.

"This isn't an idle threat, Angel. Computers weren't my only area of expertise in the military. I've killed before and if he comes after you, I'll protect you. No one is going to hurt you. And there's no way I'm letting you face this on your own."

CHAPTER ELEVEN

Angel ran her hands over Vadim's tightly bunched shoulders. The energy humming through him was palpable, his rage simmering just beneath the surface.

Barely.

"I'm not going anywhere." He calmed a fraction at that, but she continued. "And you're not going to do anything to him." She couldn't have Vadim getting in trouble because of her. Or worse. She also knew she was tired of running. She wanted her life back and that was mainly because of Vadim. He was a man she didn't want to leave. Even if her first instinct had been to flee, the time for running was over. She wouldn't live in fear forever.

"You're not leaving," Vadim said again, though this time it sounded almost like a question.

"I know." She pushed up and twisted slightly so that she was straddling him. Her knees pressed on either side of his thighs, the cushion of his chair soft. But what she felt between his legs most definitely wasn't soft.

The rage and anger seemed to dissipate from his expression, only to be replaced by confusion. And a lot of lust. The undeniable flare of heat in his eyes warmed her from the inside out.

She lifted up on her knees so that her covered mound rubbed over his growing hard-on. She didn't want there to be any doubt exactly what she wanted from him. Feeling his reaction to her was the biggest turn on there was. Knowing that she got a man like Vadim so hot made her nipples tighten in anticipation of what was to come.

"Angel." His hands settled on her thighs, his fingers flexing almost convulsively against her. When she didn't say anything, he turned his face away from her. For a moment she feared he'd reject her, but he let out a soft, very clipped command to Charlie. Angel might not understand the word, but she heard the authority behind it.

The dog let out an annoyed sound, but trotted from the room, tail waving. She was glad he'd told her to leave. Angel might adore her, but she didn't need an audience for what she wanted.

"Have you really fantasized about the color of my nipples?" she asked as Vadim met her gaze again.

He nodded, his pale eyes darkening. "Very often." His words were harsh, unsteady. And he was very still. Almost impossibly so. Which told her that he was trying to hold on to his control.

"Then why did you turn me away before?" He'd apologized, but she didn't really understand why he'd seemed almost repelled by her after they'd kissed. There was so much more she wanted to tell him about her past, but right now she wanted to lose herself with him. First, she needed to know he wouldn't reject her again.

When he finally answered, his words stunned her. "I don't deserve you."

She couldn't imagine why he would think that. "You're the sweetest, sexiest man I've ever met."

Frowning, he shook his head. "I've killed before, Angel. With my hands, with weapons, whatever got the job done." He let his hands fall from her hips, as if preparing for her to slide off him. The expression in his blue eyes was so remote it clawed at her.

She didn't want anything between them. She was going to stay in Vegas and fight to get her life back. That included having Vadim in it. All of him. If he'd killed, she knew it had been in the military and that he'd been doing his job. Vadim wasn't the type of man to relish hurting anyone. She saw that in him every time they were together. If he wanted to tell her more, he could, but she wouldn't push. And if that was the only thing that had held him back from her...She reached for the hem of her sweater and lifted it off. Before it had cleared her head she heard Vadim's gasp, felt his hips roll against hers. By the time she'd pulled it fully off, his hands cupped her breasts greedily.

The feel of his rough calluses against her sensitive skin had her arching her back into his hold. Her bra was basically scraps of lace, the thin black material showing him everything, including her pale pink nipples. He groaned again and dipped his head to one of her breasts. He didn't even bother to take her bra off, just shoved the cup down as if he couldn't wait a minute longer and sucked her tight bud into his mouth.

She slid her hands into his hair, needing to hold him.

"Are they how you fantasized?" she whispered shyly.

"Better," he rasped. "Tighter. Pinker." He clamped down on one with his teeth, lashing his tongue over the tip of it, the erotic action making her inner walls clench and her clit pulse. She arched her back, letting him take more of her. He cradled her other breast, tugging that cup down as well.

His impatience was so out of character for what she knew of him that it made her even hotter. Reaching behind her back, she unhooked her bra and let it fall loose. He shuddered as he slightly pulled back and tugged the material down her arms. When he went to tease her with his mouth again, she pushed against his shoulders, sliding off the chair so that she was on her knees in front of him. She wanted to drive him crazy, and she was so eager to touch him she was practically shaking with the need. Without pause she took off his socks and shoes.

She could see the hesitancy in his eyes and knew it was because he'd be giving up control. And she was going to make sure that he did. Well, as long as he would let her. She knew he'd never give it up completely. Reaching for the top of his slacks, she freed the button and zipper and pulled his pants down. She only brought them to his knees though, not wanting to give him more mobility.

He quickly tore his sweater off and his breathing grew even more ragged when she reached for the band of his boxer briefs. The outline of his thick cock was enough to make her entire body tingle in anticipation. He slid a hand into her hair, cupping her head ever so lightly and for a moment she thought he'd stop her.

"I've been wondering if you were a boxer's man." She liked the briefs better than straight boxers. They molded to his muscular thighs and outlined his thick cock, teasing her.

When she tugged the band down over his hard length, he shuddered again, his grip on her head tightening. It had been so long since she'd been with anyone, even before she'd gone on the run, and she wanted to savor every second of this time with him. Her own breathing increased as she took in the sight of him. The man was huge, something she'd guessed from feeling his erection pressed against her abdomen before, but he was even better than her imagination. Heat flooded between her legs at just the sight of him. Not that the sight of any man would do this to her. Only Vadim.

"You are too," she murmured, more to herself than him.

"What?" His voice was rough with confusion.

"Better than my fantasies." She was unable to take her eyes off him.

The man had starred in so many of her fantasies the past five months and now she could touch him all she wanted. She didn't have to stroke herself to orgasm while imagining it was him. This time she'd come with him buried deep inside her and she couldn't wait.

Not wanting to waste another second, she took his thick length in her hand. He pulsed in her grip, his hips jerking upward, and he made the most delicious strangled sound. She stroked upward once, earning a shuddering tremble from him. She rubbed her cheek against his cock and Vadim made another strangled sound she felt all the way between her legs. She was already so wet for him it was embarrassing. It was such a turn on that she was making this tightly wound man lose it.

"You like teasing," he rasped out, the words sounding like an accusation.

With her head bent, her hair covering part of her face, she grinned. "Very much." Before he could respond, she moved upward and flicked her tongue across the small slit on the head of his cock. The taste of his pre-come was slightly salty.

She moaned against him, taking him past her lips. She flicked and teased the crown, feeling empowered each time his fingers clenched in her hair. When he eventually dropped his hand, disappointment surged through her until she realized why. As she licked him from the base of his thick length to the head, she saw that he was gripping the sides of the chair in a death grip, his knuckles white against his tanned skin.

When she went to take him in her mouth again, he grabbed her shoulders. "No." The guttural word made her head snap up. Why was he stopping her? His eyes glittered like pale blue diamonds as he shook his head. "Not in your mouth this time."

She flicked her tongue over her lips, moistening them and teasing him. He closed his eyes, letting his head fall back as he took a deep breath. When he met her gaze again she could see that he was in control. A shot of excitement pulsed through her.

His jaw tightened as he shoved his pants and boxer briefs the rest of the way off. When he stood, completely naked, she stared in awe at his beautiful body. The man was ripped and lean. Clearly he didn't spend all his time behind a desk. Before she could fully stand, he hauled her up and lifted her into his arms.

"Vadim—"

He stopped her with a searing kiss even as she felt him walking them from his office. Moments later he stood in the open doorway of his bedroom. Luckily Charlie was nowhere in sight. Striding inside, Vadim kicked the door shut with one foot and didn't stop until he'd reached the foot of his bed.

When he placed her on the end, kneeling in front of her, his thick cock curving upward in the most erotic display, she couldn't help the nerves that took hold. She'd had exactly two boyfriends in college and they'd been more or less boys. Nothing like Vadim. Hell, there was no one like Vadim anyway.

He must have sensed her nervousness because he stilled, still kneeling between her slightly spread legs. It didn't matter that he was on the floor, this man was totally in control and they both knew it. "What is it, *milaya moya*?" His voice dropped an octave, making her toes curl.

She might not understand what he said, but she could read that seductive tone and whatever he'd called her was an endearment. She started to tell him nothing, but knew he'd see through her. "I don't have much experience and I don't want to be disappointing." Damn, why did her voice have to shake? The thought of him finding her lacking shredded her.

The room was fairly dim, except for the outside light of the moon and stars shining through one of the windows, but she could see his expression clearly. He looked fierce and a little intimidating as he leaned forward and captured her mouth with his, his kisses surprisingly sweet and gentle.

As he ran a palm up her bare back, he started feathering kisses along her jaw. "You could never disappoint me, *angel moya.*"

Her nipples tightened at the endearment. One she actually knew. *Angel mine.* When he nipped her earlobe between his teeth, pressing hard enough that she jumped, she slid her hands over his shoulders, letting her fingers dance over his muscles.

She could spend hours just touching him, stroking him, learning everything about him. As his head dipped lower, his lips moving over her breasts, he freed the button of her jeans, sliding her pants off. She hadn't bothered with panties because she'd hoped this would happen tonight.

He sucked in a ragged breath as he pulled them free of her feet. Before she could blink, he'd buried his face between her legs. No teasing like she thought he'd do, he just went straight for her clit.

The sensation was deliciously jarring. She was already wet, but hadn't been ready for the intimate contact. His tongue stroked against her clit in a determined rhythm, insistent and merciless.

She fell back against the bed, spreading her thighs for him. When she did, he made a growling sound against her spread lips, the vibration moving through her, making her nipples bead even tighter.

When he lifted his head, her entire body jerked, mourning the loss of that wicked mouth. "Touch yourself," he demanded before returning to her clit.

She knew what he meant, but the thought of touching herself in front of him—even while he was buried between her legs—made her face heat up. Before she could move, he reached up with one of his hands, took the hand she'd threaded through his short hair and moved it up to one of her breasts.

Shoving her insecurities away, she cupped both her breasts and started stroking her nipples, rolling them between her fingers as Vadim continued to pleasure her. His tongue was positively wicked, flicking and circling against her clit with the most intense pressure.

She felt as if she was walking on a tightrope and any second she'd fall off, her orgasm surging through her. She was so close to finding her release but she needed more, needed to feel his fingers inside her.

"Put your fingers in me," she whispered.

He groaned against her, immediately complying, first with one, then two, stretching her with his thick digits. She bucked against his fingers as her body raced toward climax. He pushed in and out of her in a shaky rhythm, as if he wasn't quite in control, his fingers stroking against her sensitive flesh, his tongue just as fervent, when she suddenly fell over the edge.

Pleasure punched to all her nerve endings in one simultaneous shot, making her back arch as she dropped her hands from her breasts. He continued thrusting his fingers inside her.

"Vadim." It was all she could manage to gasp out as her orgasm seemed to go on forever, battering against her senses with no reprieve until she collapsed against the bed, her legs hanging limply off the edge.

Blinking up at the ceiling, she smiled as Vadim started kissing his way up her belly, all the while murmuring Russian words she didn't understand. His fingers were still inside her when he reached her mouth.

The satisfied look in his eyes stunned her because he was that happy she'd come. As if her pleasure was all that mattered. Her previous boyfriends had never looked at her like that. No one had.

"Taste yourself," he murmured in that dark way of his before he brushed his mouth over hers.

She felt her face flush as her tongue danced against his. Tasting her own release was oddly erotic. Reaching between them, she went to grasp his cock when he pulled back.

"One second," he said, his expression tight.

She didn't understand what he meant until he rolled off her and opened one of the drawers in his nightstand. Condoms, of course.

Thankfully one of them was thinking clearly. Even though she wanted to feel him inside her bare, it wasn't worth the risk when she wasn't on birth control.

She crawled up the bed, watching as he moved with impressive efficiency, tearing open the new box—the fact that it was new made her stupidly happy. When he pulled out a condom, she snagged it from him.

He turned, watching her with those pale, hungry eyes then knelt in front of her. She cursed her shaking hands as she ripped the packet open, but eventually got it free. Before she could roll it on him, he took it.

"I need inside you." His guttural words, the way his own hand shook, melted her as he rolled the condom over his thick length.

From what she knew about Vadim, she had no doubt he'd want to be on top, to be the one in control, so she laid back against the soft bed, excited for him to show her his more dominant nature. His comforter and sheets were silky and had a cooling effect against her skin even while her entire body hummed with a burning urgency.

"You are so beautiful, more than I ever imagined," Vadim murmured before moving on top of her.

Even though he had to know how wet she was, he slid a finger inside her, testing her. Closing his eyes, he let his head fall back for a moment, his body shuddering. In the moonlight, his body looked even more...savage.

It was the first word that popped into her head. Kneeling in between her legs, he looked as if he'd been cut from stone, each ridge, line, and striation perfection. And begging for her touch. She started to sit up, eager to stroke him when he withdrew his finger and pushed his erection inside her in one long stroke.

He filled her, her inner walls stretching and molding around him even as she gasped at the intrusion. Her back arched at the feel of him pushing deeper. She reached for him, needing that contact. His expression was so open, so vulnerable as he started pumping inside her. He leaned down on his forearms, caging her in as he caught her gaze, pinning her in place.

She wrapped her hands around him, stroking them down his back and over his butt, tightening her fingers into his firm muscle when he pushed all the way inside her. Each time she dug her fingers into him she squeezed her inner muscles around his cock. And each time, his thrusts became more unsteady as he started to let go of that control. And each time he slammed into her, his cock hit that perfect spot designed to drive her insane.

"Come in me," she whispered.

Her words set something loose inside him. Groaning, he buried his face against her neck, nipping her sensitive skin as he slammed into her, over and over, his tempo increasing as he found his release. As he let go of his own control, another orgasm surged through her.

Not as intense as the first, almost like an after effect of it. But it was spine-tingling nonetheless, her inner walls rippling around him as he climaxed, groaning her name over and over until he basically collapsed on her.

She could tell he was still holding most of his weight off her, but she wrapped her arms and legs around him, nuzzling against his neck. "That was amazing."

"You are amazing." He softly raked his teeth against her earlobe, making her shiver, before he raised his head and nipped her bottom lip. "And we're just getting started."

CHAPTER TWELVE

Angel jerked awake at the feel of something cold touching her feet. Rolling over in Vadim's bed, she realized he was fast asleep, his arm stretched out over her bare stomach. When she glanced down she saw Charlie half on the bed, nudging her foot insistently.

A quick glance at Vadim's slim digital clock told her it was two in the morning. And she knew what the dog wanted. Slowly, she slid out from Vadim's grip. Or tried to. Before she'd fully pulled free, his hand tightened against her belly.

"Where are you going?" he murmured sleepily.

"To get Charlie a treat. She's hungry."

Vadim grunted and muttered something in Russian before releasing her. He looked so adorable sleeping that she didn't want to leave him, but the past few nights she'd been here Charlie had woken her looking for a handout. Angel knew she'd have to stop the dog's habit because she didn't want to get woken up at two every night, but she'd indulge her for now. Charlie's schedule and home life had been changed because of Angel, so she didn't mind. Snagging a T-shirt from one of Vadim's drawers she slipped it on and hurried to the kitchen.

Just as she'd suspected, the dog didn't whine at the locked doggy door, she went straight for the pantry and nudged it with her nose.

"You are so spoiled," Angel murmured, opening the door and giving her one of the green bones.

After Charlie ran off to her living room bed, Angel hurried back to Vadim's room and slipped under the covers. The moment she did, he tugged her close and she could feel his half-hard length pressing against her thigh when she threw it over his waist.

Laying her head on his chest, she murmured, "Don't even think about it. I'm too tired." He'd been like a machine the past few hours and they'd only just dozed off about an hour ago. They'd had sex, eaten, had sex again, showered with him going down on her, then gone to bed, only to have him wake her up again for more sex—and she was exhausted. Not to mention sore, but in the best way possible.

He chuckled, his fingers sliding under the T-shirt and stroking lightly against her back as she curled into him, but he didn't make a move to take things any further.

Starting to doze, all she could think about was the first time she'd gotten the courage to talk to him. He'd always seemed so aloof, and for some reason he'd fascinated her. She'd gone out of her way to fly under the radar everywhere she worked, not making too many friends, but the man had called to her on the most primal level. As sleep started to pull her under, she couldn't help but smile as she remembered their first conversation.

"Hi, are you looking for Hayden?" she asked the tall blond man she'd seen around the casino. She'd heard a couple of the female servers whispering about him and she was intrigued. Okay, more than intrigued. This man was deliciously sexy.

He tilted his head to the side a fraction, as if assessing her. "Yes."

"Thought so. He's in the back with Sierra, helping her with something, but between you and me I don't think he's helping her so much as trying to get some private time in her office." It was no secret Sierra had started dating one of the heads of security a couple months earlier and the man was there all the time now. Of course Hayden had been hanging out at the Cloud since it opened because of the chef. No one was shocked they'd finally gotten together.

To her surprise, the blond man half-smiled. "Thank you. I'll just wait at the bar."

"Do you want company?" she asked, unable to stop herself. She was never like this with men, especially not since she'd gone on the run.

His eyebrows raised, those pale blue eyes glinting with something she couldn't define, but he nodded.

"I'm Angel," she said as she slid onto one of the bar stools next to him.

"Vadim." He still watched her curiously.

"That's an interesting name." When he didn't respond, she nervously shifted in her seat before catching the bartender's eye. The woman smiled and poured her a glass of wine without Angel having to tell her. It was impressive how the bartender seemed to remember everyone's preferred drink.

"It's Russian." Vadim's response was a little delayed, taking her off guard, but she smiled.

"I like it. Vadim." When she said his name, his eyes seemed to almost darken, but then he looked away and motioned to the bartender. The woman knew his preferred drink too, which was top shelf Scotch.

"I don't think I've seen you in here with the other security guys." But she had seen him around the hotel, usually with Hayden or Jay Wentworth. And sometimes with Iris Christiansen.

He gave what might have been a half-shrug, it was hard to tell. He just pinned her with those blue eyes, as if he was trying to see inside her head. It was a little disconcerting. Not creepy, just like he was trying to figure her out.

"So are you from Russia?"

He shook his head. "No. Chicago. My mother was an immigrant though and didn't know any English. It's why I still have a slight accent." He seemed almost surprised at himself for a moment as he spoke.

She couldn't imagine why. Snagging one of the napkins, she started folding it into origami without looking at it. She *needed to keep her hands busy. Vadim was so sexy, so absolutely male, he made her knees weak. She was glad she was sitting.* "So what do you need Hayden for?"

"Security issue." *His answer was blunt, his expression shuttered. Maybe he thought she was fishing for security information. She'd noticed that most of the security people here kept a tight lid on what they did, which was understandable.* "Where are you from?"

His question took her off guard, though it shouldn't have since she'd asked him first. She hated lying, but had gotten used to it. "Small town in Georgia." *She stuck to her Southern roots, knowing she couldn't hide her slight accent and that most people wouldn't know the difference between a Georgia and Louisiana accent.*

When he didn't respond, she started to feel weird, like she'd cornered him into this conversation he didn't want to have. God, what was wrong with her? She was so fucking lonely, that's what. And he probably thought she was weird. Feeling embarrassed, she handed him the owl then laid a bill on the bar to cover her drink. She took another big sip, not wanting to leave the full glass sitting there. "Well, I've gotta go if I don't want to miss my bus. It was nice to meet you."

When she stood, he slid off his stool. "Do you need a ride?" *He seemed to startle himself as he asked the question, which made him adorable.*

Okay, now she was really shocked, but oddly enough not uncomfortable. After she'd gone on the run she'd gotten really good at reading people and Vadim was just being nice. "Uh, no, I'm okay. The bus goes right by my apartment complex. Hopefully I'll see you around though?"

He nodded, half-smiling in that cute way of his before he sat back down.

"Angel," Vadim murmured against her ear, his light stubble tickling her face. He hadn't shaved last night and she liked the feel of it against her skin. "What are you dreaming about? You're smiling."

"Mm, you," she mumbled drowsily, not fully awake, but when his big hand cupped her mound, she moaned. "Are you on drugs or something? You're truly a machine."

He nipped her bottom lip, but she still hadn't opened her eyes. "No drugs, just you. Now that you're letting me touch you, I'm not going to stop."

She looked at him through heavy-lidded eyes. "I was dreaming about the first time we met. I was so nervous talking to you."

He snorted and nipped her lip again as he dipped a finger inside her sheath. She was tender, but he felt so good. "You were adorable. And confusing."

She arched into his hold, already growing wet from his light stroking. "Confusing?" she managed to gasp out when he added another finger.

"I didn't understand why you were talking to me." He nipped lower, raking his teeth over her jaw as he withdrew his fingers.

"Uh, because you have that whole mysterious, sexy thing going on. I couldn't help myself." She stroked her hands over his shoulders, her fingers tightening on the flex of his muscles as he moved.

He didn't comment, just started to lift the hem of her T-shirt. He paused when his cell phone started buzzing across his nightstand, but after a moment he ignored it and tugged the shirt off.

Her nipples instantly hardened under his gaze and when he dipped his head to one of them, she slid her fingers through his hair, clutching him to her. Not that she was afraid he'd go anywhere. He'd made it clear he wanted her in a way no one ever had.

It was a little intimidating to be on the receiving end of so much hunger, but she loved it, especially since she felt the same way. When his phone buzzed again, she pushed at his shoulder.

"Vadim, it could be important."

He lifted his head, glanced at the clock, then grabbed his phone. She thought he'd answer it but after he looked at the caller ID he turned it off.

She started to protest, but he went right back to what he was doing, covering her body with his as he lightly pressed his teeth against her nipple. She spread her legs, letting him settle over her. "Are you sure…you can ignore that?" She didn't want him to get in trouble at work, but it was hard to care much about anything when he'd started teasing her.

Reaching between their bodies, she wrapped her fingers around his cock and started slowly stroking him. He shuddered against her, but didn't answer so she guessed that meant yes, he could do any damn thing he wanted. Which was good because the need building inside her was growing each second that ticked by.

When he moved to her other breast, she tightened her hold on him, stroking a little faster. He still needed to put a condom on and she liked feeling him without any barrier. As she squeezed harder, he pulled back, his breathing rough. Without a word, he leaned over and reached for the open box on the nightstand.

As he moved, she slid out from under him and pushed up on her knees. "I want to be on top." The words came out in a rush. He was so damn dominating, which she loved, but she wasn't sure he'd want her to take charge.

He gave her one of those sexy half-smiles as he slowly rolled the condom over his thick length. Stretching out on his back, he placed his hands behind his head, the action making the muscles in his arms flex, reminding her how powerful he was. Not that she'd forgotten. Staring at him laid out like that, with the dawn light just starting to stream through the window, she thought he looked like utter perfection. Faded white scars nicked his chest, stomach, biceps and even his hands, though she couldn't see those at the moment. When her gaze landed on his cock, her inner walls tightened again as she thought of what it would feel like to have him pushing deep into her. Or maybe she'd take him in her mouth first.

"You gonna stare all morning?" he murmured wickedly.

"Maybe I will." But she had no willpower. And she wasn't sure if he'd change his mind about letting her be on top. She wanted to take advantage of it, wanted to ride him and be in control as they both came.

Sliding her leg over his hips, she straddled him and took his thick length in her hand. He was so hard she didn't really need to guide him to her entrance, but she liked wrapping her fingers around him.

Meeting his gaze, she slowly slid down over him, sucking in a breath at the feel of his thickness filling her. His pale eyes seemed to glitter against the increasing sunlight from outside. He arched into her, grabbing onto her hips as she sank completely onto him.

She ran her palms over his chest as she lifted up then pushed back down, slowly starting to ride him. Her hair fell forward over her breasts and Vadim's hungry gaze tracked the movements. Every inch of him felt incredible, just as intense as that first time.

His fingers tightened on her hips, his eyes going molten as he held her in place over him. Suddenly she realized that while she was on top, he was still the one in control. The thought made more heat rush between her legs, her inner walls flexing convulsively around him. When she tried to move, he held her firm.

"Touch your breasts." A soft demand.

Even though they'd made love many times over the last few hours, with the sun now coming up, streaming over the big bed, she felt almost on display for him. The sensation was exhilarating but also made her nervous. She might be comfortable with her body, but this was new to her.

With her past boyfriends she'd never had sex more than once in a night or day and no one had ever made her feel so aware of her body. Not like Vadim.

When she reached up and cupped her breasts, he shuddered and jerked his hips upward, pushing even deeper into her. She arched her back at the sensation, rolling her thumbs over her nipples, lightly stimulating them. The pleasure was connected to the pulsing between her legs. Each time she did, she clenched around him and he groaned.

To test him, she tried to move again, but he held her still, watching her with that intensely raw gaze. Slowly, he started rocking into her, but he wasn't letting her move much, just enough that his cock rubbed against that elusive spot inside she'd only found with vibrators in the past. She realized she could come just like this as he continued to rock into her.

And when he let go of one hip and started rubbing her clit with his free hand, the orgasm built faster than she'd expected. Her stomach muscles clenched as the need magnified and she increased her own stroking, pinching her nipples between her forefingers and thumbs.

Vadim's eyes narrowed on her fingers and he gritted out what she guessed was a curse in Russian under his breath. His own caresses increased and when he tweaked her clit, her orgasm slammed into her, taking her off guard.

Pleasure rushed through her to all her nerve endings, her sheath tightening around him as she let go. As her climax continued, he mercifully let go of her hip, letting her ride him.

He met her stroke for stroke, groaning as she leaned forward, her hair spreading over his chest. When he grabbed her ass, helping her move even faster over him, he shouted out his release, pumping until he was sated and she collapsed on his chest.

She wasn't sure how much time passed, but eventually he stirred beneath her, his breathing evened out. "I'm not going to get anything done with you here," he murmured.

She laughed against his chest. "I don't think that's such a bad thing." After a long moment, she asked, "Do you have to work today?"

"I'm working from home. And we still have more to talk about." He ran a gentle hand down her back, the feel of his calluses making her shiver.

She loved his hands all over her body. Unfortunately, he was right. "Yeah, I know." Sighing, she pushed up. "I'm going to shower—alone," she added when his gaze darkened. "When I get out I'd love it if there was coffee waiting."

He leaned up and brushed his lips over hers. "I think I can arrange that."

She clenched around his half-hard length still inside her. Staring down into his eyes, she realized that she'd completely fallen for Vadim. Not halfway, she was full-on smitten with him. So much so that it should have scared her. There were so many layers to him, something she'd known from the moment they'd met, and she'd only seen some of them so far. She just hoped she wasn't in over her head. And she really hoped that once she finished telling him everything about what she'd done to cover her tracks and her past that he wouldn't judge her. The thought of seeing any sort of recrimination in Vadim's eyes sliced at her insides with an intensity she couldn't even think about.

CHAPTER THIRTEEN

Angel stepped out of Vadim's bathroom to find her bag of clothes and laptop on the neatly made king-sized bed. She thought it was sweet that Vadim had brought her things over so she could change—until she saw a couple of her clothing boxes near the window. Had he brought all of her things into his room? Not sure how she felt about that, she dressed quickly in jeans, a sweater and left her damp hair down. She'd run a blow dryer through it for a few minutes to get most of the wetness out but she was craving coffee—because tea wouldn't cut it right now—and she knew they needed to finish talking about what she planned to do moving forward.

She was tired of living in fear but she'd also made a mess of things by using a different social security number. She wasn't sure what to do about that so she hoped Vadim might have an idea.

She found him in the kitchen standing next to the island frowning at his laptop. Charlie was beside him, but perked up when she saw Angel. Immediately the dog went to the pantry door and nudged it.

"You're going to spoil her," Vadim murmured without glancing up from the screen, clearly reading something.

She ignored him and opened the door. "I have no shame buying her affection with treats. Besides, I can't say no to her face," she said as she handed Charlie two little bones. One for her to hide and one to eat.

When she shut the door she looked over to find Vadim watching her appreciatively. She was dressed casually but that hungry look in his eyes made her feel sexy. "What are you working on?" she asked as she headed for the half-full coffee pot on the other side of his computer.

"Nothing that can't wait." He half-closed the screen as he leaned against the counter. "You hungry? I can cook something."

He cooked too? Oh yeah, she was done for when it came to him. "Coffee's all I need, but thanks."

He reached for her hips, tugging her close so she set her mug on the counter. "It's no problem. And I hope that's not *all* you need." Lightly, he brushed his lips over hers and her entire body pulled taut in awareness again.

Grinning, she pushed at his chest and picked up her mug as she sat at one of the island chairs. "I'm really not hungry. By the way, why did you move all my boxes into your room?"

He shrugged, reaching for his own mug. After last night she'd thought she could read him pretty well but his expression was carefully blank. "Do you want to stay in the guestroom?"

"No, of course not, it's just I won't be here that long so…" She shrugged, trailing off.

He cleared his throat and, apparently deciding to ignore her comment, slid a small, wire-bound notebook with blank paper to her. "I need your real social security number, list of former addresses, parents' names, school info, any info you have on Emile including his parents' names. Also, whatever happened with your parents' life insurance policy? Or didn't they have one?"

She took the pad and pulled out the pen attached to the wire bound spine. Tapping it against the pad, she watched Vadim worriedly. "So you know that I didn't use my social security number to gain employment at Cloud 9?"

His eyebrows furrowed together, as if that should be obvious. "Yes. The number you're using is from an infant who died—it's in the file I have. I thought you saw that."

She shook her head, relief spilling through her like a waterfall that he didn't seem to be angry. "I hadn't seen it. I thought…" She broke off, not wanting to admit her fears. "Ah, in regards to the insurance policy we got the runaround with them. They said their death wasn't covered even though accidental deaths were. My brother was the one who handled everything since I was in no state to do anything at the time. After he died, I didn't really think about it." She'd paid for his funeral, then using a college friend's contact, she'd paid for a new ID.

His frown deepened. "Include the name of the insurance company with your other notes. Do you have the policy number?"

"I've got the info on my laptop."

He seemed to relax at that. "Good. I researched the history of the social security number you've been using. I assume you bought new credentials?" When she nodded, he continued. "You only just started using the number at Cloud 9, so did you have a different ID before?"

She shook her head. "No. The year and a half before I started working at the Cloud I was working mainly in dives that were willing to pay me under the table. Things got a little dicey at the last restaurant I worked at. It was this little place out in the middle of freaking nowhere New Mexico. Things were fine at first, but a couple months into my job the owner's son started working there as a chef and started harassing me. He made it clear that he knew I was being paid under the table and basically threatened me with calling the police. He thought I was on the run from the cops, which is clearly wrong, but still, I realized that if I kept working in places like that I'd be opening myself up to harassment and worse. It was scary using my fake credentials, I wasn't even sure they'd work, but..." She shrugged, not needing to finish. Clearly it had worked. Which was good because she'd paid enough money for the fake paperwork.

As another thought occurred to her, she bit her bottom lip. "Crap. What will happen at the restaurant and with the IRS? If I reclaim my life I need to start using my real information." She was pretty sure her crime of using a fake social security number was at least considered fraud or something.

"I'll take care of it." Vadim's voice was so full of authority, it threw her off balance.

"Just like that? How?"

"You haven't worked at the Cloud long enough to file taxes. They'll be sending out the 1099s in about three weeks, and they haven't filed anything yet. I'll talk to accounting—after Wyatt—and we'll say that a wrong number was entered by mistake. Nothing that can't be undone."

Some of the tension resting on her shoulders eased, but the thought of using her real information again was frightening after living in hiding for so long. It seemed as if Emile had found her anyway, but still, her stomach twisted in knots, the coffee she'd already had seeming to turn to lead.

Vadim reached out, gently cupping the side of her face with one hand. "We're going to figure all this out."

She leaned into him, sliding off the chair and wrapped her arms around him. She'd been alone for so long, afraid to tell anyone the truth about who she was, she felt like a sponge now, just soaking up all Vadim's strength. "I'm just scared to go back to work I guess."

Vadim stiffened and pulled back to look at her. "You're not going in to work until we find this guy."

"What?" She couldn't afford to just *not* work.

"I've already talked to Sierra and you've got the next week off. At least." He sounded so freaking high-handed, as if his decision was final, that she gave his chest a little shove.

She didn't care that Vadim was right in this, it pissed her off that he'd just made the decision without asking her first. "So you called my boss and made a decision without thinking to ask me?"

For the first time since she'd met him, Vadim looked like a deer caught in headlights. Okay, more like a tiger in headlights. His expression was wary.

"It's not a trick question, Vadim." She sat back on the chair at the island and crossed her arms over her chest.

"I should have asked you first?" he said, clearly confused.

"Uh, yeah."

"But it doesn't make sense for you to be in public with Emile out there. He's likely already vandalized my car and you seem sure he's the one who spoke to Mr.

Botkin." The tone of his voice was like he was talking to a small child.

Which lit the fuse on her annoyance. "I know, I get that. But I don't want someone making decisions for me. I could have called Sierra on my own." She would have preferred it.

He looked as if he wanted to argue, but instead nodded. "I'm sorry."

Some of her anger evaporated. "It's okay. I just...I don't like anyone making decisions for me, okay?" She'd had so much control in her life taken from her that even the little things being taken away rubbed her the wrong way.

Something like concern flickered in his pale eyes, but he nodded. "Okay. I'm going to be here most of the day working on tracking down Emile. But tomorrow I've got a full day with Wyatt...and I would like to have a friend stay here with you."

Angel figured he'd already asked his 'friend' and resisted the urge to smile. "A friend?"

He lifted a shoulder. "One of the security team."

She couldn't even imagine how expensive it would be to give her a bodyguard for a day. "Your house is safe and you've got an impressive security system. Plus you've got Charlie."

The dog trotted into the kitchen then and made a soft whining sound near the pantry door. "No," Angel said to her, knowing that even if she wanted to spoil the dog, she couldn't do it every time.

Vadim gave her a ghost of a smile as Charlie headed for her food bowl instead. "I would feel better to have someone here. And I would like him to teach you some self-defense moves. Nothing too intense, just enough training to give you moves so that you can do enough damage to someone then run."

"Can't you teach me?" After seeing him take out those guys at her apartment complex she had no doubt that he was skilled enough.

"I could, but if your hands are all over my body we'll end up naked more often than not." He half-smiled, but she knew he was right.

Even thinking about those kinds of teaching scenarios with Vadim made her body heat up. She put a pin in that for now because the thought of learning more self-defense than she'd picked up in the few classes she'd taken in college was wildly appealing. But… "Won't that be really expensive? To have someone stay here?"

He blinked, as if that was the last thing he'd expected her to ask. "No."

She knew that wasn't true, at least not to her. But maybe he didn't consider it expensive. She didn't want to take advantage, but the thought of being able to actually defend herself. Protect herself. Yeah, she couldn't say no. "Okay, thank you and I'll pay—"

Shaking his head, Vadim closed the small distance between them. He cupped her face between his hands, the action so gentle it melted her. "Let me do this for you."

There was no way she could say no to that. When she leaned up to kiss him, he brushed his lips across her forehead instead.

Disappointment filtered through her until he said, "Write everything down first. Then…" He trailed off, his expression wicked as he moved down the countertop of the island and pushed his laptop open again.

She could easily fill in the rest of his unspoken thought. She grabbed the pen and started scribbling all her information down. It was time to get her life back.

Emile opened the door to his newest motel room. His private investigator had rented the place under his name so Emile wouldn't have any records of being here in Vegas. Not that his PI knew the real reason for his trip. He'd been vague, telling him that Angel had stolen his grandmother's priceless ring when she'd left him and he just wanted it back.

He wasn't sure if the guy believed him, but he was still helping him. Of course Emile was paying him a shit-load of money so he might not even care about the truth. The guy was in another state; Emile hadn't wanted anyone with ties to his own family. He'd needed to keep his search for Angel a secret because he hadn't wanted to risk his parents finding out he was still looking for Angel. Namely his father.

His father was still angry about what he'd done to her. Or maybe not so much what he'd done, but that he'd shamed the family publicly. It wasn't like he'd ever gone to trial so he didn't have anything on his record. But his father said the whole town knew about him now, that he had to be more careful or he'd end up in jail and ruin the family name.

Emile didn't care if he ended up behind bars. He just wanted Angel all to himself one last time. Just for a little bit. He wanted her to suffer for embarrassing him, for turning him down when he'd offered her everything. He'd been there for her when she'd needed him, then she'd thrown all his kindness back in his face as if he was nothing. He was going to take everything from her, what he rightfully deserved. He hadn't pressured her about sex before but she owed him use of her body and he would take it.

But now she was nowhere to be found. He'd been watching the restaurant for three damn days and she hadn't shown up once. Fighting that sinking feeling of familiar desperation, he shut the door behind him and pulled his cell phone out of his pocket. No missed calls or texts. He quickly called his PI.

Humphrey answered on the second ring. "Yeah."

"Have you found out anything?"

"Not since we last talked an hour ago." He sounded frustrated, but Emile didn't care. He was paying the guy after all.

"Call me if you find anything," he snapped, ending the call and tossing the phone onto the king-sized bed.

His investigator had found out that the SUV Emile had briefly followed was registered to the Serafina casino and hotel. He'd also had the investigator run the plate registered to the Mercedes Angel had been driving, but had come back with nothing. Which his investigator had said was odd. Emile didn't care, he just wanted Angel and if his PI couldn't find her, he'd hire someone else.

At least Humphrey had come through with locating Angel. He had to give the guy that. Emile would have never found her in the first place without him. Using her personal history as a guide, the man had gone to New Orleans and managed to track down multiple forgers in the area. Eventually he'd found the one who'd provided false credentials for people. It had been a shot in the dark, but he'd managed to narrow down a forger with ties to the university. Then he'd blackmailed the guy into giving up Angel's information. From there, he'd found out where she lived. Not that that did Emile any good right now.

Emile shoved his hands through his hair as he stared blindly at the nearest wall. He hadn't slept in days. Now that he was so close to having her again, he couldn't believe she might have slipped through his fingers.

No, he refused to believe that. He would have her again. He just needed sleep. And a shower. He knew he smelled. Even though it had been a risk, he'd asked the hostess at Cloud 9 about Angel, wanting to know when she'd be working next. The woman had said she'd taken time off work and that's all she'd known.

But the hostess had seemed almost stressed by his question so he'd left immediately. And as soon as he'd gone, he'd seen her calling someone. Maybe he was being paranoid, but she could have called Angel or hotel security.

He just didn't know. And he hated not knowing. He raked his hands through his hair again, the slight pull against his scalp easing some of the pressure building in his brain. She brought out this obsessive side to him and he hated her for it. She made him crazy. She wasn't the first woman to do this to him, but she was the worst. She'd actually been friends with him, made him believe that she loved him. In reality she was a lying whore.

At a slight shuffling sound he turned toward the cracked open bathroom door. Confusion slammed into him when the door opened. Was there a maid in here? He'd left the 'do not disturb' sign on the door.

When a man stepped out, he frowned as it registered who he was seeing. "What are you doing here?" As soon as he saw the gun, however, he knew.

His heart jumped into his throat. He stepped back, tripping over his feet as he scrambled to escape but it was too late. As a shot rang out, pain exploded in his chest for a brief moment before everything went dark.

CHAPTER FOURTEEN

Vadim hit send on his email, sending the last file Wyatt had requested to one of the man's many accounts. This one wasn't accessible by his assistant though, it was one of Wyatt's personal addresses. His boss was about to buy a pharmaceutical company in Ohio and had requested that Vadim run all the financials of the sellers. Not the typical number crunching Wyatt's accountants would do. No, he was looking at the owners' personal accounts.

Wyatt wanted to see how desperate they were since this sale had come up unexpectedly. Turned out there was a reason for it—they were about to go bankrupt due to poor money management and what Vadim was certain was fraud from two members in accounting. On the outside the company looked stellar, but Wyatt always did his homework.

After he closed out the file, he pulled up the one he'd started to build on Emile Glass. The past three days he'd been working sixteen hour days, balancing his duties for Wyatt and his own personal stuff for Angel. He was exhausted, but it was worth it to make Angel safe. She hadn't left his house the past three days either, which he felt bad about, but Roman was there with her and they'd done a bit of exploring in the desert. So far she didn't seem to be going stir crazy, which eased his guilt.

He was close to narrowing down Emile's location, he could feel it. There was a possibility that he wasn't in Vegas at all—but he'd bought an open-ended, round-trip plane ticket to Vegas and had arrived a week ago. So the man was here.

Somewhere.

Unfortunately, he wasn't using any of his personal credit cards or phone anywhere. That in itself was odd. People didn't just fall off the grid for a week. Most people used their credit or debit cards once a day, so he was definitely trying to hide. This wasn't some random coincidence that he'd come to Vegas and now suddenly Vadim's car had been vandalized right after Angel was seen driving it.

As he flipped through the massive number of files he'd found on the guy, one of the credit card payments stuck out. It was dated a month ago to a private investigative firm. Vadim frowned, scanning back through all the statements for the past couple years but couldn't find anything similar. Maybe it was the first time he'd used an investigator but Vadim doubted it if this guy was hunting Angel. He could have been paying by check before. Either way, the use of a private investigator was interesting.

He set that file on top of everything then slid his giant stack of paperwork into his briefcase. Normally he would read from his laptop, but Angel wanted to help so he'd printed everything off. And sometimes it was easy to miss things on his computer so a print version gave him a fresh perspective. It was after five, which was early for him to be heading home, but he could read anywhere. And he missed Angel.

The security room was buzzing as he stepped from his office, but he tuned everything out until Iris held up a hand, motioning for him to stop. She paused, turning back to speak to one of the security team members where they stood in front of a wall of video screens before hurrying toward him.

She didn't bother with niceties, her expression pinched. "One of the hostesses at Cloud 9 called me about half an hour ago. Sorry I didn't get up here until now. A man was asking about Angel's schedule and I knew you'd want to know."

Vadim gritted his teeth as he took in that information, but he didn't let himself outwardly react. "Thanks, Iris." Vadim was tempted to head back to his office and scan the security cameras in the right time frame to see if he could catch a clip of Emile, but decided to do that at home. Now more than ever he wanted to be near Angel, to see with his own eyes that she was safe.

When he reached the private elevators his cell phone buzzed. Gritting his teeth, he glanced at the screen, hoping it wasn't Iris calling him back for something. His heart rate kicked up when he saw who it was. Detective Cody Hurley.

Wyatt, Vadim and a handful of others at the Serafina had worked with him a couple months ago to bring down a huge criminal element in Vegas. To say the guy owed them credit for one of the biggest busts he'd ever had would be an understatement. Vadim had called him a couple days ago asking the detective to keep an eye out for Emile Glass. Didn't hurt to use all your resources and for Angel, he'd use everything at his disposal. He wanted Angel safe more than he wanted his next breath. When the time was right he planned to ask her to move in with him permanently.

He answered immediately. "Hey, Detective."

"Found that guy you were looking for." His voice was grim.

Relief punched through him at the news. "Great. Where?"

"Dead."

Surprised, he frowned. "Where? How?" He also wanted to know who had done it, but figured that could wait.

"Cheap motel, two gunshots. One to the chest, one to the head. Why'd you want me looking into this guy anyway?" A sharp note of command colored the question.

Which Vadim ignored. "You have any idea who did it?"

"No. It's a shitty part of town so I'm just surprised anyone called in about hearing the gunshots. There aren't any video cameras at this place either. None that work anyway. Looks like he surprised someone robbing his room. Come on, why were you looking into this guy?"

Vadim wasn't telling him shit about Angel, but he'd give him what he could. "There's a possibility he was the one who vandalized my car last week. And I can't tell you how I know that. Was he staying under his own name?" Because Vadim had put out feelers. The places he couldn't hack into, he'd just called. Some places he'd had to bribe with cash or favors, but for the most part, the Serafina had a good relationship with the bigger hotels. He'd used that to his advantage.

"No, a man named Glen Humphrey rented the place with a credit card," he said.

Under normal circumstances Vadim knew the detective wouldn't be telling him any of this. It was against protocol and he could get in a hell of a lot of trouble for it, but he figured Hurley was fishing for info and asking him was smarter than trying to drag him down to the station for questioning. If Hurley did that, he'd never get anything out of Vadim and neither Wyatt nor his team would work with the police department again. "Never heard of him." A lie. He'd just seen that name on Emile's credit card statement as the name of the PI the man had hired. "Thanks for the info."

"You sure you don't know anything about this guy?"

Vadim snorted. "Other than the fact that he probably keyed my car, no."

The detective sighed, his frustration clear. "All right. Talk to you later."

Once they disconnected Vadim thought about calling Angel but he wanted to tell her in person. He'd be keeping an ear to the ground for whoever killed Emile, but if the guy had been staying in a bad neighborhood and Hurley thought it was a robbery gone wrong…karma was a bitch. There was a chance it wasn't random but since he knew Angel hadn't done it and he certainly hadn't, he couldn't imagine the guy's death was connected to her.

Normally the drive home was quick but tonight it seemed endless. All he wanted was to see Angel. By the time he reached his place, raw energy hummed through him, his need growing at just the thought of sinking deep inside her.

Work could wait, especially since her problem was dead. He wanted to give her life back to her, to start a future together where she wasn't scared or looking over her shoulder all the time.

As he stepped through his garage door into the kitchen, he heard grunting sounds. Then a peal of laughter—then Roman's voice telling Angel to pay more attention.

Angel said something but it was too low for him to hear, but Vadim grinned, glad she was getting some self-defense training. When Charlie didn't greet him he remembered that Roman had said he'd needed to put the dog up in his room during training sessions because she got upset seeing Angel tossed around.

He set his briefcase on the island counter then slipped his jacket off, tossing it on top. Loosening his tie, he made his way into the living room to find Roman pinning Angel on the couch from behind.

It jarred Vadim to see her pressed against the couch wearing just a sports bra and yoga shorts and another man flush to her entire body. The coffee table had been moved and her damp shirt tossed on top of it. It was clear they were just training, but seeing Roman on top of her like that made Vadim's possessive streak flare to life.

He hadn't even realized he could feel possessive until Angel. Right now he had the irrational urge to pummel the shit out of Roman even though the other man was doing exactly what Vadim was paying him to do. It didn't lessen his internal struggle though.

Gritting his teeth, he watched her wriggle against Roman. She wasn't aware Vadim was there, but he knew Roman was. The former Marine was always aware of his surroundings and had likely heard the soft chime of the alarm turning off when he'd arrived.

"This isn't fair," Angel growled, struggling even more, pushing her butt into Roman's crotch as she fought against his hold for all she was worth.

"A real attacker won't be fair, Angel. Remember what I taught you." Roman's voice was harsh.

Fuck. He knew they were training, but Vadim's hands clenched into fists. He didn't need to watch this.

He started to head back to the kitchen when Angel looked up from her position bent over the couch. She smiled when she saw him. "Hey, baby."

God, he loved that she called him that.

Roman loosened his grip around her upper body and to both their surprise, she slammed her head back into Roman's face right before she pushed her elbows out, letting her slide out from his grip.

Roman grunted as he took the hit and immediately Angel swiveled around. "Did I hurt you?" she asked, concern in her voice.

He lifted a dark eyebrow, those different colored eyes of his amused as he pressed a gentle hand to his nose. He wasn't bleeding, but his eyes were instinctively watering from the hit he'd taken. "Uh, no. You finally did what you were supposed to do."

"How'd she do today?" Vadim asked, stepping into the room, some of his earlier tension easing.

Angel crossed the distance to him, ready to hug him, but then stopped. "I'm sweaty," she muttered, almost to herself.

Shaking his head, Vadim pulled her into his arms as Roman started moving the coffee table back into place. He didn't care if she was sweaty, he just needed to feel her against him.

"She could do better, but she did well enough," Roman said.

"*She* is right here," Angel muttered as she wrapped her arm around Vadim's waist and half-turned to face Roman.

"Okay, *you* could have done better." The other man's lips twitched, as if he was fighting a smile. "That last move? You should have done that earlier."

"I know, but...I couldn't remember which one to do. My first instinct is to scream and then you hold so tight I can't breathe and I just forget what to do."

"That's actually good. Sometimes you only get one chance to alert others so if you want to shout and scream during training go for it. It'll get you more pumped up. Of course..." He trailed off, glancing toward the direction of the bedrooms. Then Roman looked at both of them. "We'll have to train somewhere else where freaking Cujo can't attack me."

"Charlie's a sweetheart, you big meanie." Angel nudged Vadim. "Did you bring food home? I'm starving."

He loved the way she said home, as if she considered this her place. Soon enough he hoped she would, even though he knew he couldn't broach that subject just yet. It would be too soon for her—but he wanted her here on a permanent basis. "No, but I'll cook something. Let me walk Roman out."

"Okay, I'll let Charlie out through your office. She probably needs some fresh air." She dropped a quick kiss on Vadim's mouth, thanked Roman then hurried toward the bedrooms.

"Thanks for staying with her again," Vadim said as he walked Roman to the front door.

The other man shrugged. "She's easy to be around. I see why you like her so much."

Vadim stiffened at that and Roman just laughed, the sound foreign coming from the other man. "I'm not my brother—and you know he was just fucking with you the other day, right?"

"I know he asked Angel out knowing she's mine." Which still annoyed Vadim.

"Yeah, he thinks she's hot, but he thinks any woman who talks to him is. He just wanted to push you into making a move." Roman scrubbed a hand over his hair, as if the conversation was making him uncomfortable, but he continued. "We all knew how much you liked her for a while now."

Had he been that obvious? Maybe to everyone except her, apparently. "Well he doesn't need to push anymore."

Roman laughed again. "Yeah, he knows. Listen, I don't know if you're going to want Angel out in public, but this Saturday we're having some people over to watch the fight. It'll be mainly the security guys but they're bringing their girlfriends and wives too so if you want, bring Angel. Hayden and Jay will be there."

Vadim nodded. "If she wants to go we'll be there. Her problem is taken care of."

Roman's eyebrows rose. "Taken care of?"

"Not by me, but the guy is dead. Found out right before I left work."

"Good. Stupid fucker. You still want me training Angel this week?"

Vadim paused, then shook his head. "No, but I'll ask her what she wants. If she's open to the idea I want you to train her the next couple weeks or so, just until she's more comfortable defending herself."

"No prob. I actually know a guy who runs a local gym. They've got classes exclusively for women if she's interested."

"Thanks, I'll let her know."

After Roman left, Vadim locked the door then went in search of Angel. She was in the kitchen, holding the refrigerator door open staring at the interior with her other hand on her hip.

"You take Charlie out already?" he asked, taking his tie fully off and setting it on the rest of his things.

"Yes, lazy dog. She ran out, did her business, then ran back inside. She's now sleeping, again, in your room. I don't think she likes the cold," Angel said, looking over her shoulder at him. She swept an appreciative gaze over him before meeting his eyes again. "Why are you looking at me like that?"

"Like what?"

"Like you want to devour me."

"That's because I do." Slowly he started unbuttoning his shirt. Her gaze tracked his movements, the hunger in her gaze clear, flooring him. He loved how she wore her emotions right out in the open.

Shaking her head, she shut the door and turned to face him. "I'm sweaty and gross." She wrapped her arms around her middle. "We can't do anything now."

Like he cared that she'd been working out? He continued working his buttons free, his gaze dipping to the outline of her nipples. They hadn't been visible before but after she'd gotten a workout then stood in front of the fridge, the cool air clearly affected them. He wanted to taste them. Before they took things further though, he needed to tell her what he'd found out. Reluctantly, he stilled his hands. "Will you sit for a sec?"

Her eyebrows rose and she ran her fingers through her long ponytail, bringing it around to her chest, holding onto the strands in a nervous gesture that had quickly become familiar.

"It's not bad news." At least it wasn't to him. Vadim didn't think she'd celebrate Emile's death, but she could finally move on with her life.

Some of the tension eased from her shoulders and as she sat, he joined her. "First, you'll be receiving a check from your parents' insurance company for two hundred and fifty thousand dollars. They should have it to you by next week." He'd had Wyatt's legal department look over her parents' policy then sent the company a letter directly from them. It hadn't taken long for them to jump into action—no doubt they were afraid of legal action since someone had dropped the ball. Whether intentionally or not, Vadim didn't care. He just cared that Angel would have enough money to not have to worry.

Her hazel eyes widened and she jumped off the chair. "Are you kidding me!" she shouted. "That's amazing. Did you do this?" When he nodded, she grinned, smacking her lips to his noisily.

He tightened his grip on her hips, holding her close. He loved the mix of her lavender lotion or whatever she wore combined with her natural scent, especially since she'd just worked out. She might think she was too sweaty, but seeing her all natural made him even hotter for her.

"Thank you," she said, the smile on her face radiant.

It made him feel a hundred feet tall. This woman had the ability to destroy him. And she had no clue. "They never should have jerked you and your brother around in the first place. There's more." He wasn't sure if he should work up to it so he decided to go for blunt. Angel seemed to appreciate that anyway. "Emile is dead."

Her pretty mouth formed a small O of surprise as she stared at him. "Dead? You're sure?"

He nodded. "The police think it was a robbery gone wrong. He was found shot twice in his motel room. The room was under his PI's credit card, which is why I wasn't able to find him in town."

"I guess that's how he found me, hiring someone," she murmured, seeming to slowly take in the news. Angel placed her palms on his chest. "This is a lot to absorb. I feel...really relieved. Which I know is awful." Her expression was pinched as she looked at him. "Is that terrible that I'm sorta glad he's gone?"

Vadim shook his head and pulled her against him, not letting her protest about her rumpled state. "It's not terrible. You have a right to be relieved after that monster sent you on the run, fearing for your life." Vadim wasn't sort of glad, he was fucking thrilled that the bastard was dead. The guy had beat up Angel and killed her brother, her only remaining family. Emile could rot. But Vadim didn't say that to her, not wanting to scare her.

"I...don't even know what to say. I can finally move on with my life, stop looking over my shoulder all the time." The joy in her voice slid over him, pulling an immediate smile from him.

But in the back of his head he worried that when she moved on and didn't need his protection, that she wouldn't want him in her life anymore. That thought splintered through him like shards of glass. He bent his head and claimed her mouth, hungry to mark her in the only way he could. In a way that would remind her how good they were together.

CHAPTER FIFTEEN

As she pulled up to a stop light, Angel looked at her freshly buffed and polished fingernails and smiled. She hadn't done anything frivolous for herself in two long years and while getting a simple manicure wasn't much, it felt fantastic. She still couldn't believe what had happened in the past couple days. She'd gone from being Angel Johnson to her real self, Angel Flanagan, practically overnight. Now she actually had enough money to finish school and put down roots.

And Emile was dead. Really and truly gone. She only felt bad because she *didn't* feel any sorrow for him. He'd killed her brother Aaron so she was more than relieved that her brother had found the justice he deserved.

Vadim had told her Wednesday but she'd still been too shocked by everything to leave his place. But she'd taken advantage of her new freedom to reach out to former professors at Tulane. Once she'd explained everything to two of her favorite teachers, they'd spoken to the dean and were going to work with her to help her finish her last four classes online. With just twelve credits shy of graduating, all her professors had been stunned when she hadn't returned and had seemingly fallen off the face of the earth. She was just thankful they even remembered her and were willing to help. It was too late to start this semester but she was going to take two classes over the summer then two in the fall and be done by the end of the year. She was actually glad she couldn't start immediately.

Her brain needed time to decompress from everything. For the first time in two years she didn't wake up with a lingering sense of fear hanging over her head. Not to mention she had sexy, sweet Vadim in her life.

Of course she couldn't just stay with him indefinitely. Which was another reason she was out running errands today. He'd already done so much for her and now that she had insurance money coming in—thanks to his diligence—she was going to get out of his hair as soon as she could.

Even if she didn't want to leave. She loved his home, but they couldn't just go from being friends to lovers who lived together. It would be too fast. Probably. Okay, not for her, but she didn't think he wanted her just moving in all of a sudden. Not permanently anyway.

Pushing that thought aside, she steered the Serafina's SUV into the entrance of her old apartment complex. She needed to tell Mr. Botkin she wouldn't be coming back at all, even once her place was fixed. She could have called but she was nearby and wanted to thank him for being such a great landlord.

Vadim already had his Mercedes back and the hotel had let her use the SUV for the rest of the week. Soon, she'd be buying a car of her own. She'd sold hers when she'd first left Louisiana because she'd needed the money and because she hadn't wanted to give Emile an easy way to track her. She didn't mind taking the bus, but it would be nice to have her own wheels again. In college she'd been able to walk everywhere but Vegas wasn't set up like that and it could be difficult getting around.

There were a couple open spots in front of her building so she picked the one nearest her old place. She was really curious about the water damage but wasn't sure if she should go in. From what she could tell Mr. Botkin had packed up everything well, but she still wanted to do another sweep through the place if she could. As she stepped onto the sidewalk she saw her downstairs neighbor leaving her apartment.

The woman rarely talked to Angel, but she was friendly enough. She smiled at her neighbor, who was rushing to the sidewalk, keys in hand. She was wearing light green scrubs and white sneakers. Angel knew she worked in home health and had odd hours. It was clear the woman was heading to work.

"Hey, did you get affected by the flooding?" Angel asked.

The dark-haired woman stopped and frowned. "What flooding?"

"My apartment got flooded. I thought you might have been affected too since you're below me."

The woman just stared at her for a moment, then shook her head. "Ah, I'm late for work, but I didn't know there were any plumbing issues here."

As the woman hurried down to her car Angel decided to head to Mr. Botkin's place instead of her own. Before she'd taken two steps she saw him coming out of her apartment, a bucket in his hand. When he spotted her from the balcony his eyes widened in what was most definitely guilt.

What the hell? Had he found a renter willing to pay more? It didn't make sense that her downstairs neighbor hadn't even heard about the flooding; she would have been affected too. Angel raced up the stairs ready to demand an answer from him. "Was my place really flooded?" she asked, hoping she was being paranoid by that guilty flush on his face.

After a long pause, he shook his head. "No, but your friend wanted to protect you."

She blinked, not understanding. "What friend?"

He paused, just watching her with an almost panicked look on his face.

"Did you lie because you found a different renter willing to pay more?"

He shook his head and his original statement started to sink in. Her friend wanted to protect her. There was only one friend of hers that Mr. Botkin had ever met.

"Vadim had something to do with this?" The sense of hurt that slammed into her was staggering.

Mr. Botkin nodded, his expression apologetic as he sighed. "Yes. A man was asking about you. A bad man. Vadim wanted you gone from here so he could protect you. He said you'd have a place to live. Did he lie about that?"

She shook her head, gritting her teeth. No, but he was a big liar who was going to answer for what he'd done.

"You ever gonna tell me what's bugging you?" Roman asked Angel from across the high top table they were sitting at. The bar they were in was a local hangout close to the casino. The drinks were cheap enough, the atmosphere was relaxed and there was no smoking inside.

She traced her finger down the neck of the beer bottle she'd been nursing for the better part of the hour. After leaving her old place she'd been beyond pissed at Vadim. Since she hadn't wanted to go back to his house and she wasn't ready to light into him yet, she'd called a couple of girls she was friendly with at work to see if they could hang out. They'd been working so she'd called Roman. Normally she didn't mind being alone, but she'd wanted someone to talk to. "It's nothing."

"You're a terrible liar," he muttered, waving at their waitress to bring him another drink.

When her phone buzzed again in her purse she looked at it. It was a text from Vadim, asking if she wanted him to bring something home for dinner. Tears burned her eyes and that only pissed her off. She thought about ignoring him completely but didn't want him to worry. And yes, that pissed her off too. She shouldn't care about his feelings, but damn it, she did.

Out with a friend, I'll be in late tonight. Don't wait up.

Okay, her text was kinda harsh, but she didn't care. Angrily, she shoved it back into her purse, earning raised eyebrows from Roman.

"Come on, what's going on?"

She didn't want to talk about her and Vadim, especially since she knew Roman was friends with him. It felt like too much of a betrayal of Vadim and even though she was pissed, she still didn't want to talk about him. "I've just had a long week, that's all."

"So no trouble in paradise then?" Roman asked, his voice wry.

"Not like you're thinking." Yeah, she wasn't talking about her relationship with Vadim with anyone. She just couldn't. "So how is it that you and Logan are so different?" Angel hoped the change in topic would work.

Roman's lips quirked as he shook his head. "No clue. I think he was dropped on his head as a baby. My mom won't confirm it, but I have my suspicions."

An unexpected laugh tore free, easing some of her hurt and annoyance. "You want to do a shot?" Probably not the best type of therapy right now, but if there was a better one, she sure couldn't think of it. She'd just get a taxi home—to Vadim's—if she had too much.

Roman nodded. "One shot, then we're playing a game of darts. I don't think getting wasted is the answer you're looking for."

She started to protest, then nodded. Yeah, the only thing that would do was give her a freaking hangover in the morning. "Sounds good."

"For what it's worth, we're fucking stupid sometimes," he said as he waved at their server again.

"We?"

"Men. I'm speaking for all of us, including V. He likes you, a lot. I'm guessing he did something stupid. Probably really stupid knowing him. But I guarantee it wasn't intended to hurt you."

She didn't get a chance to respond as he turned to their incoming server, who Angel was certain wanted to give Roman her phone number, but she mulled over his words. It was pretty clear that Vadim hadn't wanted to hurt her, he'd wanted to protect her. She didn't mind him wanting to protect her, but he'd just taken over and made a huge decision without asking her first. She didn't like that he'd lied to her, gone behind her back and let her cry about her place flooding when all along he'd known it wasn't true. Maybe she didn't have a leg to stand on considering she'd been lying about her identity. Sort of. She scrubbed a hand over her face, not wanting to think about it now.

When she heard her phone buzz again, she continued to ignore it.

CHAPTER SIXTEEN

After a couple hours of playing darts and drinking beers with Roman, Angel was starting to feel a little better. She was still angry at Vadim, but not in the total emotional rage she'd been in earlier. "I'm done for now. Seriously, my arm is going to fall off."

"So you concede?"

"What? That you're better? Hell no. I'm just tired and since my drill instructor has been training me like a crazy person the past few days I deserve a break," she said, referring to him and his self-defense training regimen.

"That's weak. But I'm tired too," he said with a laugh. As they headed for their round top table, Roman's eyes slightly widened at something over her shoulder.

"What?" She turned around but couldn't see over most of the people. In the last couple hours the place had started to fill up with a steady crowd.

He shrugged when she swiveled back to him. "Ah, my brother's here with some of the guys from work."

"So? He's a flirt, but I don't care. Or does he actually mind that I cancelled that date?" Angel was ninety-nine percent sure he'd asked her out in some weird way to bait Vadim.

Roman shook his head. "It's not that. It's just uh, Vadim's with them."

She narrowed her eyes at him, resisting the urge to turn around and look at Vadim. "Did you tell him I was here?" He shrugged again and she wanted to punch him. "You were right, you guys really are dumbasses."

"I said we were *stupid*. And I didn't tell him, but I did tell Logan." Roman gave what she was sure he thought was an apologetic look, but she could tell he wasn't sorry at all.

Which just infuriated her. "Well I'm saying you're all dumbasses. You couldn't have given me a heads up? And if you shrug again I'll punch you."

"I've felt your punches, they're not impressive." He was clearly fighting a grin.

"And now you're insulting me?" She gritted her teeth, fighting her own smile until she saw Vadim out of the corner of her eye arriving with Logan and two of the men from the security team. Her amusement fled, knowing they needed to talk.

Logan and his brother immediately started joking with each other, their camaraderie clear and kind of adorable while the other two guys headed for the bar to order drinks. Taking a deep breath, she turned in her swivel chair to face Vadim. He was wearing dark slacks and the button-down shirt she'd buttoned up for him this morning after they'd made love in the shower. And

Lord help her, she couldn't help but think about what it would feel like to run her fingers over all his bare skin right now.

The expression on his face was remote. "Hey."

"Hey." She bit her bottom lip, unsure what to say. She hated the feeling that there was a giant chasm between them. But she didn't know how to bridge the gap of mistrust he'd created with his lie.

"Are you angry with me about something?" He shoved his hands in his pockets, seeming almost lost and some of her icy anger melted.

"I stopped by my old place today and ran into Mr. Botkin," she said loud enough for only him to hear. The brothers were laughing and talking with each other on the other side of the table, but she didn't want anyone else to be able to listen in.

Realization dawned on Vadim's face, quickly followed by distress. He was like that panicked tiger again. Which would make her want to laugh if she wasn't so annoyed.

"I wanted to tell you," he finally said. "I should have and I'm sorry."

"You should have told me, or you shouldn't have done it at all? Why'd you lie? Why not just come out and tell me your concerns and ask me to stay?" Because she would have stayed with him.

"I'm sorry I did it. I was going to tell you the truth, then you got angry when I called Sierra for you. That was small and I figured something like…"

"Like having my landlord freaking lie about the state of my apartment at your request would be worse," she filled in, more of her anger dying at his expression. He was worse than Charlie, looking so adorable and apologetic.

Damn it, she needed to hang on to some anger because this couldn't happen again. She loved Vadim and—whoa. *Loved?* Yeah, she loved him. Stunned by her internal realization, she sat back against the chair.

"Yeah, that," he said quietly.

Even though she was still hurt she slid off the chair and wrapped her arms around him. Though he was clearly surprised by the move, he wrapped his arms around her too, pulling her close. She looked up at him, keeping her voice low. "I can't be with someone who lies to me. I understand why you did it and I'm incredibly grateful for everything you've done for me, but we have to be equals. You've got to fill me in on stuff and let me make decisions that affect my life."

"I know. I just…I'm sorry." The sincerity in his voice was so real and she was smart enough to realize that Vadim had never been in a serious relationship before now. She wasn't even sure that's what they were, but she knew that's where they were heading. Hell, they'd been heading that way from the moment they'd met. She just hadn't known it at the time. Their building friendship had been working toward something more all this time.

"Vadim...I'm probably an idiot but I'm letting this go. I know your heart was in the right place but if you do something like this in the future..." She trailed off, not needing to finish. It would be a different story if he did this again, but after being on the run for so long and not being able to enjoy herself for the past two years, she couldn't hold on to any anger. She leaned up on her toes and kissed him, brushing her lips across his.

His grip on her hips tightened as he pulled her tight, deepening their kiss until their surroundings fell away. She loved the feel of his tongue stroking against hers, of his strong arms holding her close.

"Get a room," Logan said loudly from behind them, breaking the intimate spell.

Flushing, Angel pulled back and stepped out of Vadim's embrace. "You want to get out of here?"

When his gaze darkened with hunger, she grinned. Turning from him, she grabbed her purse off the table. Ignoring Logan, she looked at Roman and smiled. "Thanks for hanging out with me. I think we're gonna head out now."

He nodded and gave Vadim a half-smile. "Anytime. You two coming to watch the fight tomorrow night?"

Vadim had already told her about Roman's invitation and they both wanted to go so she nodded. "We'll be there."

Turning back to Vadim she said, "I've had one too many beers to drive. Can we leave the SUV here?" When he nodded she continued. "Good, give me a couple minutes and we'll head out. I need to use the restroom." She was finally starting to feel the effects of those beers. She dropped another kiss on his lips, glad they'd made up. As she slowly made her way through the throng of bodies she saw Iris, Ellie, Jay and surprisingly Wyatt Christiansen heading for their table. She'd never seen the billionaire outside of work. It was a little weird that he was hanging out with all of them. Or maybe it wasn't. For all she knew, he did it all the time. Just not when she'd been around.

She breathed a sigh of relief to discover the women's restroom was empty. After she was done, she washed her hands and stepped out into the small hallway—only to have the barrel of a gun shoved into her stomach.

The background noise from the bar faded away as panic slammed into her, the icy tendrils of fear sliding over her skin. Stunned, she looked up into the angry eyes of Emile's father as he shoved her against the wall, his gun never wavering. Fighting nausea and confusion she stared at him. This couldn't be happening.

"What are you doing?" she demanded, her voice sounding a lot stronger than she felt. She was a quivering mass of nerves, her legs threatening to turn to jelly as he shoved the gun tighter into her stomach. She instinctively sucked her stomach in, her flesh cringing away from the weapon.

His dark eyes looked glassy and she could smell whiskey on his breath. The few times she'd talked to the older lawyer, he'd been drunk. She'd guessed he was an alcoholic, but didn't really care right now. All she cared about was getting away from this maniac. The fear burning inside her easily negated the awful scent.

"I had to kill my son because of you, you stupid bitch." Shock reverberated through her. She couldn't believe what he'd just said. His words were slightly slurred as he grabbed onto her upper arm with a force that made her cry out. His fingers dug into her flesh, his nails biting into her bare skin. "Don't make a fucking sound," he commanded as he dragged her down the hall toward a door with an EXIT sign above it.

She dug her heels in, her fear of being taken outside worse than her fear of the gun. She'd rather get shot in this bar than be taken only God knew where with this clearly deranged man. For all she knew he planned to do more than kill her. "You killed Emile?" she asked as he tried to drag her down the rest of the hallway. She was shaking all over, struggling to contain the terror spreading inside her.

"I had to, he shamed our family one too many times. He was such a soft boy, always letting women take advantage of him. If he'd just let you go I could have ignored his last transgression. But he's been looking for you for two fucking years. Thought I didn't know about it. That investigator told me everything I needed to know and if you weren't such a whore it would have been impossible to find you. Luckily your boyfriend led me right to you tonight." He dug his fingers in again and shoved her along the hallway wall.

She stumbled and almost fell but he grabbed her upper arm again in a painful hold and dragged her to her feet, not caring that he was almost ripping her arm from its socket. She howled in pain, unable to stop her cry.

"It's your fault he's dead," he growled, starting to drag her backward to the exit door.

Angel tried to grab onto the wall but there was no traction. She opened her mouth to scream, but the man—Quinton Glass, she remembered his name—he yanked her back against his stomach. That was when she saw Vadim and Mr. Christiansen standing at the other end of the hallway.

There wasn't much distance between her and them, maybe fifteen feet. But it felt like the Grand freaking Canyon separated them. Her heart pounded a staccato beat against her chest even as her lungs seemed to shrink. It was impossible to drag in a full breath as she stared at Vadim. His expression was dark, deadlier than she'd ever seen as his eyes promised death for Quinton. His hands were at his side, but his right hand was slightly pulled back, hidden by his body with his defensive stance. She couldn't see it, but she'd bet everything she had that he was holding a gun.

His pale eyes weren't on her, they were daggers of ice pinned on the man behind her. Angel had no doubt that given the chance he'd kill the man holding her in a heartbeat. Quinton was saying something, his breath hot against her face as he pulled her tighter to him. He was so angry, his shouting not making any sense, his entire body vibrating with rage. That was when she realized the gun wasn't digging into her. He was holding her close, his meaty arms crossed over her chest as he kept her in place. He was holding the weapon in one of his hands, and with the way he was securing her arms, the gun was pointed at the wall as he continued to rage nonsensical words.

Roman's training moves clicked into place and she knew she'd only get one chance to do this right. If she didn't, she was dead for sure, but this bastard could also hurt Vadim. Something she refused to let happen.

She could hear Roman's frustrated voice in her head. *Shove your elbows out hard, loosening your attacker's grip. At the same time let your legs go lax, your body becoming a dead weight. It will take them off guard long enough for you to duck out of their embrace.* From there he'd given her different options of how to either attack or attack then flee. She wasn't going to do either of those right now.

No, she was just going to fall to the floor and get out of the line of fire she knew was coming. Without thinking about it a second longer, she grunted, shoving her elbows out to the side.

Quinton stumbled behind her, clearly taken off guard as she dropped to the floor like a stone.

Before her palms had hit the ground two loud booms echoed through the small hallway. She screamed, covering her head as she waited for the ripping pain. When nothing happened she started to get up, but found herself being hauled to her feet by two strong hands instead.

For a moment the instinct to fight kicked in until she saw Vadim's face. His expression was terrified as he dragged her away a few feet. He ran his hands over her face, then her arms and hips.

"You're okay?" he rasped out, his voice shaking as she nodded.

"I'm good." Unable to stop the tremble snaking through her, she glanced over her shoulder.

Wyatt was crouched down next to Quinton's body. He looked up at both of them, his expression grim as he shook his head. So Quinton was dead. Angel didn't know what to feel other than confusion and relief that none of them had been injured. She turned back to Vadim and clutched at his waist, needing support. "He killed his son. He told me that it was my fault he'd done it. He didn't say the words, but he was obviously going to kill me."

Vadim pulled her close as Wyatt came to stand next to them. That was when she heard the panicked voices of the patrons from the bar and grill area. It was as if her surroundings suddenly rushed back all at once. Iris appeared in the entry at the end of the hallway with a weapon in her hand. Hayden and Jay were right behind her. They all put their weapons away at once when they took in the scene.

To Angel's surprise, Wyatt waved everyone back before focusing on her and Vadim. "The cops will be here soon. Just tell the truth about what happened here, but don't give them any more information than they ask. And whatever you do, don't say a word about using a fake social. They don't need to know any of that. It's not their damn concern. I'm putting in a call to one of my attorneys now. They're going to separate the three of us for individual questioning. Angel, do *not* answer any questions without my attorney present. He is your official representation." His low voice held a commanding edge to it.

Blinking in surprise, Angel looked at Vadim then back at the billionaire she'd never said more than two sentences to. "Why?"

"Because you're part of the Serafina family and because you're with Vadim."

At that she promptly burst into tears. She didn't care how weak she appeared, she couldn't seem to hold the tears at bay as she buried her face against Vadim's chest. It was strange to have people actually give a shit about her after so long. She'd felt so alone for so many years that all this support was beyond overwhelming.

Vadim stroked a gentle hand down her back, murmuring nonsensical words, the sweet tone of his voice and the feel of his arms around her taking away most of her frayed nerves. By the time the cops showed up her tears had dried, but she had a new set of fears. What if Vadim went to jail for the shooting? What if he got in trouble because of all her baggage? It was self-defense so she wasn't sure why that would happen, but the fear lodged its talons deep inside her, refusing to let go. If he was taken from her now, then she would lose everything that mattered.

CHAPTER SEVENTEEN

"She's going to be fine," Wyatt murmured, casually sitting in one of the chairs next to Cody Hurley's desk.

Instead of making them wait in the lobby, the detective had told them to sit tight in the bullpen of Vegas PD. Vadim stood instead of sitting, his arms crossed over his chest as tension hummed through him with the intensity of a thousand buzzing bees. He couldn't stand still, much less think straight. He and Wyatt had both finished with their questioning and filled out their reports before being let go. Angel was still in with Wyatt's lawyer and Hurley. While Vadim was glad the detective was the one talking to her, since he was a good man, every second that passed made him itch to storm in there and find out what was going on. "Easy for you to say. That's not your wife in there," Vadim snapped.

To his surprise and annoyance, Wyatt grinned. "You really like this girl."

"I fucking love her." The words were out before he could stop himself. He hadn't told her, but it was true. No sense denying it even if he wanted to. Which he didn't. Angel was his.

Wyatt straightened from his casual position, his dark eyebrows raised. "Seriously?"

Jaw tight, Vadim nodded.

His friend didn't say anything, just leaned back again in his chair. Vadim turned away from him, ready to start pacing when he spotted Angel walking out with Wyatt's high-priced attorney standing between her and Hurley. The older man with sprinkles of gray peppered throughout his otherwise dark hair was speaking in clipped tones, but Vadim ignored the men. All his focus was on Angel.

Her dark expression lifted when she saw him. She hurried from the others, sidestepping two uniformed officers as she made her way to him. "Everything's okay," she whispered as she hugged him tight.

"Thank God," he murmured as he returned her embrace.

As the other two men reached the desk, Wyatt stood and let himself be pulled aside by his attorney. Hurley nodded once at Vadim. "Can I talk to you for a sec before you go?"

Even though he didn't want to let Angel go, Vadim nodded and stepped away. "Will you wait with Wyatt?"

She nodded, giving him a small smile that eased all his worry about her. Everything was going to be fine. Once she was out of hearing range, Hurley leaned against his desk, crossing his arms over his broad chest.

Vadim knew the guy had played football in college and guessed he used his size to intimidate suspects. He better not have tried that crap with Angel.

"What?" Vadim asked more harshly than he'd meant to sound, but he didn't want to stick around here. He just wanted to be home alone with Angel. They'd been at the station for hours.

Hurley raised a dark eyebrow. "Your girl isn't under suspicion of anything. While we were questioning you three, our team ran the ballistics on Quinton Glass's weapon. It's the same that killed Emile."

Vadim nodded; Angel had told him what Emile's father had said.

"Everything is pretty clear cut with both cases and we get to close one murder investigation, but don't think I buy that you called me about Emile because he vandalized your fucking car. Why didn't you just tell me he was stalking your girl?"

Vadim shrugged. "I didn't need your help."

The detective gritted his teeth before he pushed up from the desk. "Cops aren't the enemy, dumbass."

A ghost of a smile touched his lips. "Yeah, I know. You guys have your uses."

Hurley rolled his eyes, but his defensive stance relaxed. "Whatever. I'm just glad that fucker is off the streets one way or another. I put in a call to Angel's hometown and it turns out she's not the first woman he stalked. She's just the first he harassed who actually filed charges. According to the sheriff, all the other women dropped the charges, likely because they'd been paid off or were too scared."

Vadim nodded. He'd figured Angel hadn't been the first, but when Emile had been killed he hadn't looked any further into him. Now he wished he had. Maybe he'd have discovered that the guy's dad was a fucking psycho too. At least Angel was safe now. That was all that mattered. "Thanks for handling Angel. If you need anything from either of us, just call me."

"Will do."

Vadim went in search of Angel—he just wanted to get her home where she'd be safe. It was almost three in the morning and he knew she had to be exhausted. He planned to take care of her if she'd let him. She'd been through enough and deserved a damn break.

Vadim placed his hand on Angel's shoulder, lightly trying to rouse her.

Her eyes opened and she jerked once, as if startled. She blinked, staring at him in confusion. The soft dome light from the interior of his car highlighted her exhausted, beautiful face. "Did I fall asleep?"

He nodded. She'd passed out from almost the moment she'd slid into the passenger seat of his car. "Yeah."

She shook her head, as if clearing her mind. "Can't believe I did. I was so wired."

He stepped back from the passenger door, letting her get out on her own, guessing that she'd want some control right now. "A lot happened, it's your body's way of decompressing." Sleep was a fucking cure-all sometimes.

She met his gaze as she stepped out, her expression serious. "I never got a chance to thank you, but thank you for saving me."

He blinked, surprised. "You don't have to thank me for that. Besides, your quick thinking gave me an opening." And he didn't even want to think about what could have happened if she hadn't remembered the moves Roman had shown her.

As if reading his thoughts, she laughed, the sound tense more than amused, as she shut the door behind her. "I should probably send Roman a fruit basket or something. I'll never call him names again after tonight."

Vadim just nodded, not trusting his voice as he looped his arm around her shoulders. He could have lost her tonight, something he was having a hard time wrapping his mind around. Hell, he didn't think he'd ever get over seeing her being held by that gun-wielding asshole. It was a stark reminder that no matter what he did to protect her he couldn't keep her safe all the time. Even though he wanted to.

But he *could* give her the tools to protect herself. And after tonight he planned to enroll her in self-defense classes five days a week—if she let him.

When they stepped inside Charlie was lying near her empty water bowl whining. He squeezed Angel's shoulders once. "Let me get her taken care of. I'll be in our room in a sec." It belatedly registered that he'd said 'our', but she didn't seem to notice as she nodded and headed toward the bedroom. He knew she still had to be angry at him for the lies he'd told about her old place and that they'd have to talk about it. He just hoped she'd actually forgive him once all the dust from this settled. She might have said it was okay at the bar, but he figured she'd still want to talk. Something he wasn't looking forward to. He was so used to taking control of things that he knew it would be an adjustment remembering he couldn't just make decisions for her. Because she was right, they had to be equals and he had to trust her in the way she trusted him.

He still didn't feel like he deserved her, but hoped he'd get over his own shit. He had to if he wanted to keep her, to claim her. And he did, in every way possible. He loved her and planned to tell her tonight, even if it was too soon. After almost losing her, he wasn't going to hold back the words he'd never said to another woman.

Once Charlie was settled on her beanbag in the living room, he reset the alarm, locked the doggy door and went looking for Angel. The bed was empty, but she'd left a trail of clothes to his bathroom.

The shower was running, steam billowing out from the cracked open door. He hadn't thought she'd want anything physical tonight—this morning—but the string of clothes was a not-so-subtle hint. Instantly hardening at thoughts of her bare, luscious body, he stripped and rolled a condom on before he stepped into the bathroom. Even though he couldn't see her, his entire body tightened with need as he imagined taking her up against the shower wall.

"You better be naked," Angel called out, making him grin as he reached the frosted glass enclosure.

He stepped down the one step into the big shower. Angel was standing directly under the shower head, her wet, red hair seeming almost brown and her pale, pink nipples beaded tight. Her hungry gaze nearly killed him.

"Aren't you too tired?" he asked.

She rolled her eyes before her hazel gaze raked over him, flicking down to his erect cock and back up to his face. "Are *you*? Because if you are, I can just take care of myself." As if to prove her point she reached one hand between her legs and started stroking her clit very slowly.

His cock, which was already rock hard, pulsed as he watched her. While he wanted to take over, he loved watching her like this. Their first time together he'd sensed she'd been a little nervous, whether about her body or him, he wasn't sure. She clearly wasn't now. And it was fucking hot.

She spread her legs a fraction, fully cupping herself and he couldn't stand it anymore. He closed the short distance between them, placing his hand directly over hers.

Angel immediately arched into him, rubbing her breasts against his chest as she removed her hand, letting him take over stroking her. She was warm and slippery against his caressing fingertips. "Have I told you how much I love this shower? All the glass makes it seem bigger," she murmured as he dipped one finger inside her. She closed her eyes, her lips parting as he slid another in, pushing deep. It thrilled him how wet she already was.

Bending down, he nipped at her earlobe, tugging it between his teeth as hot water rushed over him. He stilled with his fingers inside her, wanting to tell her something important about himself. He'd been more open with her than he had with most people, but he wanted her to know all of him. And if he didn't say it before the lust took over, he knew he wouldn't be able to tell her for another few hours. "After my mom died—

overdosed—I got moved around to different foster homes. They were always crowded." It was why he craved space so much.

Leaning back, she slid her hands from his shoulders to his chest, her touch perfect, gentle. "Is that why you live in the desert instead of closer to the city?"

He nodded, loving that she understood what he was trying to say when he couldn't get all the words out.

She smiled softly, the action taking his breath away. "I love you, Vadim."

Her sudden words made him still, unsure he'd heard right. He'd been ready to tell her the same thing, but hadn't expected her to return the sentiment. Not this soon.

"You don't have to say anything," she continued, arching against him, rubbing her hard nipples over his chest. "I just wanted you to know."

He pumped his fingers into her once, earning a low gasp of pleasure from her. "I love you too." No way was he holding back the truth, not when she'd been brave enough to tell him first. Not when he didn't want to go another second without telling her how much she meant to him. "I know I fucked up with your apartment, but I swear I'll never do anything like that again." Gently he brushed his lips over hers as he continued his slow thrust into her tight body.

She shuddered, her grip on him tightening. "I know and even if you do something stupid like that again, I'll still love you. I'm not going anywhere." She playfully nipped his bottom lip.

He wasn't sure how she knew he'd needed to hear those exact words, but what she'd said eased the tension that had been humming inside him nonstop since the bar. Hell, since he'd made his first move on her. Angel was everything to him. She was so sweet and affectionate and he still couldn't believe she'd chosen him.

He withdrew his fingers from her and clutched her hips. "Do you want gentle?" he murmured against her mouth. Because the way he was feeling he wasn't sure he could give her that right now. He needed to claim her, fast and rough, right fucking now to satisfy the primal need inside him.

She shook her head as she continued kissing him, stroking her lips against his teasingly. He loved the way she nipped him with her teeth.

His hips rolled against her as he dug his fingers into her soft skin. Without warning he lifted her up. She immediately wrapped her legs around him, her kisses growing more fervent.

"In me, now," she panted as she started feathering kisses along his jaw, her fingers digging into his shoulders.

She didn't have to tell him twice. Pulling his hips back, he pressed her back against the wall and repositioned their bodies so his cock nudged her slick entrance. Water rolled down them, but he had more than enough traction with his feet to take her the way he wanted, the way his body demanded.

When he thrust into her, she moaned his name, her head falling back as she met his gaze. He held her still against the wall, his cock pulsing inside her, her inner walls clenching around him. Her breathing was ragged, matching his own as he slowly pulled back out, then slammed into her, letting her feel his need and the power that drove him.

She arched, another moan tearing from her lips. "Faster," she rasped out, her hazel eyes dark with need.

Hell yes. While he wanted to touch all of her, to cup her breasts and tease her clit as he fucked her, he was barely hanging onto his control as it was and he couldn't hold back the dark tide of need inside him a moment longer. He held her hips tight as he began thrusting hard and deep. Each time he slammed into her, her eyes grew more heavy-lidded, her inner walls tightening around him.

Oh yeah, it wouldn't take her long. When she reached between their bodies and started stroking her clit, he jerked harder against her. Just the sight of her touching herself was enough to set him off.

Crushing his mouth to hers, he continued thrusting, savoring the feel of her hot, tight sheath squeezing him with every stroke. The pleasure intensified until it became a burning agony inside him. His heart was pounding out of control and he could barely breathe, desperate to mark her in this primal way. When her fingers dug into his shoulder and she dropped her hand from her clit, she tore her mouth from his and cried out his name as her climax slammed into her.

He felt it ripple around his cock, her inner walls tightening as her heat rushed over him. Vadim slid his arms fully around her back and crushed her to him. Burying his face against her neck, he inhaled that lavender scent and found his own release, his orgasm making his legs shake as he continued thrusting into her tight body. As she wrung everything from him.

Angel kissed his neck then his jaw as he came down from his high. "I love you so much, Vadim."

His throat clenched with too many emotions. After growing up alone, Angel was someone he'd never imagined having in his life, but always hoped for. She was more than worth the wait, and he was never letting her go. Wrapped around each other, the warm water rushed over them, the heat enclosing them in a safe cocoon. "I love you too."

EPILOGUE

Four months later

Angel nudged open the door to Vadim's office with her foot. She had a hot cup of coffee in one hand and a binder in the other. Summer school started in a week and Vadim had set up a desk and work station for her in his office.

Well, now it was *their* office according to him. The man was just too damn sweet for his own good. She knew this work space was a sanctuary to him so the fact that he was sharing it with her meant so much.

She set her stuff down on her new desk and pressed the button on the panel for the drapes. It was early and she wanted all the natural light she could get while she set all her school files up. She'd been out of college so long she wanted to be ahead of the game when her classes started. Even if she was only taking two, she'd already cut her schedule at the Cloud to three days a week. It wasn't like she had to work while she finished school, not with her parents' insurance money, but the thought of not having a job at all was too weird.

As the drapes settled into place, revealing the beautiful desert landscape, she saw Charlie standing outside the ceiling to floor length glass windows with something dangling from her mouth. But she didn't see Vadim anywhere.

Frowning, she opened the door and Charlie trotted inside before sitting perfectly still in front of her. Vadim had gone out with Charlie to get the dog some fresh air earlier so they should be together. Even though Charlie rarely went far, he was so protective of the dog—another reason Angel loved him. The sun was already up and the gentle breeze of the seventy degree weather felt good. Bending down, she affectionately rubbed Charlie's head. "Where's your master?" she asked as she started to pull what she saw was a tiny basket from Charlie's mouth.

The dog let go of the basket with a soft whining sound and Angel realized there was a small, square blue box nestled in the basket. She pulled it out but could only hold and stare at it.

Charlie nudged her hand but Angel ignored the dog. Her heart skipped a beat as she realized what it was. But it couldn't be what she thought...could it? She'd only been living with Vadim for four months—thankfully he hadn't wanted her to find her own place and she'd happily taken over more than half his closet. But this...No way.

"Only one way to find out what's in there," a sexy, familiar voice said.

Lord, how long had she been kneeling here staring? Her head snapped up to meet Vadim's pale gaze as he stood in the doorway. The smoldering look in his eyes made her entire body flare to life. Thankfully there was no doubt there. Sometimes she saw a flicker of worry in his eyes, at the most random of times, as if he was afraid she wasn't real or was going to leave. Hell freaking no. Not in a million years. Vadim was the man for her.

Swallowing hard, she looked back down and opened the box to find a huge, sparkly engagement ring. Tears blurred her vision as she smiled, pulling it from the box.

When she looked up again Vadim was kneeling in front of her, reminding her how quiet the man was. Batting away her tears, she grabbed his shoulders and lunged at him, kissing his lips, cheeks and all over his face. "Yes, yes, yes!" she shouted.

Giving her one of those rare full-on smiles, he held onto her hips, holding her steady. "I don't think I asked a question."

"You don't need to. The answer's still yes." Laughing, she kissed him again as he plucked the ring from her hand and slid it onto her left hand ring finger.

Dear Reader,

Thank you for reading Sweetest Surrender. I hope you enjoyed the newest addition to the Serafina series. There is more to come soon! If you'd like to stay up to date on my new releases feel free to join my newsletter. I only send out messages for new releases or for a special sale. There's an easy sign up on my website: www.katiereus.com

I'm often asked why some of my novellas aren't in print. Because of the shorter length it's difficult to put all of them into print format so as a thank you to my wonderful readers, I'm including a novella of Killer Secrets with this book. It's not related to this series (or any for that matter), but it's a light romantic suspense with a sexy cowboy hero and a very fun heroine so I hope you enjoy this bonus.

Katie

Killer Secrets
Copyright © 2011 Katie Reus

CHAPTER ONE

Eve Newman pressed her back up against one of the stone pillars at the entrance to the Underwood's long, winding driveway. She wasn't exactly sure what she was doing here but for the tenth time in the last hour she regretted her decision to put any credence to that anonymous email. *'Want the story of the year? Underwood mansion. Nine o'clock. Tonight. Don't trust anyone and don't be seen.'*

The cryptic message annoyed her. As one of the few journalists in the small town of Hudson Creek, Texas, she'd had no choice but to follow up on the lead. She certainly wasn't going to give the story to someone else and her curiosity wouldn't let her ignore it.

Since she'd grown up here—and had attended a few high school parties at the mansion courtesy of Tara Underwood—she knew exactly where the security cameras were and how to avoid them.

Squashing the twinge of guilt at using that knowledge against her friend's parents, she peered around the pillar. A full moon hung in the sky illuminating only one car. The District Attorney's Mercedes. Made sense Richard Underwood would be home. She doubted he'd sent her the email because what could Richard be doing to warrant such a mysterious message?

Frowning, she glanced down the long street. The upscale neighborhood was quiet tonight. Still she tucked her long hair into the thick, knitted cap she'd brought and pulled it down low on her head. Without it, her strawberry blonde hair would be like a beacon for anyone to see. Wearing all black and feeling like a thief, she gritted her teeth and sprinted toward the closest oak tree on the property.

Using the darkness and shadows as her friend, she hurried toward the six foot wall surrounding the property. Her heart pounded wildly and her palms were clammy inside her gloves. She hadn't even told her boss where she was going. But she wasn't totally unprepared. Her Glock 33 was tucked into the back of her pants as a precaution.

As she crept down the length of the brick wall, the sound of a male voice shouting made her pause. She was right in line with the main house but the voice was farther away. Almost like it was outside, but too muted. *The pool house.*

Careful to dodge two of the security cameras, she moved fast until she was hunkered down by a couple of overgrown bushes. The lights from the pool house were on, but the blinds were shut. She could see two silhouettes moving around inside. The shapes were too blurry to make out whether the people were male or female.

After glancing around the back of the large property to make sure she hadn't missed any more video cameras, she pulled her cap down lower and began making her way across the grass. It was almost nine o'clock so maybe this meeting was what her anonymous email had been talking about.

A man started shouting again and her curiosity surged higher. She couldn't understand what he was saying but his tone was angry. As she started to move closer, the very distinctive sound of gunshots erupted.

Pop. Pop. Pop. One shot right after another.

Then silence. Adrenaline surged through her like a raging river.

She was standing right in the middle of the yard like a freaking target. Not caring if any of the cameras caught her, she ran toward the cluster of bushes lining the pool house and jumped behind them. She needed to call the cops, but hiding was her number one priority. Eve held her breath and when there were no other sounds she raised her head and tried to look in one of the windows.

The blinds were drawn shut and she could barely see through the sliver between the edge of the blinds and the edge of the window. Immediately she spotted a pair of male dress shoes. Expensive shoes. From the awkward angle it looked like they were attached to someone lying on the ground. Someone not moving.

Slowly, she reached down to grab her cell phone out of her pocket. When she patted nothing, she inwardly cursed. Sure, she'd remembered her gun but she'd left her damn phone in her purse...which was in her car a few blocks over. A lot of good that would do her now.

If someone was dead or dying, she had to get help.

The sound of a door opening then slamming shut made her duck back down into the bushes. She hoped her dark clothing would help conceal her. Even though she hated to move, she withdrew her gun.

Her hand shook slightly but she'd spent countless hours on the range. When the time came, she knew she could use it if she had to. At the sound of footsteps running away, she inched above the foliage only to see the French door that led into the main house slam shut.

A light went on in one of the rooms downstairs then a few seconds later a light upstairs flipped on.

Taking a chance, she hurried from her hiding place and ran to the front of the pool house. Eve cringed as her boots thudded against the stone patio at the front of the small structure but she couldn't do anything about it.

Her time was limited.

Easing the door open with her shoulder, she kept her gun tight in her hands. Her gut roiled at the sight in front of her. Next to the splatters of blood on the slick tile floor, the pale yellow walls seemed garish and too bright. Right beside the billiard table in the corner of the room, Allen *freaking* Martin lay on his back. His dark, unblinking eyes were wide open, and a look of shock covered his handsome face. Her gut told her he was dead.

Eve hadn't exactly liked the guy but, *damn*. She quickly peeked back out the door and when she saw no one was there, hurried over to the body. After spending months embedded with the troops in Afghanistan, she'd seen her share of dead bodies and she had a feeling he was gone, but she checked his pulse anyway.

Nothing.

Crimson slowly seeped out from the three gaping holes in his chest and was beginning to pool on the tile floor. The coppery scent of death filled her nostrils.

Instinctively she started to step back. She didn't want to contaminate the crime scene and she really didn't want to leave any evidence behind. She had no business being here but she did need to call the cops—even if she didn't have much faith in their abilities. Her car was blocks over and she couldn't waste that much time. She hoped Martin had a phone on him.

Avoiding the growing pool of blood, she felt the front of his jacket pocket until she found his cell. Once her fingers clasped around it she hurried back to the door. When she looked out she saw the light upstairs in the main house shut off.

Crap!

Whoever had done this was probably coming back. She just couldn't wrap her mind around the fact that Richard Underwood had shot Allen Martin. Sure, Martin was sleazy, but Underwood was a good, honest DA. Or she'd thought he was. Now it looked like he might be a killer.

Hurrying back the way she'd come, she paused once she was outside the fenced yard to use Martin's phone. She dialed 911.

As soon as the operator picked up she started whispering into the phone. "There's a dead body at the Underwood mansion. 685 Kent Ave."

"Ma'am, can you please repeat that address?"

"There's a dead body in the pool house behind the Underwood mansion on Kent Avenue. Allen Martin has been shot three times in the chest and he's not breathing. Hurry!"

"Ma'am, are you telling me that Allen Martin is dead in the DA's pool house?" Eve doubted the operator was supposed to let her disbelief show, but in a small town the woman would have no doubt where the Underwood mansion was and exactly who owned it.

She sighed at the woman's question. The dispatcher should already be contacting a patrol car. Another strike against the police department of Hudson Creek. They'd screwed up the prosecution of the man who'd killed Eve's parents. Why not screw this up too?

"Yes, that's what I'm telling you. Send someone *now*. The killer is still here." It was hard to keep her voice a whisper when she wanted to shout at the operator.

"We're sending a patrol over but I need to know who I'm speaking to."

Not freaking likely.

Instead of answering, Eve hung up. She couldn't afford to say anything else. She'd trespassed on the property and admitting that to the sheriff would give him an excuse to waste hours interrogating her.

As she glanced around she realized no one must have heard the shots because the street was deathly quiet. She desperately wanted to wait around and make sure the cops showed up but knew she couldn't. If they found her here she'd be in a world of trouble. Hurrying, she continued her escape down the sidewalk.

When the phone she'd taken started ringing, she jumped. The caller ID screen said restricted.

"Hey, I hear it," a thick, accented male voice said from behind the fence of the Underwood's place.

Panic jumped in Eve's chest. She pressed the end button, effectively silencing the call as she started running down the sidewalk. Her boots thudded loudly but there was nothing she could do about it. She wanted to turn the phone off completely but didn't have time to waste.

"Hey! Stop!" the same voice shouted behind her a few moments later.

A sharp pop blasted through the air and the trunk of one of the trees lining the street splintered. The pop sounded again and Eve felt a gush of air rush past her face. Someone was shooting at her!

Taking a sharp right, she darted across the Hawkins' lawn. Even though they had an incredible house their security was shit and she knew they had an opening in their wrought iron fence in the backyard. If she could just make it.

Her leg muscles strained and for the first time in years she was thankful for her daily jogging routine. Pumping her arms and legs, she cleared the edge of the house. A spotlight on the side of the house flipped on—likely motion sensors—but she didn't pause.

It almost felt as if someone was breathing down her neck, but she knew it was fear and adrenaline surging through her. Then she heard a muttered curse farther behind than before. At least they weren't still shooting. Probably because whoever it was didn't want to draw more attention to themselves.

She needed to make it to the opening and hoped no one saw her slip through. Her car was on the next street over. Her heart pounded that erratic tattoo against her chest as she dove over a cluster of bushes lining the back fence.

Blood rushed loudly in her ears as she began to slowly crawl toward the opening. When the phone started ringing again, her chest tightened. They were trying to track her using the sound. She silenced it again then slid the back casing off. She'd only have a few seconds to do this. Sliding the SIM card out, she put it in her pocket then left the phone lying in the dirt.

As she continued crawling, she pulled her gun out. When she reached the small gap in the fence she shimmied under it. Ignoring the dirt coating her hands and the underbrush caught in her cap and clothes, she shoved up and ran through the neighboring backyard.

After risking a brief glance behind her, she saw she wasn't being followed. She allowed herself a small measure of relief but didn't stop running. Even if they were still looking for her, they weren't going to find her. She wouldn't let them.

Unfortunately she couldn't go home. She hadn't recognized the accented voice, but she couldn't be sure whoever had been chasing her hadn't identified her. That left one place to go.

Macklin wasn't going to be happy to see her, but Mr. Tall, dark, and too-sexy-for-his-own-good would have to deal with it. He was one of the few people on the planet she would trust with her life.

CHAPTER TWO

Mac paused as he ran a towel over his damp hair. Then he heard the sound again. Someone was banging on his front door. Insistently. He glanced at the watch he'd left on his bathroom counter. It was almost ten. Normally he'd be in bed by now and so would most of his men, but they'd had trouble with some of the cattle getting out after a section of one of his fences had been intentionally knocked down. By drug smugglers no doubt. They were getting worse in this area and he was fed up with it.

Without bothering to put on clothes, he headed toward the front door. That's when he heard the one voice that had the ability to make him go rock hard in seconds.

"Macklin Quinn, I know you're in there! You better open this door right now!" Eve's shouts were followed by three more bangs.

For such a petite woman she had a loud knock. Shaking his head, he jerked the door open.

"Damn it, Mac..." She trailed off as she stared at him. Unabashedly her eyes tracked down his bare chest to the damp towel hanging on his hips.

Her peaches and cream complexion often gave away her emotions and now was no different. Those dark eyes of hers flared with momentary interest as they reached the top of his towel. When her gaze landed on his growing erection, her cheeks tinged an adorable pink and she quickly looked up. "Uh...do you have company?"

"No." The only company he wanted was her. In his bed. But that wasn't going to happen. So why was she here?

She sighed and visibly relaxed. "I need a place to stay tonight."

Mac wouldn't mind accommodating her but he knew her well enough that she wasn't looking to jump into his bed. If only. He frowned as he took in her appearance. "What the hell happened to you, Eve?" The question came out harsher than he intended. Her hair was hidden by a dark cap and she wore all black, like some sort of cat burglar. Dirt smudges covered her face and...were those leaves sticking out of her collar?

She bit her bottom lip and eyed him nervously. "Aren't you going to let me in?"

Sighing because he couldn't say no to her, he stepped back. When he shut the door behind her, she wrung her hands in front of her stomach. "I did something stupid tonight but I'm not going to tell you what it is if you're going to give me a lecture."

Oh, shit. If the stubborn woman was actually admitting she'd done something stupid, he'd no doubt need a shot of whiskey. Stepping further into the foyer, he motioned with his hand. "Come on. Let's go to my office."

Once they reached his office she tugged the cap off her head and all those gorgeous strawberry blonde waves fell around her face and shoulders. He resisted the very real urge to reach over and run his hands through her hair. To cup her head tight, pull her close, and—

"Can't you put on a shirt or something," she muttered as she sat on the cushy chair across from his desk.

He stiffened at her words. Instinctively he rubbed a hand over his left side and all the hideous, scarred skin. It didn't hurt anymore and most days he forgot about it but now...he wished he *had* put on a shirt. He didn't like her seeing this deformed side of him.

Before he could respond she continued. "Don't get that hurt look on your face. You *know* I didn't mean it because of your scars."

"Then why'd you say it?"

Her cheeks flushed again as she found a spot on the wall behind him to stare at. "Because I can't think with you half-naked." The way she spoke through gritted teeth told him she meant it even if she didn't want to admit it.

It shouldn't please him, but it did. Probably too much. He bit back a grin because it would only annoy her. Eve was one of the few women he knew who didn't focus on superficial stuff. And she'd been one of the few people who hadn't acted like she felt sorry for him when he'd moved home injured, scarred and pissed off at the world. No, she'd told him to get over himself and be thankful he was alive. "Stay put and don't get into trouble for sixty seconds, okay?" Without waiting for a response he hurried to his room and tossed on a pair of faded jeans and a sweater. He found her sitting in the same spot with that worried expression on her face. "What's going on?"

"I just saw a murder," she blurted. As she launched into a crazy story he was torn between shaking her and hugging her. When she finally finished she tucked a wayward curl behind her ear and stared at him with wide eyes.

"You really think Richard Underwood killed Martin?" Underwood was the squeaky clean DA of Hudson Creek whereas Allen Martin was one of the sleaziest men Mac knew. Martin owned five car dealerships around the immediate area and lived up to that greasy car salesman cliché. But that didn't mean he deserved to be shot.

"I...I don't know who killed him, but Richard's car was outside the house. Whoever chased after me wasn't him. That much I'm pretty sure of. The guy had an accent."

"How do you know?"

"When he called the phone—"

"That you *took*." It was smart she'd taken it to call the police, but stupid that she'd been there by herself in the first place.

She gritted her teeth. "Don't interrupt. When he called Martin's phone he said 'I hear it' or something like that."

"Then he was probably talking to someone."

"Yeah." Her eyes glazed over for a moment and he could practically see the wheels turning in her head.

"What is it?"

Instantly she jerked out of her trance and cleared her throat. "Nothing. Can I stay here tonight? I don't think whoever it was recognized me but just in case I'd feel safer here."

"You need to call Sheriff Marcel," he said mildly, knowing it wouldn't make a bit of difference in convincing her.

She shook her head. "No way. Those jerks don't know what they're doing. They'll probably think it was me or something."

Mac bit back a sigh because he understood her anger. Her parents had been killed by a drunk driver and the current sheriff's predecessor had botched the entire process. It had gone to trial but when they'd lost the blood test results with the other driver's blood alcohol content, it had been over before it began. And it didn't help that the attending officer had been a new recruit and had gotten so flustered on the stand, the defendant's attorney had ripped him apart.

"You can't lump Marcel and his guys in with...his predecessor." Mac didn't even like to say Frank Reed's name. It only made pain flash in Eve's eyes and seeing that was like someone stabbing him.

"I can do whatever I want," she said, though she'd lost most of her steam. "Besides, Marcel's mad at me because he thinks I got in the way of his last investigation. I don't want to give him more ammunition against me."

"He's pissed at you because you keep turning him down for dates." How did she not know that?

Eve blinked twice then frowned at him. "He's not *serious*."

Mac snorted. Oh yes, the sheriff was. He'd been after Eve since she'd moved back to town a couple years ago. And he wasn't the only one. It shouldn't bother Mac. He had no claim on her. But damn if he didn't want her for himself. Things between them would be too complicated though and he couldn't travel down that road with her. "Fine, I'll place a call to him tomorrow and—"

She jumped out of her seat. "No! I already have a plan and I don't need your help. Tomorrow I'm going to head to the station and act like I'm following up on a lead about Allen Martin. I can't accuse the DA of anything until I'm positive he's involved in this."

"You don't think showing up at the station is suspicious?"

Her lips pulled into a thin line as she shook her head. "I'm a journalist. I'm always bugging the sheriff about stuff."

Mac scrubbed a hand over his face. It took all his self-control not to call the sheriff but in his gut he knew it wouldn't do much good. She'd already called the cops and if he told the sheriff what he knew, Eve could get in a lot of trouble. Not to mention it would break her trust. Not something he could do and live with himself. Standing, he pushed his chair back. "I'm beat so…"

"Sorry, I know I barged in on you. If you have a T-shirt or something I could borrow to sleep in I promise I'll stay out of your hair."

His lower abdomen burned with need at the thought of her wearing something of his. Instead of responding—because he didn't trust his voice—he grunted something incomprehensible and motioned for her to follow him.

Hating how tight his skin felt and the uncomfortable sensation coursing through him, he stalked down the hall to his room. The five bedroom house was big for just him and now he felt as if it were taking forever to make it across the house.

As he finally entered his room he cringed. A pile of unclean clothes lay in one corner and he'd tossed his dirty work clothes at the end of his unmade bed. Nice.

Behind him, Eve chuckled under her breath and muttered something about him being 'such a guy' but he ignored it. He was definitely feeling like a guy right now. Being near her was making his brain short-circuit and giving him a raging hard-on. It was embarrassing that he couldn't control himself.

He shifted uncomfortably as he jerked open one of his dresser drawers and rummaged around until he found one of his old Marine Corps T-shirts. It was about a decade old and he'd gotten it when he'd first enlisted. Since that first year in he'd put on a lot of muscle so while it would still be big, it wouldn't completely swallow her. Next he grabbed a pair of sweatpants that would definitely be too big but it was all he had.

When he handed the bundle of clothes to her, their fingers brushed and they both froze. An undeniable electric arc of energy sparked between them and made him almost jerk back.

Staring into her dark eyes, he fought that familiar drowning sensation he experienced every single time she was near. She made him feel like a randy teenager. Out of control and horny all the time. He could lose himself with her. His brain struggled to think of something—anything—to say but she beat him to the punch.

It vaguely registered that this was exactly why he avoided her.

She mumbled 'thanks' as she took the clothes but she still didn't make a move to leave. Just stared at him as if she wanted him to kiss her. Ten years ago it wouldn't have surprised him, but it did now. She wasn't a teenager anymore. She was a beautiful, grown woman and shouldn't want anything to do with a roughneck like him.

But damn, did he ever want to follow through with this kiss.

More than just a kiss. He wanted to taste her, dominate her, make her forget anyone but he existed... The flare of lust in her eyes was too much.

Reaching out, he cupped her cheek. When he did, she sucked in a shaky breath but didn't pull away.

He wanted to tell her to go but the words wouldn't form. And her skin was so soft and *female*. He rubbed the pad of his callused thumb over her cheek. Her eyes grew heavy-lidded for a moment.

He could practically feel the heat rolling off her. Stepping forward slowly, he gave her time to back away as he closed the distance between them. But she didn't.

She met him halfway. Before he could react, her hands slid up his chest and around his neck.

He was so screwed. The thought rang in his head crystal clear. Once he kissed Eve he knew there'd be no going back for him.

As he leaned down, her mouth parted invitingly. When their lips touched he felt the reaction straight to his center. Her tongue stroked against his, playfully at first. But he didn't want playful.

Something primal burned inside him. He wanted to invade her senses. Make her feel the way he did every time he got close to her. He started to thread his fingers through her thick hair when she froze.

With wide eyes, she pulled back and out of his embrace. She swallowed hard and shook her head. "I can't…we can't…goodnight, Mac." Before he could think of a response, she turned on her heel and hurried out of his room.

After she'd gone he realized he hadn't shown her to a guestroom, but he knew she'd figure it out and pick one. If she didn't, he hoped she'd crawl into bed with him. He scrubbed a hand over his face at the thought. That was definitely wishful thinking.

The only thing he knew was that she wasn't going to the sheriff's by herself tomorrow. The woman could fight him all she wanted but after what she'd told him, he wasn't letting her out of his sight.

Eve, more than anyone, had the ability to drive him insane. He'd known her practically his entire life and he'd been half in love with her for most of it. Things would never work out though. Too many complications and baggage. She was too good for him. Way too good. Part of him was glad she'd realized it before they'd done something stupid tonight. He sure as hell hadn't had the common sense to pull back.

CHAPTER THREE

Eve pulled her damp hair back into a ponytail as she stared at her closet. It was weird to have Mac waiting in her living room while she was getting dressed, especially after that kiss last night. She'd been ready to jump in bed with him right then and there. But that would have been insane. Taking things further would completely ruin their friendship. A man like him didn't settle down and it would be foolish to think otherwise.

She didn't understand why the stubborn man had insisted on following her home. And then he'd decided to wait while she showered and got dressed. After getting a solid night's sleep she felt better about the fact that no one had seen her. She'd kept her face hidden and she'd worn gloves. By now the police probably had someone in custody and since she'd already copied Allen Martin's SIM card, she was going to give it to the sheriff anonymously. She felt a little bad about that but chances were, if she'd left it, it would be destroyed by now. Someone had wanted it for a reason so that had to be important.

She finally settled on a pair of dark jeans, a plain black shirt and a black fitted jacket to go over it. She had a few stops planned today and if she dressed up too much, people always seemed to be uncomfortable. Maybe it was a Texas thing, she wasn't sure. After grabbing a pair of flat boots and her purse, she found Mac in her living room.

He was staring at a twelve-year-old picture of her and her brother. It had been taken on Mac's ranch, back when his father had run the place. She'd been sixteen at the time and just growing into her body. And she'd developed a massive crush on Mac that summer. He'd noticed her body and her crush.

As she sat on the couch and slid on one of her boots, he turned those ice blue eyes on her and her heart stuttered. "Sure you don't want to fix breakfast or anything before we leave?" he asked.

She shook her head and zipped up the first one. And she didn't want to talk about mundane stuff either. "You remember that summer?" She nodded toward the picture.

He shrugged stiffly but at least he didn't avert his gaze. Yeah, he remembered all right. She could see it on his face.

"You almost kissed me that summer. Would have been my first kiss too." Instead she'd gotten her first one from Billy Johnson later that year. He'd been all tongue and slobber. Not the best experience. Even thinking about it now grossed her out.

"I almost lost my head that summer," he muttered as he shoved his hands into his jeans pockets.

She remembered that day well. Barely eighteen, Mac had been horrified he'd almost made a move on his best friend's little sister. He'd told her he was sorry for what he'd done. She hadn't wanted his apology, she'd wanted him. But after that they'd never talked about it and that summer he and Daniel had enlisted in the Marine Corps together. She hadn't seen Mac much after that but when she had, nothing had ever happened between them—or *almost* happened—again.

Not that she wouldn't have liked it. He'd filled out in all the right places after joining the military. He'd been good looking before but he'd come back ripped and toned and not in that gross gym rat way. Even today he wore his dark hair cropped close. And those blue eyes of his still had the ability to make her melt. Sometimes it felt like he could see right through her, all the way to her fantasies. She wasn't sure why she'd even brought up the almost-kiss when she should be doing everything in her power to avoid talking about anything that involved their lips meshing.

When he didn't say anything else, she plucked her purse off the coffee table and stood. "I appreciate everything you've done for me but you don't need to follow me into town today."

"I'm not following you. You're riding with me. I know you're busy so you can take my truck and do whatever it is you need to do." He spoke as if she had no choice in the matter.

"That's stupid. Besides, what are you going to do for a vehicle?"

"After we go to the sheriff's station you can drop me off at the feed store where I'll catch a ride with Griffin. I've already talked to him." He'd lost a lot of his drawl after being gone for almost a decade, but it came back in full force when he was being extra bossy.

"Mac, that makes no sense—"

"For all we know, Martin's killer is still on the loose. I'm not taking the chance someone recognized you…or saw your car leaving the scene. They could have gotten your license plate number. It's not that hard to track someone that way. I don't want you driving around in your car today. Not until we have more information." By the firm set of his jaw she knew it would be pointless to argue, but sometimes the man riled her up.

"Look, I know I came to you for help last night, but—"

"It's not up for discussion, *darlin'*."

At the word darlin', the argument died on her lips. Didn't he know how to take all the wind out of her sails? "Fine." She might not like his domineering attitude, but a part of her she didn't want to admit existed, kind of liked the way he was insisting on taking care of her.

Over the years they'd butted heads a few times but the way he was acting now was somehow different. Grunting something incomprehensible, he palmed his keys and strode for the front door.

As he trailed in front of her she couldn't help but watch that tight, firm butt. She'd fantasized way too many times what it would be like to grab onto him. Just once. Okay, maybe more than once. Spending more time with him was going to make those cravings worse. Especially now that she'd had a taste of him.

Eve lived in a ranch-style house in a small subdivision right on the outskirts of town so it took less than ten minutes to reach downtown.

Mac hated everything about what they were doing, but he didn't see another option. At least she hadn't balked too much at driving his truck around today. He might not be able to keep an eye on her all the time but until they figured out who was responsible for Martin's death, it would have to do.

As Eve sat inside Sheriff Marcel's office not-so-subtly drilling the man with questions, Mac took his time pouring a cup of coffee at the table directly outside the office. From what he could tell, the sheriff had an open door policy and kept the coffee stand next to his office for a reason. He wanted to keep a pulse on his officers, something Mac appreciated.

"You can tell whoever your source is that they're mistaken. We followed up on a bogus lead last night to the Underwood's and found nothing there," the sheriff said.

Mac frowned as he stirred sugar he didn't want into the coffee. Anything to drag out his excuse for loitering.

"My source is impeccable," Eve snapped back.

"Not this time, they're not. The pool house was clean. No blood and certainly no body. I wasted good manpower checking out that bogus call."

"No blood?" Eve sounded incredulous. She'd told him that it had been all over the tile floor.

But Mac knew a fast clean up job would have been easy if the cops hadn't been looking too hard. If they'd already gotten it in their minds that it was a prank call then they wouldn't have brought in anyone to check forensics. By now any blood evidence would be wiped clean. Unless of course they decided to go back and check for traces with luminol.

"That's right. The only thing we discovered is that Richard Underwood's car has been stolen. Maybe you can write a story about that." His voice held an edge of sarcasm.

"Stolen?" Eve asked, disbelievingly. "And what about Allen Martin? Anyone see fit to check up on him?"

The sheriff sighed loudly and Mac knew he was reaching the end of his rope. "I did receive a call last night about a prowler roaming around the exclusive Ranch Rock subdivision. A couple houses down from the Underwood's place. Maybe I should be asking where you were last night."

And that was Mac's cue. Grabbing the second Styrofoam cup he'd poured, he casually strode into the office. "Hey, Rob."

Tearing his gaze away from Eve, the sheriff slightly faltered. "Uh, hey Mac. Haven't seen you around in a while. Everything all right?"

Mac nodded as he handed a second cup to Eve. For effect he winked at her and held back a grin as she blushed. "Everything's fine," he said to the sheriff. "I'm waiting on Eve to take me down to the feed store."

"Ah…oh." His frown deepened.

"She had some car trouble this morning so we decided to ride into town together." The way he said 'we' made it obvious that something was going on with them. He wasn't sure she'd out and out lie to the sheriff about last night, but Mac didn't want her saying something that could come back to bite her in the ass later. He would rather divert the subject regarding her whereabouts last night than have her lie.

Next to him Eve choked on her coffee but didn't argue. She grabbed her purse from the floor and stood. "Sorry to have bothered you."

The sheriff stood, eyeing them suspiciously. "Eve, is there something you need to tell me?"

She snorted softly as if that was the last thing she'd ever do then took another sip of her coffee. "Thanks for your time, Sheriff."

Putting his arm around her shoulders, Mac steered her out of the station.

Once they stepped out into the bright sun, she elbowed him. "What was that? Now he thinks you stayed over at my place."

"So?"

She gritted her teeth and tossed the cup of crappy coffee into the trashcan outside the building. "Now everyone is going to think we're together."

And would that be such a bad thing? He followed suit with his cup. The stuff was swill. "It's better than him questioning you about your whereabouts last night."

Immediately she switched gears as they strode across the parking lot toward his truck. "What was that bull about the DA's car being stolen? I *know* what I saw last night. I certainly didn't conjure up a dead body. Or someone chasing me. Or *shooting* at me. I guarantee the patrol cop only glanced at the pool house—if he even did that at all."

Mac didn't respond as he slid into his seat. Eve might be a lot of things but she wasn't crazy and she wasn't a liar. If she said she'd seen Martin's body, she'd seen it. With the less than stellar record of the Hudson Creek P.D., he didn't blame her for not having faith in them.

"I left one tiny detail out about last night," Eve said as he steered out of the lot.

His stomach dropped at her words. "What?"

"I took Martin's SIM card out of his phone before I escaped."

He swore under his breath. It was actually a pretty smart thing to do. "What are you going to do with it?"

"I already copied the numbers this morning. I was going to anonymously mail the card to the police station but now I wonder..."

"It's evidence. You *need* to turn it over." It wasn't necessarily hard to make a body disappear in west Texas so if someone had taken Martin out to the desert to bury him, Mac doubted they'd ever discover his corpse. But if Eve could get the cops riled up enough to dig into things, maybe it wouldn't be a bad thing. He glanced at her as they pulled up to a stoplight.

"I'll do it today." She chewed on her bottom lip as she stared out the windshield.

"What *else* are you thinking of doing?"

"Nothing. I'm simply wondering if there's a way for us to get his phone records."

Mac shook his head and made a right turn when the light switched to green. "Not without a warrant, you know that."

She was silent as he steered into the feed store parking lot. Something that worried him. When she shifted in her seat to face him, he couldn't help himself.

Reaching out, he cupped her cheek. Apparently he really was a masochist. No good could come of this, but feeling her soft skin against his callus, roughened palm was like holding silk. Her mouth parted slightly, invitingly. If he kissed those pink lips now he'd never want to stop. Instead he kissed her forehead lightly and drew back. "Please don't do anything stupid today, Eve."

"I won't." Her voice was raspy and sexy.

"I'll have one of the guys drop me off at your place later tonight. Call me and let me know when you'll be heading home. I'll try to get there at the same time."

For a moment she looked like she might argue but she nodded. "Okay."

Getting out of his truck and leaving her was the last thing he wanted to do but he ordered his body to obey.

CHAPTER FOUR

Eve stupidly lifted her fingers to her forehead after she pulled out of the parking lot. She didn't understand Mac. Since he'd moved back to town he'd kept his distance from her. Not physically, but she could almost feel him withdrawing from her sometimes when they saw each other. And now he wanted to be all sweet and concerned. Not to mention he'd freaking kissed her last night.

She so didn't need that right now. Allen Martin was dead and no one knew about it. Since she obviously couldn't count on the police to do their job, she needed to find out what was going on and find the killer. The DA's car had 'suddenly' been stolen. More likely it had been used to transport a body then disposed of.

She had to get Martin's phone records. If she could find out who he'd been in contact with lately, she might get a lead. A small part of her wanted to tell the sheriff, but she wasn't sure he'd believe her. And if she opened up that can of worms and he didn't, the whole town would know about it by sunset and the killer would have no doubt she'd been the one at the Underwood mansion last night. She'd become a walking target, she *still* wouldn't have a clue who had killed Martin and the police wouldn't be concerned if they didn't think Martin was dead.

Her money was on the DA, but what if it was his wife? Or someone who worked for them? And who was the guy with the accent who'd chased her?

Shaking her head, she put her hands-free earpiece in and called her boss. After letting him know she planned to run down a few interviews, she was almost to her destination. When she steered into Iris Bunwell Martin's driveway she braced herself. Iris, or Bunny, as she liked to call herself, was nice enough. Sometimes she was a lot to take in though. Big blonde hair, big voice, big…other assets.

Bunny opened the door a few seconds after Eve rang the doorbell. Her blue eyes widened a fraction, then surprising concern filled her expression. "Hi, Eve. Is everything all right?"

Eve cleared her throat, hating that she had to question Bunny. They weren't friends but they were acquaintances. Bunny and her mother had been on a few charitable boards together. That was the one bad thing about living in a smaller town. She didn't literally know everyone but some days it felt like it. "I wondered if you had a few minutes to talk about Allen."

Instantly Bunny's features hardened. "Why would I want to talk about that snake?"

And that's when Eve noticed Bunny wasn't wearing her wedding ring. Interesting. "I was curious if you'd talked to him lately."

Her eyes narrowed. "Tell me you're not sleeping with him too."

"Ew...Uh, sorry, I mean *no*. I'm following up on a lead for a story and wondered when you'd seen him last." Her stomach ached knowing Allen was dead and she had to question Bunny, but she wasn't sure what else to do.

Bunny relaxed and stepped back. "If you're not sleeping with him would you like a cup of tea?"

Nodding, she followed Bunny inside past a sweeping staircase, through a tiled foyer, and into a formal-looking room with all white furniture. When Bunny motioned for her to sit, Eve took a seat on one of the high-backed, uncomfortable-looking chairs and crossed her legs. Discretely she wiped her palms on her pants. She wanted to run for the front door and never look back. Talking to Bunny like this was not only awkward but her insides were all twisted up. Before she could think of something to say, a woman in black pants and a starched white shirt appeared with a tray of tea and an assortment of pastries.

Eve didn't want to make small talk but she'd have to if she wanted her answers. She also knew she'd get more cooperation if she was semi-honest. "Bunny, I'm here about a story dealing with Allen. This isn't a social call so I want to make sure that's clear so you don't get the wrong impression."

The other woman smiled wryly. "Sweetheart, I'm not stupid. I haven't seen you since your parent's...ah, well, whatever you're here for, feel free to ask. I might not answer but you can ask anything you want."

That was her go ahead, even if she did feel like crap asking Bunny these questions. As Eve took one of the cups she decided to start with a bolder question. "So you and Allen aren't getting along?"

Bunny snorted in an out of character manner. "That's an understatement. I got tired of him screwing his female staff and God knows who else behind my back."

Well that was certainly motive for murder. Though why she'd commit it at the DA's house was a little weird. "So you haven't seen him lately?"

She shook her head. "I saw him about a week ago before I had the locks changed. He packed a few bags but I have no idea where he is. Probably with one of his tramps. I can't believe I stayed with the bastard so long. Thank God my daddy insisted he sign a pre-nup," she muttered.

Allen might have made a lot of money in the past decade but Bunny came from old money. Even if that left a financial reason out as a motive—and Eve couldn't completely rule it out—revenge was always a classic.

"What kind of story are you working on exactly?" Bunny asked as Eve took a sip of her tea.

"I can't say yet. It's sensitive, but...I wondered if you knew who he'd been in contact with lately?"

Her blonde eyebrows rose. "You mean who has he been sleeping around with?"

Eve shook her head even though she was *very* interested in that. If there was more than one woman, talk about motive. "No. I'm referring to business associates." She cleared her throat and decided to plunge ahead. She couldn't lose by asking. "If you have any of his old phone records or anything that would be great. I'm trying to put together some puzzle pieces for a story."

Bunny eyed her curiously for a second. "Are you going to screw him over?"

Eve sat back at the question. "I don't intend to." She wanted to find out who his killer was. Even if he was a snake, he didn't deserve to be murdered and forgotten about.

The blonde half-smiled and stood. "Well if you can, I'd appreciate it. I can give you a copy of the last few months of his phone records but that's all I've got."

Surprise must have shown on Eve's face because Bunny's toothpaste commercial smile widened. "I don't know why you want the records but if you can stick it to the lying bastard, you have my blessing."

Before Eve could respond, she disappeared from the room. A few minutes later she returned with a stack of papers. "These are all copies and they date back about three months. Whatever you plan to do with them, good luck."

After slipping the papers into her purse and thanking Bunny, Eve made a hasty exit. The second she got to her office she was going to pore over these records. She wasn't sure what she was going to find but if she could figure out who he'd been in contact with recently she might have her first big lead.

As Eve pulled out of the quiet, upscale neighborhood she spotted a black SUV behind her. She thought she might have seen one on her way here but she couldn't be sure. She'd been too focused on that stupid kiss Mac had left on her forehead. She still tingled all over thinking about it and it wasn't even a real kiss. Not like what they'd shared last night.

Steering on to the two lane road that led back to town, she shook those thoughts away. She didn't have time for that right now. When a bright flash caught her attention in the rearview mirror, she frowned.

Why had that jerk turned on his brights? It was daylight. They flashed a couple times so she slowed down. She was already going five miles over the speed limit but if he wanted to pass her, she'd let him. The cops around here didn't give speeders a break so either he was passing through and didn't know any better or he was stupid.

The moment she slowed down the other vehicle rammed into her. She gasped as her head and body jerked forward but she managed to hold onto the wheel.

A surge of adrenaline roared through her when the SUV rammed into her again. She jolted forward again. The sound of metal crunching was unmistakable, but Mac's truck was tougher than her little car would ever dream of being. The big truck took the impact of the hit without crumpling. Her throat seized as her grip on the wheel tightened. Someone coming after her in the middle of the day was insane!

She floored the accelerator and risked a glance in the mirror again. The windows were too tinted to see inside. Even the windshield had a dark strip across the front.

Her heart pounded wildly. With shaking hands she grabbed her purse from the passenger seat. As she tried to dig her phone out, the SUV clipped her again. The truck fishtailed wildly.

Eve struggled to keep a grip on the wheel as her purse slid across the bench seat and slammed into the passenger door.

Sweat bloomed on her forehead. Whoever was doing this was serious and she was out by herself with no way to defend herself.

If this guy managed to run her off the road... No! All she had to do was hold on another couple minutes and she'd be closer to town. And other cars and people.

She watched the rearview mirror as he slowed down then zoomed up again. Taking her eyes off him, she floored the truck again. Hating the high speed and the out of control sensation swelling through her, she held on tight and kept her foot on the gas.

The needle point on the speedometer steadily rose— higher than her car could. When she spotted another car coming toward them on the opposite side of the road, she felt a tiny spike of relief.

She was almost to a local gas station that was always busy. All she had to do was get away from this guy. Whoever it was couldn't be stupid enough to attack her in public.

Easing her foot off the gas, she held her breath and glanced in the rearview mirror. The other driver was doing the same. Looked like he didn't want an audience after all. Now she had a dozen other questions. Maybe someone had seen her last night after all. This attack couldn't be random. Not in a small town like Hudson Creek. Her last story had been about the struggling real estate market. Not exactly motive for murder.

Taking a chance, she ducked down and swooped up her fallen phone from the floorboard. The other car flew past and she knew her window of opportunity was closing. Scrolling to Mac's number—after this she was *so* putting him on speed dial—she pressed send. Calling the cops in a situation like this was laughable. If she knew Mac, he'd be able to help her a heck of a lot faster than anyone else.

The second she hit send, she felt another shock from behind. This one was stronger, harder, and she lost her grip on the phone. And on the wheel.

Crying out, she fought for control but it was no use. The truck tilted on its side as she flew off the side of the road.

Trees flew at her. Blood rushed in her ears so loud it was all she could do not to scream. She tried the brakes but it was useless. The tires weren't even on asphalt.

As the truck hurtled forward she heard the sickening crunch of metal a split-second before she felt the harsh impact throughout her entire body.

Her head slammed into the exploding airbag. She instantly jerked back against the headrest. Her neck ached something awful.

Then silence.

She blinked a few times as something dripped down across her right eye. Blood? She reached up and gingerly touched her forehead. The slight contact made her wince in pain.

Blinking again, she looked around. The truck was still on its side. When it had tipped, her purse and phone had slammed back to the driver's side. The vehicle must have slid sideways because she couldn't see the main road anymore. Just a tree and underbrush.

Clutching onto the strap as if it were her lifeline, she held her purse because it gave her a weird sense of comfort. When she heard male voices nearby, her heart pounded harder and she snapped out of the haziness threatening to overwhelm her.

Escape!

She needed to get out of this death trap. She scrambled to get the seatbelt off. When it finally snapped free she fell sideways onto the driver's window and door. No way out here. The door was pinned against the ground.

Her arms and legs ached as she pushed up and tried to crawl toward the other door, but at least her bones weren't broken.

"I hear movement. Hurry!" a male voice shouted.

It registered that there must be two of them. Maybe the same two who'd killed Allen Martin.

They were close now. Eve stopped trying to climb higher and crouched back down. Even if she managed to get out there was no escape.

They were going to kill her!

CHAPTER FIVE

Eve shrank back against the door. Fear blossomed in her chest with a painful awareness that she was probably going to die. Her heart pounded loudly and blood rushed in her ears. She had no clue who was after her. There would be no witnesses either. A burst of anger surged through her, overwhelming her fear. She wouldn't die without a fight.

Looking around the cabin of the truck, she frantically searched for a weapon. Anything to defend herself. Though if they had guns it wouldn't matter much.

Before she could move, a middle-aged man wearing a Stetson appeared at the top of the broken passenger window. He actually looked concerned. "Ma'am? Are you okay? We saw what that SUV did."

She blinked at him, trying to comprehend what he was saying. *Wait, what? He was here to help her?*

"Ma'am, can you hear me?" His voice was louder this time.

Eve nodded. "Yeah. I think I'm okay." She could at least move.

"Hold on." He shouted orders to someone else that she couldn't see. Then another man appeared next to the front of the truck by the windshield. He had a big stick in his hand.

Fear jumped inside her again and she tried to move back. *What was going on?*

Sirens sounded in the distance but if these two planned to kill her it wouldn't matter. She doubted anyone would make it in time to save her.

Her vision hazed for a moment and she realized more blood was dripping down her face. She tried to wipe it away but her hands shook along with the rest of her.

"Try not to move. We're going to pull the windshield off and get you out!" the second man shouted.

That's why he had the stick. She allowed a kernel of relief to blossom inside her. Staying put—not that she had anywhere to go—she watched as he slid it into the small opening where the windshield had broken away from the frame. Using it as a lever, he pushed it down and the whole windshield started to peel up, frame and all.

The other man grabbed the frame. "I'll hold this, you get her out."

Understanding what they were trying to do, Eve hooked her purse across her middle and held her arms out. As she struggled over the steering wheel, the man dropped the stick and looped his hands under her armpits. Reaching up, she wrapped her arms around his neck and let him pull her out.

Once she was free, he bent and picked her up under her knees. "What are you doing?" she mumbled.

"We've got to get you away from this truck. I doubt it'll explode but we're gonna get you closer to the main road. The cops are on their way."

"Cops?" She didn't remember calling them.

"Yes, ma'am. Don't you worry, help is on the way. We couldn't get the full license plate number for that SUV but we got part of it." The man continued talking as he carried her across the dried grass and spots of bare dirt.

Unbidden tears started streaming down her face the farther he walked. It finally started to register what could have happened if it hadn't been for these two men. "Thank you so much for helping me," she said on a choked sob.

"Ah crap, please don't cry, ma'am. You're going to be fine. I don't think you have any broken bones at least." He stopped near what she assumed was his four-door truck on the side of the road and gently sat her on the crunchy, dried grass. Then he also sat and turned to face her. "Can you understand what I'm saying?"

She glanced at his friend who stood next to them looking just as concerned, then looked back at him. "Yes. The cops are on their way and you don't think I'm hurt."

"Good." He nodded then pulled out a plaid handkerchief. Putting it against the top of her forehead, he asked. "Can you hold this in place?"

Nodding, she replaced his hand with her own and held it. Awareness of the stinging sensation skittered across her face at the contact but it was bearable. She was alive. At this point she figured anything was bearable.

"Can't you go any faster?" Mac asked Griffin through gritted teeth.

"I can't pass the ambulance." Griffin was so calm, Mac wanted to slug him. He'd gotten a call from Eve then heard what sounded like a horrific accident. From the sound of things, some men had apparently helped her out of the truck but he didn't know if she was okay.

His foot tapped against the floorboard impatiently as they flew down the road. He'd called in a favor from a friend at the sheriff's station and found out that a single car accident had been reported around the same time he'd gotten the call from Eve.

As the ambulance slowed down, all his muscles tensed. When he saw his mangled truck turned on its side off from the main two-lane road his heart jumped wildly. *Eve had been driving that.*

Before Griffin had fully stopped Mac jumped out and ran past the two paramedics pulling a stretcher out. He heard another siren in the distance—likely a police car—but he ignored it and sprinted toward another truck sitting on the side of the road. When he cleared the front of it, he almost tripped.

Eve sat next to the truck on the small incline with two ranchers he recognized. "Eve." All he could manage was her name.

Holding a handkerchief to her head, she looked up at him. When her eyes started to water, he lost a decade of his life. The only time he'd seen her cry had been at her parents' funeral.

He ignored the other two men as he knelt in front of her. Taking him completely by surprise, she lunged at him and threw her arms around his neck. "I'm so sorry about your truck," she mumbled against his neck.

"Forget the damn truck." His grip around her waist tightened as he pulled her close. All he cared about was her. She might mess with his head like no other woman could but the thought of Eve hurt...he shuddered. Lightly, he stroked his hand down her back, hoping to soothe her. Though he hated to do it, he slightly pulled back to look at her. Mascara smudged under her eyes and blood had dried on her forehead but she seemed to focus on him without any trouble. "Are you okay? What happened?"

Before she could respond the two EMTs appeared out of nowhere barking orders. He understood he needed to move and let them take care of her, but the most primal part of him didn't want to leave her side for even a second.

Feeling helpless, he stepped back as they helped Eve to her feet. "I'll follow you to the hospital."

"But your truck…"

He shook his head. He didn't give a shit about that. "Don't worry about that. I'll see you in a little bit."

With watery eyes, she nodded as the two men helped her stand and put her on the stretcher. Since she was moving on her own he doubted she even needed it but he was glad they weren't taking any chances.

Once she was out of earshot he turned to the two ranchers. He nodded politely at them but didn't bother with small talk. "DJ, Derek. What the hell happened?"

Derek took off his hat and shook his head. "Don't know exactly. Saw a dark SUV run her off the road. I think the driver started to slow down until they saw us coming from the other direction. We thought it was you in the truck at first until we got to the accident."

He frowned at their words. "Was it intentional?"

The two men glanced at each other, then Derek nodded. "I think so. It could have been someone passing through being an asshole but it didn't seem that way. I got part of the license plate at least."

As the sound of a siren grew louder, Mac glanced over his shoulder. Sheriff Marcel was pulling up. Mac quickly looked at Derek. "Can I see what you wrote down?" He wanted to look at it before the sheriff took it.

Derek nodded and handed it to him. He memorized the few numbers and letters before giving it back. Mac wasn't sure what was going on, but if someone had intentionally tried to hurt Eve, they were going to pay.

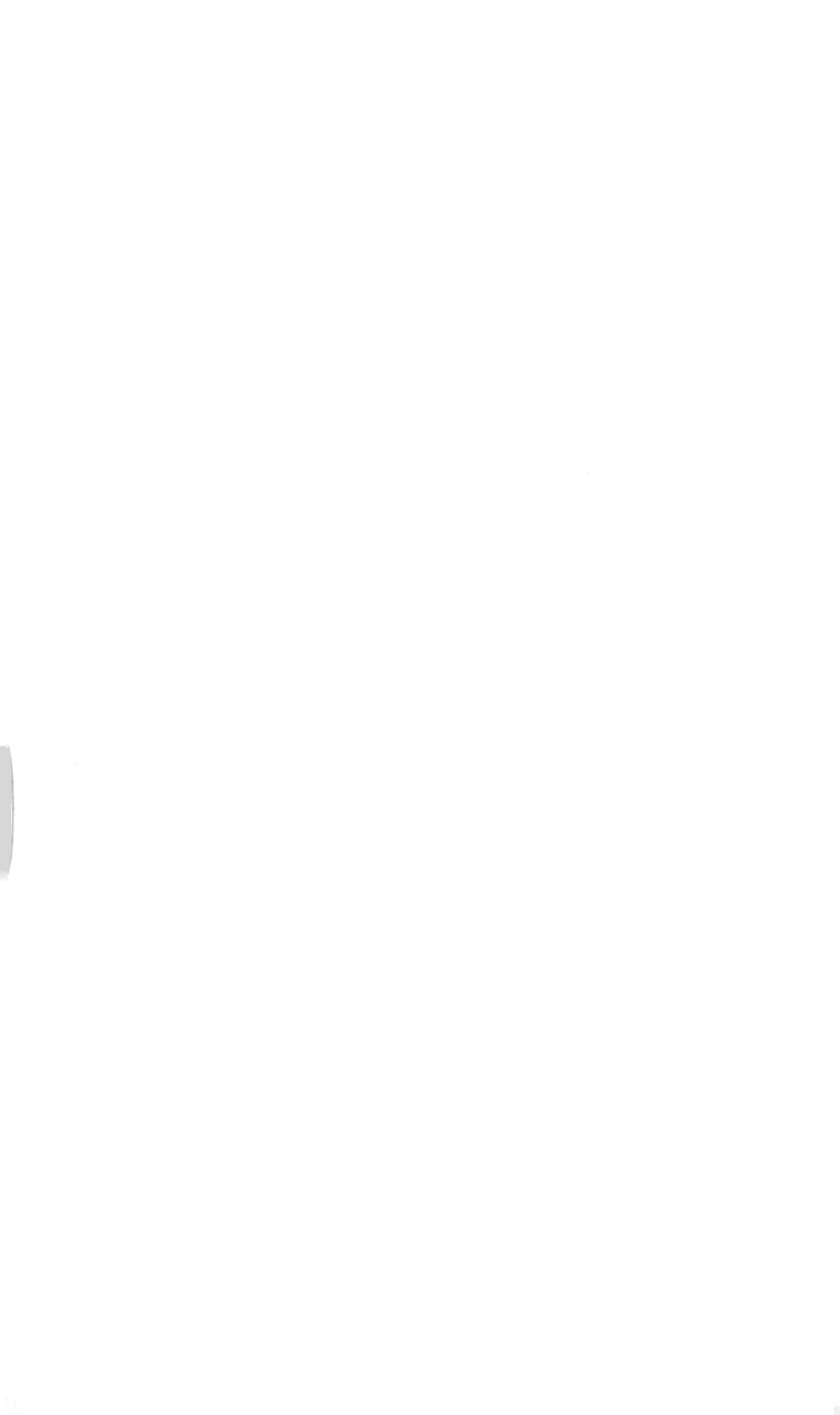

CHAPTER SIX

After dealing with the tow truck company and talking to the sheriff, Mac managed to get away from the scene. All he wanted to do was check on Eve at the hospital. The sheriff would be on his way there soon to question her and he wanted to arrive first. He'd rescued her phone from the cabin of his truck so he didn't have a way to contact her until he saw her.

From what he could tell she'd looked fine but his truck was totaled—and it wrecked him that she'd been driving the mangled mess.

"I've never seen you like this, man." Griffin shook his head as he headed toward downtown.

"What do you expect? My truck's totaled," he growled at him.

Griffin snorted. "This has nothing to do with that truck and everything to do with one very petite, very cute blonde."

"It's strawberry blonde," he muttered, not sure why the distinction mattered. But it did. Everything about Eve mattered.

At that Griffin laughed, but Mac ignored him. "I don't know why you don't get it over with and ask her out."

"Are you still talking?" He and Griffin had been in the Marines together and he loved him like a brother but right now, he didn't want to hear it. He just wanted to make sure Eve was okay.

"Well if you're not interested, maybe I'll ask her out myself."

"Do it and I kick your ass," he growled softly without looking at him.

Griffin laughed again so Mac kept his mouth shut. He didn't feel like being baited and that's all his friend was doing.

The rest of the drive to the hospital was quiet and thankfully short. Without having to tell Griffin to drop him off at the ER entrance, his friend pulled through and stopped.

"I'll park and meet you inside."

"Okay." He jumped out and hurried to the entrance. As he was walking through, Eve was walking out. She jerked to a stop when she spotted him. "Uh, hey."

"Are you leaving?" he demanded.

Her hair was pulled back in a ponytail and other than the small bandage on her forehead, she actually looked okay. She must have washed her face because she didn't have a scrap of makeup on and all the smudged mascara was gone. She nodded as her cheeks tinged bright pink. "I can't stay here and I'm fine."

While he wanted to hug and protect her, he simultaneously wanted to throttle her. "How were you planning on leaving?"

She bit her bottom lip. "Um..."

"Damn it, Eve, you never think things through. You don't have your car or a phone." He fished hers out and handed it to her. "And you need to make a statement to the sheriff. He's on his way here now. I know you were run off the road intentionally and so does he. What the hell is going on? I know this wasn't an accident."

"I honestly don't know. I went to see Bunny Martin and—"

"You *what?*"

Her lips pulled into a thin line. "I didn't tell her anything and according to her she's leaving her husband. Though I guess that doesn't matter now...Anyway, she gave me his phone records for the past few months and—"

"Why the hell did she do that?" He couldn't stop interrupting her.

Her shoulders slumped. "Look, I'm hungry and I feel like crap. Can you take me to Brick's Diner? I'm starving and I promise I'll call the sheriff on the way there. I'll stop by the station as soon we leave."

Stubborn woman was in no shape to be going anywhere. "You need to stay here, Eve. After what happened—"

She shook her head and wrapped her arms around herself. "I'm scared to stay here!"

His eyebrows rose at the raw terror in her voice. "Are you serious?"

She nodded, eyes haunted. "Whoever ran me off the road must have been following me or something. They know I'll be here and it's not that I don't trust Hudson Creek P.D., but…"

"But you *don't* trust them."

"Well, what if the sheriff doesn't believe me? I haven't exactly been truthful with him and here I'm a sitting duck. *Please*, I don't want to stay."

The pleading note in her voice did him in. Well, that and the way she looked at him with those big brown eyes.

Sucker. That's exactly what he was. A big one. Knowing he was going to regret his decision, he shook his head and put a protective arm around her shoulders. "Come on. Griffin's parking the truck."

Oscar Perez tightly gripped the wheel of the SUV. He wasn't sure what the nosy little journalist knew, but she had to know something. Why else would she have stopped by Allen Martin's house? He'd been randomly staking out Martin's residence for the past few months. The car salesman had been acting odd lately and their operation was too big to risk him getting cold feet and bailing. And the reporter woman had *never* stopped by before.

Maybe Allen had talked to her before he'd died... No, he'd been neck deep in their operation. He wouldn't have contacted a journalist.

After glancing in the rearview mirror to make sure he wasn't being followed, Oscar pulled out his cell phone.

His contact answered on the second ring and she sounded annoyed. "What's wrong? We're not supposed to be in communication today."

Rolling his eyes, he shook his head. He'd set up the schedule. "I saw that blonde journalist, Eve Newman, leaving Martin's house. She talked with his wife for a while."

"What did they talk about?"

"Hell if I know." He hadn't been in the room. "I ran her off the road after she left. Thought I'd be able to intimidate her into telling me what she knows, but I didn't get a chance to question her. Someone stopped to help her."

She sighed loudly, which only made him grit his teeth. "She's a nosy little bitch. Did you kill her?"

"I don't think so."

"Then she's probably at the hospital. I can't risk running into her there but you should stop by. I'm sure you can *convince* her to talk to you."

He didn't like the idea of going to the hospital and exposing himself like that. Especially not when they were so close to bringing in more money than he'd ever dreamed of. Cops would likely be at the hospital and he didn't exactly fit in there. "The hospital is too public. I'll wait until she's released."

"That's fine. I actually have a better idea. I'd planned to use it on Allen but I can use it on her instead." She sounded a little too excited.

He knew exactly what she meant and the idea was stupid. "That will bring too much heat down on us and we're not even sure if she knows anything yet."

"Someone saw Allen's body last night and we were lucky enough to clean up the blood before that patrolman showed up. If he'd looked around a little harder..." She trailed off and he could picture her tapping her fingers against her desk. "Well, whatever. If Eve was there, I don't think she saw us or she'd have told the cops. But if she keeps nosing around, she might figure something out. This needs to be done immediately."

This was going to be violent and explosive. Normally he didn't mind a little violence but right now he wanted to play things safe. Fly under the radar. But arguing was stupid. She would do it anyway because she liked to push boundaries. He'd only gone into business with her because she'd been able to help him make contacts he otherwise wouldn't have. And he'd bought into her dumb routine too easily.

She was anything but stupid. Sharp and savvy most of the time, she expertly pushed his product and kept people coming back for more. But she got too excited sometimes and tended to act rashly. "Fine. Get rid of her but keep it contained to *only* her. I don't want anyone else hurt or involved."

She muttered something then hung up.

Something Oscar wouldn't tolerate from anyone else. And one day soon he wouldn't tolerate it from her either. He planned to build his own empire and she was a stepping stone.

CHAPTER SEVEN

Eve knew Mac was annoyed with her but after she'd called the sheriff, he'd settled down. Well, sort of. There was still an edginess about him. He'd been quiet at lunch, just giving her hooded stares that made her blood heat up and only served to confuse her. She shifted in the back seat of Griffin's truck as he drove them to her place.

"Whatever your insurance doesn't cover, I'll pay for," she said, mainly to break the silence. Since leaving the diner, he'd agreed to let her get her car. But he didn't seem too happy about it. It's not like she had a concussion. Sure she was achy and her neck hurt but she was fine to drive. And if she went home now and took the nap that her body craved, she wouldn't be able to follow up on her lead. She was obviously on to something and truth be told, she was scared to be home alone anyway.

"Enough with the damn truck." He didn't turn around to look at her.

"Then what's the matter with you? You were moody all through lunch," she snapped.

Griffin cleared his throat from the driver's side, as if reminding them he was there. But she didn't care.

Mac whipped around in his seat. "*You're* what's the matter with me. You should still be in the hospital. Or talking to the sheriff right now. At the very least you should be at home resting!"

"I am going to talk to the sheriff, but I need my car." Since the sheriff had the partial license plate already he'd been pretty accommodating in letting her come in later.

"Someone tried to hurt you, maybe even kill you, a few hours ago. You should be more concerned."

"I *am* concerned." Actually, she was *terrified*, but that only meant she needed to figure out who was after her that much faster. And she couldn't trust the cops to do it for her. She could only depend on herself for this and she didn't want to drag Mac into whatever mess this was.

He muttered something under his breath, then said, "I'm driving you to the sheriff's station."

"I'm more than capable of taking myself and you need to go to work anyway." Now he was starting to put her on edge.

"Don't tell me what I need to do." His voice was a low growl.

"Then don't tell me you're going to be chauffeuring me around like I'm incapable." She wasn't sure why she was arguing with him. The thought of him staying with her was nice but she didn't like his whole bossy attitude.

"I've got your keys so deal with it." He turned around in his seat, effectively cutting her off.

Frowning, she patted her jacket pocket and then looked in her purse. She couldn't remember where she'd put her car keys this morning but she'd probably left them in her purse after locking up her house. She wasn't sure when he'd managed to snag them though. Maybe when she'd gone to the restroom at lunch. Which meant he'd been expecting an argument from her.

She scowled at the back of his head but didn't say anything else. She knew when to pick her battles. After they pulled up to her place, Mac jumped out and opened the extended cab door for her.

His expression softened as he helped her out and she pushed down the guilt she experienced for fighting with him. He also didn't let go of her hand as they stood there. "I don't want to fight with you. Are you sure you're okay to head to the station?"

She nodded and decided to keep it to herself that she planned to head to her office afterward. He really wouldn't like that. And after the way he'd raced down to the accident site to check on her...she wasn't quite sure what to make of that. "I promise I'm fine. And I'm sorry...well, for everything."

He nodded then looked over at Griffin. "Did you see anyone follow us?"

Follow them? Before she could ask what he meant, Griffin said, "No. But I'll still tail you to the station."

"What are you talking about?" she asked as they headed to her parked car.

"Someone wanted to hurt you today and I made sure they didn't follow us from the hospital or the diner. After what happened last night you and I both know that probably has something to do with today. You need to tell Sheriff Marcel. He can help you in ways I can't."

She snorted.

"Damn it, Eve. He's not—"

"Please don't say his name," she murmured.

Because it was her and because she'd had a rough day, Mac shut his mouth even though every instinct inside him told him to argue with her until she conceded. She headed for the passenger side, which said a lot about how bad she was feeling. She wasn't even trying to argue with him again.

As he got into the front seat, he glanced at her to find her clutching her purse possessively in her lap. No doubt protecting those phone records she'd gotten. Sighing, he slid the key into the ignition and turned the engine over. When it clicked, he frowned. "Have you had any problems with your battery?"

"No. I just got a new one."

The hairs on the back of his head tingled. A feeling he'd never ignored before. "Get out now!"

With wide eyes, she didn't question him. She grabbed her handle and yanked the door open before jumping out.

He did the same and ran.

A deafening blast ripped through the air. Heat licked at his back as he felt himself being lifted off the ground. The only thing he could think of was Eve as he flew through the air.

With a thud, he landed chest down on a patch of grass. All the air rushed from his lungs at the impact. He covered his head at the sounds of glass shattering. When her bumper slammed into the ground next to him, ripping out a chunk of grass and dirt, he pushed up and stumbled a few more feet, trying to stay out of the line of fire. His knees buckled and he hit the ground.

His ears rang as he tried to move again but he couldn't gain his balance. When he felt a hand on his shoulder, he rolled over ready to fight until he saw Griffin's anxious face.

"Are you all right?" Griffin sounded like he was talking from a mile away.

Mac shook his head, trying to clear it, but it was no use. He tried to push up but his world spun. As he stared at the burning car, his heart dropped.

Eve!

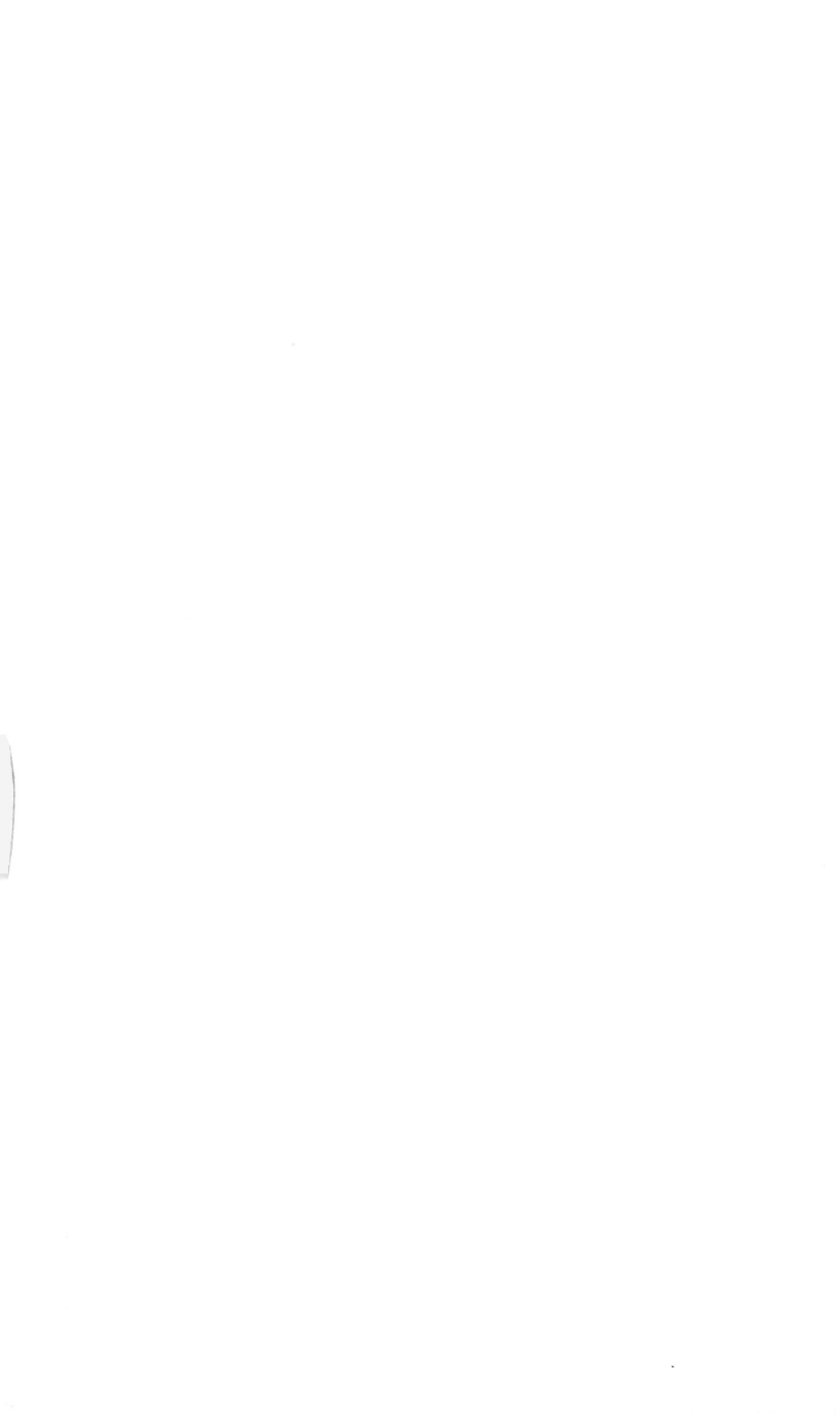

CHAPTER EIGHT

Eve felt like someone had shaken her until her bones rattled. She tentatively opened her eyes and realized she was face down in the grass. She'd jumped from the car like Mac had told her and then tried to run. She didn't think she'd gotten very far though.

All she remembered was a loud explosion then the sensation of being lifted through the air as a smoldering heat lapped at her back. Stretching out one arm, she tested her strength and pushed up. There was a slight buzzing in her ears. Almost like a phone ringing from a long distance.

She was shaking but at least she could move. More than anything she needed to find Mac and make sure he was okay.

As she started to sit up, two strong arms lifted her under her armpits from behind. "I've got you." Mac's steady voice had never sounded so wonderful.

A second later she was sitting on the ground and he was crouched next to her. "Are you all right?"

She managed a slight nod. "I think so."

"Stretch out your arms and move them." After she did what he said, he instructed her to do the same with her legs. Then he made her take a couple deep breaths and tested her ribs for pain. She was sore, like she'd run a marathon or something, but she didn't feel broken. When she did everything he said, he pushed out a sigh of relief.

Eve blinked a couple times as she tried to focus on his face. For a moment he was blurry but cleared up when she shook her head. Someone had tried to kill her. And Mac could've been killed too. That thought alone made her see red. "Are you okay? Did you get hit with any flying debris?"

"I'm fine." He brushed her questions away as if she hadn't spoken. The muscles in his jaw stood out. "You're going to sit here and wait for the ambulance and the sheriff. When Sheriff Marcel gets here you're going to answer every damn question he has for you. You have to tell him what you saw last night."

He spoke to her as if she was a child and she didn't blame him. Maybe she should have told the sheriff earlier but she couldn't go back and change that now. "Okay."

The tension in his face melted into shock. "You...wait, okay? You're not arguing with me?" He arched a dark eyebrow.

"Someone tried to blow me up." She might not like or even trust the local police department, but she couldn't hide the fact that someone had tried to kill her—and almost killed someone she cared about in the process. "I'm sorry I dragged you into all this. If you'd gotten hurt..." Her voice broke off as her throat tightened unexpectedly. If she could go back she'd have never stopped by Mac's place last night. Unfortunately he was the first person she'd thought of because she'd known he'd help her. Now he was paying for her mistake.

"I'm not." He reached out and brushed the pad of his thumb across her cheek. Probably to wipe off some dirt or grass but she liked the way his touch felt. Way too much.

"Mac..." Staring at his lips she leaned in closer. He could provide the kind of strength she desperately needed right now. The ringing in her ears was gone but she was suddenly hot all over. His blue eyes darkened to something she'd only seen a glimpse of last night. A sound rumbled deep in his throat as he moved forward.

"Sheriff is pulling down your street. You sure you're okay, Eve?" Griffin hurried toward them holding his cell phone.

His question jerked her back to reality and away from Mac's touch. That's when she heard it. Sirens. For the second time today. "I think I'm okay." Holding out her hand to Mac, she let him pull her to her feet, but she didn't let go right away. The sensation of his callused hands on hers sent a strange tingling sensation down her spine.

When she swayed, he put an arm around her shoulder and let her use him for support. His spicy, masculine scent wrapped around her like a warm, comforting blanket, almost making her forget what had happened.

As she focused on what was left of her smoldering car, bile rose in her stomach. The front doors were blown off, all the glass was shattered and the two front seats were practically obliterated. Dancing embers flickered across the remains. "Holy shit." She and Mac could have been in there. When unexpected tears pricked her eyes, she tried to turn away but he pulled her tighter and murmured soothing sounds against her hair. Not caring what anyone thought, she buried her face against his chest. She was so glad he was with her now.

She almost never cried and today she couldn't seem to shut off the waterworks. When she finally got her control back, she drew away from him. "Can we sit down somewhere?" *Away from the wreckage.* She didn't say it but she knew he'd understand. She wasn't nauseous but her knees were weak.

As he started to help her toward his truck, the sheriff, three patrol cars and an ambulance all screeched to a halt in front of her house, blocking half the street.

Sheriff Marcel was out first. Concern filled his expression as he hurried toward them. "What the hell happened? Are you two okay?"

"Someone blew up Eve's car." She was thankful Mac answered for her.

The sheriff eyed her cautiously. "Does this have anything to do with your 'accident' earlier today?" He didn't sound exactly sarcastic—probably because she'd almost died—but he obviously knew she'd been holding something back from him.

She nodded. "I think so."

Two male paramedics—different than the ones who'd helped her earlier—quickly descended on her and Mac.

As the men steered them toward the back of the ambulance, the sheriff followed them. "What's going on?"

"I'll tell you everything, but..." She nodded at the two paramedics. "Not around anyone else."

He gritted his teeth before turning to one of his patrolmen and barking out orders to cordon off the explosion site. He also told everyone to stay away from her house. From the sound of it, he'd called in a bomb squad from the next county and they were going to check her house before anyone entered it.

Smart, she thought hazily. Her head began to pound as one of the paramedics helped her into the back of the ambulance. After she answered a dozen questions geared toward making sure she didn't have a concussion, he checked her completely over but other than the gash she'd gotten from the car accident earlier, she was fine. Sore everywhere and definitely shaken up, but she refused his insistence to take her to the hospital. It would be pointless and they couldn't make her go. From her eavesdropping of Mac's conversation with the other man, he wasn't going either.

Once they were finished, the sheriff guided them toward his car and away from everyone else. She leaned against the back door for support.

"What have you gotten yourself into, Eve?"

She bristled at his question. This wasn't her fault. Well, maybe some of it was but she hadn't asked to be almost blown up. "You know that anonymous call you received last night?"

His eyes narrowed as he nodded.

Suddenly she lost some of her steam. She cleared her throat. "Hypothetically, let's say it was me who called. Let's say I received an anonymous email advising me to head to the Underwood mansion for a good story. When I got there, I might have—hypothetically—seen Allen Martin's dead body in the pool house."

He swore softly but Mac stepped closer and put an arm around her shoulders. The silent show of support made her stomach flip-flop.

Finally Sheriff Marcel spoke. "Did you see who did it?"

"No, I...you believe me?" Her eyebrows rose.

He nodded. "Yeah. Despite what you might think, we follow up on leads. Martin hasn't been to work in a few days and while that isn't exactly odd, the call came from his cell phone and it's been turned off ever since. No one has seen him, not even his wife. Right now I'm working on getting a warrant to search the DA's pool house."

"Martin's wife is leaving him, so..." Eve trailed off as she realized what she was admitting.

"How do *you* know?"

She sighed. Might as well admit it now. "I went to see her today."

He swore again but didn't look surprised. "Before or after someone tried to run you off the road?"

"Before."

"Damn it, Eve—"

"If you believed me at the station, why didn't you tell me?"

"You're a journalist." He said it so clear cut, as if the reason should be obvious.

Which in hindsight, it was. He'd never been very forthcoming with her. Still, it annoyed her. "Do you think the DA is involved?"

"I'm not going to discuss any more details of this case with you. I will need you to make an official statement and after this I'm putting you in protective custody until we figure out what the hell is going on. And where is Martin's phone anyway?" He spouted off everything with machine gun fire speed.

She stepped closer into Mac's embrace. Not because he happened to be there, but because it was him. The man who'd been there for her too many times to count. Even when they'd been kids. When she was eight and he'd been ten, she'd broken her arm on his father's ranch after falling off a horse. He'd helped her back to the house and hadn't made fun of her for crying. Unlike her brother who'd teased her mercilessly. Not Mac though.

When she realized the sheriff was staring at her, she felt her cheeks redden. "I'll make a statement but I don't have Martin's phone. After I took it..." She glanced at Mac who nodded for her to continue. When she looked back at the sheriff, she cringed. He was so not going to be happy with her. "After I took it, someone chased me and shot at me. I didn't see his face but I heard his voice. He had a Spanish accent, that's the only thing I know for sure. I ran and ditched the phone, but I did take the SIM card out of it before I got rid of it. I doubt you'll need it since you can probably subpoena Martin's records but I swear I was going to give it to you guys."

"She was." Mac's deep voice cut through the conversation, causing both of them to look at him. "And she wanted to tell you everything but I wasn't sure that was the smartest idea. I didn't want her to become a target, but it looks like it doesn't matter anyway. Someone knows she saw something."

Her mouth fell open at his blatant lie but she quickly shut it. She wasn't sure why he was lying to protect her. She'd be responsible for withholding evidence if the sheriff decided to prosecute her either way.

Sheriff Marcel sighed and scrubbed a hand over his face. "I don't care why you withheld this info. I'm not going to bring charges against you only because I know you're not involved in this and I understand why you held back. But remember I am *not* my predecessor," he said, as if reading her mind. "Where's that SIM card now?"

She fished it out of her purse and handed it to him. She didn't tell him she'd made a copy of it and she didn't say anything about the phone records she'd gotten from Bunny. The cops would be able to get those records easily—and they probably already had them. Just because he believed her didn't mean she was going to stop investigating this story. Someone had tried to kill her twice and Mac had almost gotten killed in the process. She wasn't going to let that slide. "Thank you for everything, Sheriff, but I'm not going into protective custody."

He started to argue when Mac interrupted him. "She'll be staying with me. The ranch is about as secure as anything. I've got guys patrolling 24/7 so I'll increase my numbers." When the sheriff tried to interrupt again, Mac shook his head. "I'm not letting Eve out of my sight, so save it. You could try forcing the issue but you and I both know what she's like. You won't be able to keep her anywhere for long. It'll be a waste of manpower I'm sure you don't have. Keeping her with me will be better."

Eve gritted her teeth that he talked about her like she wasn't even there but she was grateful when the sheriff finally nodded. "Damn it, you're right. Do me a favor Eve and don't harass the DA, okay?"

"So you *do* think he's involved?" His non-answer earlier had been a giveaway but she wanted to hear him say it.

He shook his head. "I didn't say that. Just…stay out of trouble and keep a low profile. If I find out you're not staying under lockdown with Mac I'll lock you up myself."

She wasn't sure if he meant it or not so she bit back a response and nodded. "Okay."

CHAPTER NINE

Mac pulled Eve's suitcase from the back of Griffin's truck. After the bomb squad had cleared her house, she'd packed a bag and they'd headed to the police station to make a statement. That had taken another hour and a half.

Dusk had already fallen and he was beat. More mentally than anything. But at least Eve was alive and unharmed. He'd nearly lost a decade of his life during those moments he hadn't known if she'd been all right.

When he'd found her lying face down in the grass, he could have sworn his heart stopped beating. Until she'd moved. Then something foreign had twisted inside him. Something he didn't want to admit existed for her. That sharp burst of adrenaline and the need to protect her had nearly overwhelmed him. That need had always been there. Since they were kids in fact. But this was different. It wasn't simply a need to keep her safe. He wanted to claim her so that every male in the damn state knew she belonged to him.

After Griffin headed toward the bunkhouse where he stayed during the weeks he was on night rotation at the ranch, Eve cleared her throat nervously. "I never got a chance to ask you, but why'd you lie to the sheriff?"

"What are you talking about?" Enough hours had passed that he'd hoped she'd forget about it. Should have known better. The woman forgot *nothing*.

"When you told him you convinced me not to tell the police about what I'd seen."

He shrugged as they reached his front door. "I didn't want you to get in any trouble."

"I don't need a big brother." She sounded testy and he wasn't sure why.

He sure as hell didn't have *brotherly* feelings for her. After last night she should know that. "And I don't want to be your brother," he muttered. He wished that was all he wanted. Sleeping under the same roof would be a hell of a lot easier if his feelings were platonic. He might not *want* to want her, but that burning deep-seated need for her wasn't going away any time soon. The longer he was around her, the more obvious that became.

She said something he couldn't understand but he wasn't going to ask her to repeat it. He wanted a cold beer and a hot shower. "Which room do you want?" he asked as they reached the beginning of the hallway.

Eve took the bag from his hand. "I'll stay in the one I did last night if that's all right?"

He'd rather her sleep in his bed. He told himself it was simply because he wanted to hold her. To convince himself she was okay. But that was bullshit. He wanted to bury himself inside her and make her come so many times she didn't remember the touch of anyone before him. The offer was on the tip of his tongue but somehow he reined it in. Damn, he really did need sleep. "It's fine. I'm going to grab a beer."

She nodded. "I'll be there in a sec."

For a moment he watched the sway of her ass as she strode down the hallway. What he wouldn't give to slide his hands down her back and cup that perfection. The woman was soft and curvy in all the right places. Just once he wanted to feel all that womanly softness pressed up against him when she was stripped bare to him. No clothes, no barriers and the only thing in her eyes would be desire and heat.

He shook himself out of his trance and headed for the kitchen. Eyeing the contents of his stainless steel fridge, he frowned. There wasn't much there. The men who lived on the land ate supper at his house during the week but they always took the leftovers back to the fridge in the bunkhouse.

"Got any beer for me?" He turned at the sound of Eve's voice.

"Yeah." He grabbed two and handed her one. "I don't have much food but you're free to take a look." As he popped the top of his bottle he tried not to stare too hard. She'd taken off her boots and jacket and looked two of his guys watching the house. If Mac trusted the men then she did too.

Before he'd left he'd looked like he wanted to say more but she'd been too tired to press him. The conversation she wanted to have with him wasn't an early morning kind anyway. After that kiss and the gentle way he'd held her last night, she was even more confused and wasn't sure what she should be feeling. The feel of his erection pressing against her back had been unmistakable and he hadn't tried to hide it. Nope, he'd been content to hold her.

Shaking those thoughts free because they'd only distract her, she started a pot of coffee and went back to the table. First, she cross-referenced the numbers from Martin's SIM card and the call log. The ones that weren't on the call log, she disregarded for the moment. If he hadn't called a number in the past three months, it could wait. Out of the almost two dozen numbers that he'd called with a decent amount of frequency, three were called with a surprising regularity and at odd hours. She highlighted the three numbers and the call times.

The one with the most calls was the number she called first. According to his SIM card, it belonged to a Beth Woods.

A woman answered on the first ring. "Hello?" She sounded out of breath and nervous.

"Beth Woods?" Eve asked.

"Yes. Who is this?"

Eve hadn't used her personal cell phone, but a backup she used when working on stories. "My name is Eve Newman. I'm calling about Allen Martin and—"

"Is he hurt? Where is he? I need to see him." Her voice was frantic and it was obvious her interest was personal.

"When was the last time you saw him?"

"A week ago...why are you asking me that? Wait, *Eve Newman*, I recognize your name. You work for the Hudson Creek Gazette don't you?"

"Yes. I was wondering if—"

"Do you know something about Allen? He hasn't called or stopped by in days and that's not like him. We had plans last night and..." She broke off and started softly crying. "Something must have happened to him. I just know it."

"You're sleeping with him," Eve said softly. Immediately she wished she could take the comment back. She hadn't meant to come off as callous but it had slipped out. If Martin's wife was correct, this was probably one of the women he'd been seeing. Considering the number of times he'd called this woman, it was definitely more than casual.

"It's more than that. We love each other. Why are you calling me? Has something happened to him? Why aren't the police involved?"

"I don't know that anything has happened to Mr. Martin." She swallowed the lie. This was her job and finding out the identity of Allen Martin's murderer was important. "I'm simply following up on a lead for a story so if you have any information about him you think might be important—"

"I don't know anything! If something has happened to him you should be calling the police, not me. Why aren't you questioning his wife? He was leaving her for me. Maybe she did something to him." Her voice rose with each word, nearing hysteria.

"Thank you for your time, Ms. Woods. I'm sorry to have bothered you." She ended the call and sighed in a combination of irritation and guilt.

It was obvious Martin and Bunny were headed for divorce court, but why would Bunny kill him at the Underwood mansion? And who was the man she'd heard that night? Eve was usually a pretty good judge of character and his wife hadn't seemed homicidal. No, she'd appeared almost relieved to be rid of him. And it was pretty obvious Beth didn't know anything. While Eve felt bad she hadn't been able to tell the woman her lover was dead, that was the least of her worries. Finding Martin's killer and her would-be killer was the most important thing right now.

Next she called the other two numbers on the call log but they both went to an automated voicemail after a few rings. After tallying up the next batch of the most-called numbers she discovered one was his lawyer and the other his bank. She marked those off. The third was supposedly the DA's house. When Betsy Underwood—the DA's wife—answered, she immediately hung up. She'd only called to clarify it was the right number and now she knew for certain. Even if she wanted to talk to her, she had nothing to say. For a brief moment she thought about calling the sheriff but knew it wouldn't do any good. She didn't have proof of anything. Sure, she had proof he'd called the DA a lot. Which meant they were friends. Big deal.

While she felt slight elation at Martin and the DA's connection, it was tiny and short-lived. All she knew was that they talked on the phone at odd hours. She didn't know why Martin was dead or what he'd been involved in to get him killed. She was back to square one. Hell, she'd never really left it.

After she organized her notes, she pulled up another article on her laptop that she'd started on the upcoming parade next month. Not exactly riveting stuff but she had to do something. If not, she'd go stir-crazy stuck in Mac's house. She couldn't go to work and she couldn't go anywhere else unless she wanted to worry about someone trying to kill her.

As she finished the first draft of her article, her cell phone rang. She glanced at the number and frowned. It was Tara Underwood. The DA's daughter. Eve's heart rate quickened as she answered it. "Hey, Tara."

"Hey! How have you been? I heard some craziness about you almost getting yourself blown up. Is it true?" She sounded way too excited and intrigued. Which meant whatever Eve said would be spread like wildfire moments after they got off the phone.

Word traveled too fast in this town. Not that she'd expect anything less from the kind of event yesterday. "Where'd you hear that?"

"*Everyone* is talking about it. My father is in a tizzy trying to get the sheriff to talk to him about it. He wants charges pressed against whoever did this and…" She continued droning on, but Eve frowned.

Yeah, she bet Tara's father really cared about who'd tried to blow her and Mac up. She hadn't talked to Tara in a while and Eve couldn't help but wonder if Tara's father had put the idea in her head to contact Eve.

"… And I hear you and sexy Mac Quinn are a hot item now. Every time I see that man in town I want to jump him, lucky girl. Are you bringing him to the fundraiser tomorrow night?"

Crap. She'd forgotten her boss had given the staff tickets weeks ago for the *Find a Cure for Lymphoma* fundraiser. "I'll be there," she said before she could stop herself. The sheriff might have made her promise not to harass the DA, but he couldn't stop her from attending a public event. The sheriff and Mac were going to be pissed she was going to the fundraiser but she didn't care. She wanted to see the DA's reaction to her and if she got to talk to him, maybe he'd slip up. She wasn't worried about her safety, especially since she'd be dragging Mac along with her. He wouldn't like it but she knew how to convince him otherwise.

Eventually she managed to get off the phone with Tara and when Eve saw how late it was getting, she cleaned up the table and headed back to the guest room. Mac had let her know his cook would be coming in around dusk to prepare the evening meal for the men and she didn't want to get in the way. Smiling to herself, she stripped and jumped in the shower. She might be a little sore from the accident, but things were definitely going to change between her and Mac tonight. She'd had strong feelings for him for over a decade and they obviously weren't going away. If anything they'd only gotten stronger the last couple days.

What she'd been forcefully keeping at bay for so long had bubbled to the surface and she could no longer deny she had completely fallen for Mac. Now that she knew he felt something for her, she wasn't waiting any longer. Even if things ended between them, she couldn't risk not taking a chance.

Mac was tired, cranky and horny. The cold shower jets pummeling his body weren't doing a damn thing to ease his discomfort. Eve hadn't joined him and his men for dinner—not that he'd exactly expected her—but he hadn't seen her once since he'd gotten home. All day he'd felt anticipation humming through him. At first he'd chalked it up to being worried about the unknown and who was after Eve. But he knew better. He'd been excited to see her. All day he'd been distracted to the point that Griffin had noticed and given him shit for it. Not that he cared about that.

He wanted Eve so bad he ached for it with alarming need. For a moment he wrapped his callused hand around his hard cock and began to stroke. The feel of his rough palm made him wince. He didn't want his hand. He wanted what only Eve could give him.

Sighing, he turned the shower off and stepped out onto the bath mat. After drying off, he didn't bother with clothes. Pulling boxers over his hard cock would only agitate him more.

When he opened the bathroom door and stepped into his bedroom, he froze. Eve was stretched out on his bed, blonde hair framed around her face in seductive waves.

And she was completely naked.

"Hi." She sounded nervous and her cheeks were as pink as her nipples.

He couldn't find his voice. Could only stare. His gaze tracked from her full, lush breasts down the flat planes of her stomach to the juncture between her thighs. Fine, blonde hair covered her mound in a neatly trimmed strip.

His abdomen clenched as he stared. What he wouldn't give to bury his face and cock there. He didn't remember moving but suddenly he was kneeling at the end of the bed. Eve sat up but didn't make a move to cover herself. Her hands were at her side, tightly clutching the covers beneath her.

"Do you want this?" He barely recognized his raspy voice.

She nodded. "Yes."

"Are you nervous?"

She nodded again. "A little."

Hell, he was nervous too. But he wouldn't let anything stop this from happening tonight. She obviously didn't care about talking since she'd come to his room like this. He wasn't a big talker, especially in the bedroom, but at least he could alleviate some of her nerves. All he needed to do was touch her sweet body and show her what she meant to him.

He wanted to take his time but right now his cock throbbed with the demand to be inside Eve. Grasping one of her ankles, he placed a soft kiss to her inner calf. She shuddered lightly and opened her legs farther. It was almost imperceptible but the action wasn't lost on him. She was opening herself up to him.

As he moved his way up her legs, the subtle scent of her desire surrounded him. She smelled like a fresh spring rain. When he reached her inner thighs, he slowly kissed and teased above her mound, but never directly stroking her pussy. Her fingers threaded through his hair and she gripped him hard.

It was hard to believe what they were about to do, but there wasn't anywhere else Eve would rather be at that moment. The feel of Mac's lips on her body had turned her into a raging inferno of heat and longing.

Her fingers tightened on his head in a silent plea. She didn't want him to tease her anymore. She wanted to feel that thick length inside her. When he'd walked out of the bathroom with that gorgeous rock hard cock, her inner walls had tightened with the desire to feel him inside her. She appreciated foreplay as much as the next woman but she'd wanted him for too long.

She was tired of being patient.

When he flicked his tongue over her clit, her hips rolled against his face. Such a slight touch and she was ready to combust. He chuckled lightly against the sensitive area, which only enflamed her more.

As he teased and stroked her with his tongue, tingles skittered across her entire body. She'd only fantasized about this and now that he was actually doing the things she'd imagined, the real thing was definitely better.

A moan escaped her when he delved his tongue inside her. The graze of his tongue had her legs clenching tighter around his head and her panting harder and harder for relief.

He suddenly pulled back and she froze. Was he going to stop?

"I need to be inside you," he growled softly. His dark eyes were filled with promises she hoped he fulfilled.

Before she could react he grabbed a condom from the nightstand table and quickly ripped it open and sheathed himself. As he rolled it over his cock, her eyes grew heavy-lidded watching him. Next time she planned to do that herself.

Unable to stop herself, she reached out and grasped him. When her fingers closed around his hardness, he made a throaty, almost animalistic sound.

He settled between her spread thighs but placed a hand between their bodies. Covering her mound, he slid a finger inside her. She automatically clamped around him.

"You're so wet," he murmured.

"Please tell me you're going to do something about it." Her voice was playful but she wasn't joking.

The slight trace of humor on his face melted away as he withdrew his hand. Without pause, he thrust inside her.

He filled her completely. Her inner walls molded around him, but before she'd fully adjusted to his size, he pulled out and slammed into her again.

She rolled her hips, meeting him stroke for stroke until their bodies found a sensual, rhythmic dance that had her clawing at his back for release.

When he nipped her earlobe with his teeth, her orgasm slammed into her hard and fast. It was almost unexpected. She knew her body and had thought she was still building to her climax.

Pleasure raced throughout her, sending tingles to all her nerve endings as she rode that high and finally crested into a numb freefall. As her orgasm slowly subsided, Mac's slammed into him with unbridled force.

He groaned loudly in her ear while his once steady thrusts became harder and uncontrolled. Reaching lower, she grabbed on to his butt and dug her nails in. That set him off. Another, more primal sound tore from him until his thrusts slowed and he relaxed and settled on top of her.

Thankfully he used his arms to prop himself up as he stared down at her. His dark eyes glinted possessively. She wasn't sure what the right thing to say was after something like this. Instead of sticking her foot in her mouth like she often did, she reached up and clasped her fingers around his neck.

As she did, he met her mouth and kissed her softly. The tenderness of his tongue stroking over hers was in direct contrast to the hard, fast coupling they'd just had. She sighed in contentment as their tongues continued the sweet, gentle kisses.

Now that she'd been with Mac like this, the fantasies she'd had in the past seemed dull and lifeless. Since she wasn't sure what their future held or even if they had one, she was afraid that if he walked away from her she'd never be able to settle for anything less than him in her bed. He was pretty closed mouth about what he wanted from her and she didn't want to broach the subject. The thought of being that vulnerable to him was too scary.

No, she decided to enjoy what they had without worrying about the future or asking questions she wasn't sure she wanted to know the answer to. When Mac threaded his fingers through her hair and she felt him begin to lengthen inside her again, she knew she'd made the right decision.

Talking and questions could wait until later.

CHAPTER ELEVEN

Mac tugged at his collar and shifted uncomfortably in the driver's seat of his rented car. Eve had somehow convinced him to take her to a fundraiser tonight. The cause might be a good one but he knew that wasn't why she wanted to go. Despite the sheriff's warning, she wanted to see the DA and gauge his reaction to her being there. She hadn't said it in so many words but he knew her well enough by now to know that's what she was up to.

The last place he wanted to take her was anywhere public, but especially not to the Underwood mansion where the fundraiser was being held. After what they'd shared together last night, it was hard to say yes to her when all he wanted to do was lock her up tight and keep the world at bay. At the same time it was also hard to say no to her.

For the briefest of moments last night he'd wondered what she thought of his scarred side but it was almost as if she didn't even see it. All he'd witnessed on her face was lust and need and something else he couldn't put his finger on. Being around her was like a breath of fresh air—even when she was driving him crazy.

He shifted in his seat again and rolled his shoulders. At least it was only semi-formal. Black tie would have been too much. It was bad enough he was wearing a regular suit and tie.

"Stop it. You act like you're escorting me to your own execution," Eve muttered from the passenger seat next to him.

"I don't like this."

"I know. You've only said it a hundred times. It's not like Richard Underwood is going to attack me in front of everyone." She smoothed a hand down her simple black dress, momentarily distracting him.

The strapless gown molded to all her curves and slit up one side to her thigh, revealing too much skin for his taste. He didn't like the thought of anyone else seeing what was his. Barbaric? Totally. He just didn't give a shit.

"It's not like it's a sit down dinner," she continued. "It's cocktails and hors d'oeuvres and a bunch of expensive stuff going up for auction."

Which would be followed by dancing and more mingling. And more time Eve was exposed to whoever wanted her dead. Which was why he didn't plan to let her out of his sight. Not for a moment. Hell, he'd follow her to the restroom if need be. "I don't care. Leave it alone, Eve. I agreed to go."

She mumbled something under her breath about him being a bad date but he ignored it and focused on the road ahead. So far he was sure they hadn't been followed since leaving the ranch. He'd rented a sports sedan so he wouldn't have to take her to the fundraiser in Griffin's truck. He'd also let the sheriff know they were going. The man was livid, not that Mac blamed him. But he'd waited until the last minute to tell the sheriff and there wasn't much the man could do short of taking Eve into custody.

To do that, the sheriff would have to confront her at the fundraiser and Mac didn't see that happening.

They arrived half an hour late so the line of cars wasn't that long. After releasing his car to the valet driver, he headed inside with Eve. A lot of people he recognized, but some he didn't. Their town had grown in the past few years, gaining transplants from some of the bigger cities in Texas.

Most men wore suits and ties though there were a few in tuxedos. All the women wore long gowns and most of them had on too much glittery jewelry that probably cost a fortune. Not Eve. Her hair was pulled back into some sort of complicated twist and she wore simple diamond earrings, but nothing else.

And she looked gorgeous. Frowning as he looked down at her, he realized he hadn't told her. He'd been too pissed she'd roped him into this thing. "You look beautiful," he murmured loud enough for only her as they crossed the threshold into the mansion.

Her head jerked up. Surprise covered her face but was quickly replaced by a megawatt smile. She blushed lightly as she said, "Thanks." When her grip on his arm tightened, he inwardly smiled.

After this thing was over he was going to have her flat on her back again and they wouldn't be leaving his bedroom all weekend if he had any say. Security on his ranch had been ramped up thanks to drug runners trying to smuggle their product across his property and the neighboring one so he might have to make a few runs with his men. But other than that, he planned to spend all his time buried deep inside Eve's tight body.

A giant chandelier hung overhead and to their right was the auction room. From his vantage point, he spotted the DA immediately. Not wanting Eve to see Richard Underwood yet, he stroked his hand down her arm to distract her. He nodded toward the giant room on the left where servers were walking around with trays of champagne and food. "Want to grab a drink?"

Eve nodded absently. "Sure." She didn't care about getting a drink, but knew a small one would probably calm her nerves. She'd thought coming here was the perfect idea and she didn't regret it, but the stark realization that the person who'd tried to kill her might be under the same roof was more than a little frightening. She couldn't help the way she sized up everyone who got too close. Even people she'd known since she was a kid.

An hour and a half later, she still hadn't had a chance to talk to Richard Underwood, but she had seen him. Once the auction had started most small talk had stopped. Now there was a short break in the auction and it was back to mingling for half an hour or so. She'd spotted the DA but he was engrossed in a conversation with the head of one of the local banks and she didn't plan to interrupt him. She could wait him out.

The champagne she'd had earlier had gone right through her. "I need to find a restroom," she whispered to Mac.

Silently, he led them down a hallway with marble floors, custom crown molding and a few paintings she was sure cost more than her house. All from old family money.

She heard female voices inside so when Mac went to open the door, presumably to check out the room, she tugged him back. "I'll be fine," she whispered. She'd been inside years ago and remembered the setup. Two sinks with a giant ornate mirror hanging over them, a settee bench by one wall and the actual toilet and another sink were part of an additional enclosed room. The dark wood plank flooring was a perfect contrast to the rich gold and cream colored hues.

"Be quick or I'm coming in to get you," Mac said before planting a surprisingly heated kiss on her lips.

Before she had time to react, he nudged her toward the door. Her lips tingled from where they'd touched and she was sure anyone could read all the hot thoughts running through her mind. He'd been slightly annoyed all night but he hadn't been paying attention to her at all. Nope, he'd been scanning everyone as a potential threat. The little kiss was a stark reminder of what they'd be doing later that night. Despite her tension, the knowledge of what was to come in a few hours sent a thrill twining through her.

As she entered the large room, a woman she didn't recognize was leaving, but Leslie Gomez was washing her hands at one of the sinks. She hadn't seen the other woman since high school, but she hadn't changed much. Very pretty, petite brunette with dark eyes and perfectly bronzed skin thanks to her Mexican heritage.

When she made eye contact with Eve in the mirror, her eyes widened almost unnaturally. She glanced behind Eve, then breathed out a sigh of relief. "Are you alone?" she whispered.

Eve nodded. She wasn't going to tell her Mac was waiting outside for her. "Yeah."

Leslie glanced in the attached room then stepped back out. "I need to talk to you. In private."

Eve leaned against the counter and crossed her arms over her chest. "*This* is private."

"I was going to try to talk to you after the party, but you're here now and... I sent you that email. I didn't know who else to turn to." She twisted her hands in front of her. "Once I overheard what she was planning I wanted to go to the police, but who would believe me? She's practically royalty around here and her father—"

Eve's heart rate increased. "Slow down. What exactly are you saying?"

Leslie took a deep breath. "I overheard her talking to someone about Allen Martin and from the sound of it, they were going to kill him. I know she's in to some shady stuff but I've never really known what for sure. But I had to tell someone. You were the first person I thought of. The police would never believe my word over hers and I remember how you wrote that story about corruption in the Mayor's office a year ago. I know you're honest and I was hoping you'd be able to help." She picked at the silk material of her dress as she stared expectantly at Eve.

"Who is the woman you're talking about?" Blood rushed loudly in Eve's ears. She figured she already knew the answer from something Leslie had said, but wanted to hear it out loud.

"Tara Underwood," she whispered.

Eve's palms dampened, but she remained still. "Tara? Not her father?" She wanted to deny what Leslie was saying, but how well did she really know Tara? Eve hadn't seen her in years and the woman in front of her had no apparent reason to lie.

Leslie nodded again in that frantic manner. "I haven't been working at her boutique very long, but I've overheard some strange conversations and I've seen her talking to a very scary man on occasion. Usually later when I'm getting off work he'll be arriving. I don't know if it's drugs or what or even how Allen Martin is involved, but she said he was a problem and that she was going to take care of him. Something about the way she said it…" She shuddered as she trailed off.

"We need to go to the police." Something Eve never thought she'd say with such sincerity.

Leslie shook her head. "I don't know anything."

"Allen Martin is dead and the police are currently running down leads. You need to tell them what you know." Even if Leslie was wrong and Tara wasn't involved, they had to tell the police about it. This could be the lead they needed to catch the killer.

Leslie's face paled. "I—"

The door swung open, cutting her off. Eve turned at the sound and nearly stumbled when she saw Tara walking in. Pasting on her game face, she smiled brightly. "Tara. How are you?"

With a thick diamond choker, matching teardrop diamond earrings and a gold shimmery dress, the blonde woman looked stunning. Eve couldn't help but wonder if she'd paid for any of it with illegal money. From what Leslie had said, Eve guessed Tara was definitely into drugs. Dealing or smuggling, she couldn't be sure.

Tara smiled but it looked more like a cougar baring its fangs. "Eve. So glad you were able to make it." She glanced back and forth between Eve and Leslie curiously.

Eve didn't dare turn around. She could only pray that Leslie didn't act nervous or give herself away. When Tara's eyes narrowed at Leslie almost accusingly, Eve knew they were screwed.

It happened so fast, she didn't have time to react. The blonde pulled a snub nose .38 revolver from her clutch purse and pointed it directly at Eve, but directed her attention to Leslie. "You stupid bitch. I wondered how Eve had gotten involved in this. Now I know. I pay you well, give you good benefits and this is how you repay me?"

Behind Eve, Leslie was silent other than a few sniffles that almost sounded like she was crying.

"What are you doing, Tara?" Eve asked, trying to keep the woman's focus away from Leslie. Her heart pounded erratically and sweat bloomed across her forehead, but she didn't dare make a move.

Tara's eyes narrowed dangerously. "You two are going to come with me. The auction is about to start up again and no one will know you're missing."

Mac will. Eve thought it, but didn't say it out loud.

But Tara must have read her mind. "Say a word and I'll kill your boyfriend too," she whispered as she slowly backed toward the door. Keeping the gun trained on them with one hand, she opened the door a fraction. "Mac, sweetie, Eve started her period and I don't have anything. Will you be a doll and go ask one of the servers or better yet, find my mama."

"Uh, Eve?" Mac sounded hesitant.

She hesitated for only a moment. "Hurry up, Mac. I don't have all night." Eve tried not to let her panic show as she spoke. She didn't want Tara to hurt Mac because of her stupidity. On another man the excuse might work but she really hoped Mac wouldn't buy this, even for a female issue.

He sighed heavily. "Give me a few minutes. I'll be right back."

Tara waited a few moments then eased the door open. After peering out, she motioned to them with her gun. "Come on."

"Stay calm," Eve murmured to a trembling Leslie as they exited the room. Her palms dampened even more when she realized Mac wasn't waiting in the hall to ambush Tara. They were alone.

"This way." Tara motioned them in the opposite direction Eve had originally come from.

Following her orders they reached the end of the hallway, made a left and headed for a door that led them into the backyard. They were on the opposite side of the large property from the pool house. Tara dug the gun into her back. "Head for the tennis court."

Eve winced at the slight pain in her back, but didn't say a word. The lights were off and even though she could faintly hear partiers and what was probably some of the valet guys from the front of the house, she didn't dare turn around and look anywhere. Raw fear and the steel digging into her spine was enough to make her cautious of any sudden moves.

"Why'd you kill Allen Martin?" Eve asked quietly. Her heels clicked along the stone patio as they rounded the pool.

"Martin was an idiot. We had a perfect system and he wanted out." She dug the gun in harder and shoved Eve.

When Eve stumbled, Leslie gasped and reached out to help her, but Tara shoved her too. "Don't piss me off anymore, Leslie, and I might make death quick for you."

Eve might not have talked to Tara in a while, but the one thing she knew for certain about the tall blonde was that she liked to talk about herself. So, she decided to fish for information. If she was going to die she wanted to know why. "What would your parents think if they knew what you were doing?"

Tara snorted behind her. "My parents cut me off a year ago so I don't give a damn what they think. My daddy thought he was teaching me a good lesson and it turns out he has taught me something very valuable. There's a whole lot more money in drugs than in a stupid little boutique that barely covers my costs."

Eve's heels sunk into the damp grass as they finished the rest of the trek to the tennis court. She wasn't sure what the woman planned but whatever it was, she and Leslie weren't coming out of this alive unless Mac figured out what was going on in time. She thought about trying to overpower Tara for the weapon, but until she had more leverage she couldn't risk it. If she did, she feared she or Leslie would be shot for sure.

"Where are you taking us?" Eve doubted she'd kill them on the tennis court so she had to have some other sort of plan.

"The same place I took Martin's body. No one will ever find you. Don't worry, I'll be sure to comfort that sexy rancher of yours while he's mourning your disappearance." There was such a malicious edge to her quiet laugh that it sent a shiver slithering down Eve's spine. "Now open it," Tara demanded when they reached the court.

Eve unlatched the green, fenced door and let Leslie walk in first. "Are you going to kill us right here?" She risked a glance over her shoulder to find Tara pulling the door shut behind them.

The woman smirked. "Of course not. Head that way." She motioned to the back left side of the court and that's when Eve saw it. There was a small wooden structure attached to the fenced in area, no doubt a storage shed. "You're going to stay right in here until the fundraiser is over. I'll tell Mac you took poor Leslie home because she was feeling ill. When you two go missing, nothing will point to me. Even if he's suspicious, he'll never be able to pin anything on me. Not with my daddy being the DA."

Eve reined in a snort of derision. Tara obviously didn't know Mac very well. Eve tried to think of anything to say to convince the other woman to let them go but knew it was useless. Why would she? She'd caught them and—

"Ahh!" Eve spun around at Tara's sharp exclamation and the sound of a gun clattering to the concrete surface.

She lifted her hands defensively until she saw Mac. He stood over Tara's fallen body, a gun in his hand and a grim expression on his face.

Heart racing, Eve gaped at him. "How did you..."

"I'm not stupid," he said wryly as he picked up Tara's gun. The other woman wasn't moving. "I waited around the corner until she came out with you two and followed. The cops are already on their way. Turns out Sheriff Marcel has already been watching Ms. Underwood on suspicion of transporting illegal narcotics."

Eve glanced at Leslie who'd wrapped her arms around herself and was trembling uncontrollably. Eve's insides were shaky and her knees felt wobbly but she managed to stay calm. After living in a war zone for months on end, having a gun pointed at her sucked, but she'd been in worse situations. "It's okay, Leslie. All you have to do is tell the police what you know. You're fine now."

"I can't believe Tara was really going to kill us. I always thought she was so perfect and..." She trailed off and shook her head but didn't continue as more tears tumbled down her cheeks.

The sound of sirens in the distance made Eve's heart sing. There were still some unanswered questions, like who was the man Eve heard the night she found Allen Martin's body? No doubt it was Tara's partner and something told Eve that as soon as Tara was taken into custody she'd tell the cops everything. She'd be desperate to cut a deal and Eve really hoped the sheriff didn't go easy on her. But more than that, Eve was just happy to be alive. Everything that had happened the past few days was too surreal. Maybe it would all sink in later.

Eve went to Mac and slid her arm around his waist. "Thank you for saving us." The words didn't seem like nearly enough but they would have to do for now.

His entire body was tense as he murmured something she didn't understand against the top of her head. He pulled her into a tight hug and gripped her so tight, it was almost hard to breathe. His strong arms were like steel bands, locking her in with his warmth and strength, both of which she'd gladly take right now.

Sagging against him, she buried her head against his neck, grateful to be alive and safe and in Mac's comforting embrace.

Oscar sped away from the police station and reviewed his options. He still couldn't believe that bitch Tara had gotten caught. Considering their arrangement, he didn't expect any loyalty from her.

She'd always looked out for herself and had made that perfectly clear from the beginning of their arrangement. He'd needed her because she pushed their product to the wealthy clients of Hudson Creek and with Martin's help they'd been transporting cocaine to various cities around Texas using his vehicles. It had been the perfect arrangement. Three people with almost nothing in common able to make a fortune and fly under the radar while doing so. The fact that Tara's father was the DA had always struck him as ironic. Now it pissed him off. Her father would be sure to let her cut a deal if she flipped on her partner.

If Martin hadn't been so stupid, everything would have been fine. And now Tara was caught. For what, he couldn't be sure, but he did know she wouldn't leave his name out of it for long. After driving to one of his safe houses, he loaded up the pound of coke he'd stashed along with fifty thousand dollars of his emergency money and a couple fake passports.

Always have an exit strategy. Unlike Tara he had few ties to this town. While he didn't want to head to Brownsville, his cousin lived there and could set him up temporarily with a place to live. Brownsville saw too much violence from all the border skirmishes and the law was much tighter there than in Hudson Creek, but it would be a perfect place for him to lay low until he could figure out his next move.

Before he left, he had one more stop. Eve Newman's house. He still wasn't sure if the bitch had seen his face but he couldn't take the chance. If Tara decided to cut a deal and testify against him, he'd take care of her later. But he wasn't going to wait to kill that journalist when he could tie up loose ends now.

CHAPTER TWELVE

Mac glanced in the rearview mirror before switching lanes even though he was fairly certain no one else was on the road at this hour. After dealing with the police, giving their official statement and then making sure Leslie Gomez made it home all right, it was well after two in the morning and he and Eve were dog tired. Instead of driving all the way out to his ranch they'd opted to go to Eve's place. The drive was barely ten minutes but for how he felt it was almost too long.

When he'd seen Tara pointing a gun at Eve he'd gone completely numb. That feeling had quickly morphed into rage though. His fingers tensed around the wheel, digging into the leather. Knocking Tara out and not strangling her was a testament to his self-control. If anything had happened to Eve... *No.* She was alive. He looked at her sitting next to him and was able to breathe normally as he was reminded of that fact.

Eve let her head fall back against the headrest and closed her eyes. "I'll be glad when this mess is over."

"Me too," he grunted. Sheriff Marcel had still been questioning Tara when the DA had shown up demanding answers so he and Eve had quickly left the station.

There wasn't anything they could do there anyway and all he wanted right now was to crawl into bed with Eve and hold her tight. He wanted to feel her every breath and heartbeat as he cradled her. To remind himself she was okay.

Once they made it to her place, he reset the alarm to stay mode and stripped out of his suit. Leaving his boxers on, he fell onto her bed without bothering to pull the comforter back. She didn't bother either. She shimmied out of her formfitting dress to reveal she hadn't been wearing a bra, but she didn't take her panties off before curling up next to him. In the morning he knew exactly how he'd be waking her up. He smiled at the thought and closed his eyes.

She threw her leg over him and sighed contentedly as she settled her head against his chest. The way she snuggled up so tight in his embrace made his chest tighten. Especially after what had happened only hours ago. He'd seen too many friends die when he'd been stationed overseas, but almost losing Eve would have been too much to bear.

The realization that he couldn't walk away from her hit him with the intensity of a semi-truck. He wanted her in his bed and his life all the time. If anything had happened to Eve, he'd never have forgiven himself for not protecting her. And the thought of living without her? He shuddered, not able to even think it.

She'd always been in his life and in his thoughts. Even when he'd been overseas, her face had often been the one he dreamed of before drifting off to sleep. *She was alive*, he reminded himself for the hundredth time that night. Tightening his hold, he let the blackness of sleep overtake him.

Mac's eyes flew open to a quiet darkness. His heart pounded loud in his ears as he slowly sat up, every sense on alert. Something was different.

It took a moment to realize that the numbers of the digital clock on Eve's nightstand no longer illuminated the room in a dull, green glow. And the low hum from her refrigerator he'd all but tuned out was now silent.

Slowly, he reached for where he'd set his gun on the nightstand and slipped out of bed. No one was going to hurt Eve.

She murmured something, but otherwise didn't stir. He crept toward her window and slowly pulled the gold curtain back a fraction.

The back porch light of her neighbor's house was on. Which meant only her power had shut off. Or more likely it had been turned off by someone. He pulled the curtain back farther to give himself a little more light.

Silently he hurried back to Eve's sleeping form. He rustled her awake and put his free hand over her mouth when she started to speak.

He leaned forward so that his mouth was practically on her ear. "Someone's here. Call the cops and stay in the closet until I come get you. Tell them to leave their sirens off." His clipped instructions were lower than a whisper, but she heard him.

With wide eyes she nodded and sat up. Before she headed to the closet, she pulled out a small case from under her bed and withdrew a gun of her own. Then she plucked her cell phone from her nightstand.

He breathed easier as he watched her move to the relative safety of her closet. Once the door slid closed behind her, he eased open her bedroom door. The hallway was dark, only illuminated by slim streams of moonlight coming in from the guest bedroom door that was ajar. When he heard slight movement from somewhere else in the house, he paused.

It sounded like it came from the living room. His feet were silent as he stole down the hallway. Once he reached the end of it, he pressed his back against the wall and listened again.

An almost imperceptible squeak pulsed through the air. Eve's living room was carpeted but the attached hallway was plank wood floors. That hallway connected with the one Mac was now in.

Instead of moving against the intruder—or intruders—he stayed where he was and waited. Whoever was here expected the element of surprise.

They would have had it too if they hadn't turned off the power. The sudden quiet had been damn near deafening to him. Of course if they hadn't turned it off, they wouldn't have gotten past Eve's security system.

They weren't getting past him.

A scant shadow stretched across the floor in front of Mac. As it grew wider, Mac tensed, ready to fight more than one assailant if necessary. If Eve had already placed the call he hoped it wouldn't be long until the cops got here.

But he wasn't counting on them. He was the only defense between Eve and whoever was in her house. And he'd be damned if he let anyone hurt her.

There was another soft squeak and Mac crouched slightly. He clutched the gun in one hand and when the shadow grew wider he knew the intruder was close. The faint breathing of someone grew louder and louder so he made his move.

Gun in hand, Mac kept his stance low as he jumped out from his hiding position.

A dark-haired man wearing all black jerked back in surprise but started to raise a gun. Mac lashed out with his foot, kicking the intruder's arm and taking him off guard. If he didn't have to kill him, he didn't want to.

If there was more than one person after Eve, Mac wanted to know their names. She couldn't live in a state of constant fear of being targeted. And he wouldn't allow it.

The man cried out as his gun flew through the air. It clattered against the wall but instead of retreating, the intruder lunged at Mac. With his free hand, Mac hauled back and slammed his fist against the other man's jaw. He knew how to fight and shoot with both hands and relished the feel of his fist connecting with this bastard.

Another cry rang out as the man flew back and this time he slammed against the wall. When he made a move to dive for his fallen weapon, Mac fired off a shot near the gun. Immediately the man held up his hands in surrender. He cursed under his breath before he said, "Don't shoot."

"Face down on the floor and keep your hands behind your head." There was a deadly edge to his voice that left no doubt he'd kill the man if necessary. After the man did as Mac ordered, he used his foot to kick the gun back behind himself. "Why are you after Eve?"

When the man didn't answer, Mac kicked him in the ribs. He'd never been one to abuse a prisoner but this guy had come after Eve with the intent to kill her. Maybe worse. There weren't many reasons someone broke into a woman's house in the middle of the night armed with a gun. This guy was lucky he was still breathing.

"She was a loose end," he grunted.

A loose end? Mac growled softly under his breath. As flashing red and blue lights filtered through the slats of the blinds in the living room, they lit up the hallway. Even though blood rushed in his ears from the rage building inside him, his breathing evened out as it sank in that this was hopefully almost over. Once the police got this guy into custody, it would only be a matter of time before Tara and this intruder fought over who could make the better deal.

"Eve? You can come out now! It's safe." And he planned to make sure she stayed that way.

CHAPTER THIRTEEN

One Week Later

Eve looked at her packed suitcase and fought the sadness welling up inside her. She should be happy. Tara and a man named Oscar Perez were both going to jail on so many charges it made her head spin. They'd both tried to make deals but with murder, kidnapping, breaking and entering, distribution of narcotics and a whole mess of other stuff they were being charged with, neither one of them was walking away without doing some serious time. Tara had given up the location of Martin's body, which she'd left abandoned in the desert in the back of her father's 'stolen' car.

It also looked like the cops would be making more arrests they hadn't planned on. Oscar agreed to testify against some of his thugs in exchange for a shorter sentence. Eve didn't think he'd last very long in prison once word got out he'd flipped on his own guys but that was his problem.

Now that she was safe, she could move home. She and Mac had spent every night together at his place since the cops had arrested Oscar Perez breaking into her home, but after a week she knew she couldn't stay here indefinitely.

Mac hadn't said anything about a future and even though she knew this wasn't casual, she couldn't very well move in with him. It was way too soon. Not for her, but he'd been a bachelor for a long time. If they moved too fast she'd probably scare him off and that was the last thing she wanted.

She rolled her suitcase into the foyer and left it there before heading to the living room. It was Friday night, which meant Mac's cook wasn't coming in. The guys who were off for the night would likely head into town to one of the local bars. Mac hadn't said it, but she guessed he probably wanted some guy time. They'd practically lived and breathed each other for the last week and she didn't want to smother him. Even if her heart ached at the thought of leaving, she didn't want to screw up the best thing that had ever happened to her by forcing her way into all aspects of his life.

While she waited, she flipped on his giant, flat screen television. She shook her head as the surround sound came on, nearly deafening her. He might be a roughneck rancher but the man sure liked his toys.

As she turned the volume down she heard the door to his kitchen opening. Fighting the dread that burned through her, she pressed the mute button and went to meet him.

Wearing a long-sleeved flannel shirt, dirty jeans and dusty boots, he looked good enough to eat. His face broke into a smile when he saw her. "Hey, darlin'." He dropped a brief but searing kiss on her mouth before grabbing a beer from the fridge. As he popped the top, he frowned at her. He looked her over from head to toe and suddenly looked nervous. "Did we make plans to go out tonight?"

Smiling, she shook her head. She wore a formfitting V-neck sweater and tight jeans that showed off all her assets because if she was headed home tonight, she wanted to leave him with a nice picture of her. "No. I figured it was time to give you your house back. I appreciate you letting me stay here all week. The thought of sleeping in my house after that man was in there creeped me out, but knowing he's going to jail makes me feel better. I cleaned up your bathroom and I think I got all my clothes but if I forgot something I can grab it later." She snapped her mouth shut when she realized she was rambling.

Nervously, she cleared her throat. He stared at her with those icy blue eyes, not saying a word. She'd thought he'd be relieved to have his space back, but he looked almost angry. Finally he spoke. "Have I made you feel unwelcome here?"

"No."

He set his beer on the counter next to him and took a step toward her, his expression growing darker. "Do you want to go home?"

She shrugged. Of course she didn't want to. "I'm sure you want your place back to yourself."

"That's not an answer." His words were a soft growl that sent a shiver down her spine.

"I...what do you want me to say? I didn't think you'd appreciate me shacking up at your place indefinitely. I thought I'd save you the trouble of having to awkwardly ask me to leave." She figured he'd be relieved she'd taken this step but his face said otherwise.

He stepped closer until they were a foot apart, his blue eyes blazing. His spicy, earthy scent surrounded her. "So you're walking away from us?"

"No. I'm going home." She crossed her arms over her chest defensively.

He made a strangled, annoyed sound. Then he cursed, loudly and abrasively. She stared at him as he let loose a string of words she'd never heard him utter before.

"*Stay*, Eve."

She bit her bottom lip, unsure exactly what he meant. "I'm not leaving for good or anything. I still want to date you and—"

"Fuck that. I want more than dating. Move in with me."

Her eyes widened in shock. "What?"

He pushed out a long, frustrated sigh. "I thought you understood how I feel about you. I don't want to do the back and forth thing with you, especially when I know you're *it* for me. I don't want to just date because I don't want to see anyone else. I want to see you every morning when I wake up and every night when I come home. I don't live that much farther from town than you do. You can keep your house if you want. Hell, I'll pay the mortgage on it. Just don't leave."

At his declaration, all the air sucked from her lungs in a whoosh. Mac had never been particularly vocal about anything. Of course she hadn't said anything about the future either so maybe she was to blame too for assuming he'd want his house back to himself.

For a moment she wondered if it would be a mistake, but she knew what she craved from him. She'd wanted the man since she was too young to even know *what* she wanted. Her attraction and love for him hadn't waned in over a decade. A slow smile broke out over her face. "I have a lot of clothes and shoes. You'll have to make room in your closet if you're serious."

At her words his face relaxed. He grabbed her hips possessively, pulling her tight against him. Through their clothes, his erection was hard and insistent. "I'll give you the whole damn thing if you'll move in here. I love you, Eve. Have for a long time. This past week I've been working up to telling you and hoping you didn't throw me out on my ass."

She snorted softly. "I love you too, Mac."

She'd barely gotten the words out before his mouth crushed over hers. His fingers clamped tighter around her hips and he lifted her until she wrapped her legs around his waist. As their lips and tongues danced in a hungry erotic rhythm, she felt him walking them back to his room.

No doubt they were in for a long night. And she couldn't wait.

ACKNOWLEDGMENTS

As usual, I owe a huge thanks to Kari Walker and Carolyn Crane for their help with this book. Carolyn I owe a double thanks to for her valuable technical help. I'm also incredibly thankful to Joan Turner and Tanya Hyatt for all their behind-the-scenes help. For my readers, thank you guys for reading my books! I appreciate your e-mails, tweets and Facebook messages more than you all know. I'm also grateful to Jaycee with Sweet 'N Spicy Designs for her beautiful design work. And I'm eternally thankful to my patient family who puts up with my insane writing schedule. Last but never least I'm grateful to God for being there through the good and rough times.

Complete Booklist

Red Stone Security Series
No One to Trust
Danger Next Door
Fatal Deception
Miami, Mistletoe & Murder
His to Protect
Breaking Her Rules
Protecting His Witness
Sinful Seduction

The Serafina: Sin City Series
First Surrender
Sensual Surrender
Sweetest Surrender

Deadly Ops Series
Targeted
Bound to Danger (2014)

Non-series Romantic Suspense
Running From the Past
Everything to Lose
Dangerous Deception
Dangerous Secrets
Killer Secrets
Deadly Obsession
Danger in Paradise

His Secret Past

Paranormal Romance
Destined Mate
Protector's Mate
A Jaguar's Kiss
Tempting the Jaguar
Enemy Mine
Heart of the Jaguar

Moon Shifter Series
Alpha Instinct
Lover's Instinct (novella)
Primal Possession
Mating Instinct
His Untamed Desire (novella)
Avenger's Heat

Darkness Series
Darkness Awakened
Taste of Darkness (2014)

ABOUT THE AUTHOR

Katie Reus is the *New York Times* and *USA Today* bestselling author of the Red Stone Security series, the Moon Shifter series and the Deadly Ops series. She fell in love with romance at a young age thanks to books she pilfered from her mom's stash. Years later she loves reading romance almost as much as she loves writing it.

However, she didn't always know she wanted to be a writer. After changing majors many times, she finally graduated summa cum laude with a degree in psychology. Not long after that she discovered a new love. Writing. She now spends her days writing dark paranormal romance and sexy romantic suspense. For more information on Katie please visit her website: www.katiereus.com. Also find her on twitter @katiereus or visit her on facebook at: www.facebook.com/katiereusauthor.

Made in the USA
Lexington, KY
28 October 2016